SWEEP IN PEACE

Sweep In Peace

Ilona Andrews

Contents

ACKNOWLEDGMENTS

A book isn't made in a vacuum, and we would like to thank many generous people who helped us bring this project to completion. Huge thanks to Lora Gasway for her editorial guidance, Anne Victory for her expertise with all things copy edit. We are grateful to Doris Mantair for the fantastic cover and interior art. We also would like to thank Shannon Daigle, Sandra Bullock, and Kristi DeCourcy for their incredible patience in correcting the manuscript as it was written and wonderful suggestions that helped us make this book much better. Without them, Sweep in Peace wouldn't have been possible.

Finally, thank you to all of the readers who gave Clean Sweep a chance and followed our free fiction experiment at Innkeeper website. We are planning on continuing the Innkeeper series in winter of 2015 with the third installment of our free serial and we hope you will join us again.

PROLOGUE

A man walked into a darkened room, moving on silent feet. He stopped by the round table, poured a glass of red wine from a bottle, and drank. A refined, slightly oaky taste washed over his tongue. He savored it, watching through an enormous window as the stars rose above a stone balcony. Muffled sounds of a ball filtered through the floor from below. It would be a good twenty minutes, perhaps half an hour, before anyone discovered the body in the office, neatly tucked behind the desk. By that time he would be long gone.

He almost never did fieldwork himself anymore. But this one, this one was special. Politically insignificant now, but personally deeply satisfying. A hint of a smile curved his lips. He supposed some would call him cruel for killing an old man ravaged by magic and disease, and some would call him kind. He was neither. It was simply a thing that had to be done, and he'd done it.

If his old mentor still ran things, he would have caught heat for this little outing. The smile dripped down into a narrow, sardonic frown. Nobody told him what to do anymore. Nobody had the right to berate him. Not even the Crown. He had accomplished far too much to suffer any rebuke. In fact, if the current ruling family had any ambition, they would murder him out of principle, just to maintain power. Thankfully, they were far too civilized and complacent.

At twenty-eight he had climbed the ladder of his chosen profession as high as he could. Life was no longer a challenge.

He was so mercilessly bored.

A pale star detached itself from its neighbors, curved over the sky, and rained down in a shower of pale glow onto the balcony. A dark-haired man stepped out of the light. Interesting. The spymaster sipped his wine. Either it was laced with a remarkably potent hallucinogenic, or he'd just witnessed a new kind of magic.

The man wore jeans and a tattered cloak. Not from around here.

"I'm so glad I caught you," the dark-haired man said. "You're a hard man to get alone."

Interesting choice of words. "Wine?"

"No, thanks. I'm on the clock. I'll come straight to the point. Are you bored?"

The spymaster blinked.

"With this, I mean." The man indicated the lavish room. "Shifting the future of countries and colonies. Rather small potatoes, don't you think?"

"It has its moments."

"How would you like to raise the stakes?" The dark-haired man smiled. "I represent a small but powerful organization. We're known as Arbitrators. We specialize in dispute resolutions. You're aware that Earth is but one of the planets in the solar system. There are many star systems and many planets out there. Many dimensions, many different realities even, to be specific. Once, these inhabitants of the Greater Beyond decided to have an interstellar war. It went rather badly, so when the proverbial nuclear explosions settled, it was agreed that a neutral body for settling conflicts should be established. We would like to recruit you to be member of that fine body."

Perhaps the man was insane. But if he wasn't...

"You will receive extensive training and be granted funds to maintain your own staff. Sadly, you will be forbidden from seeking independent sources of income until your term of service is over. Nor can you return to your home planet until the expiration of your contract."

"How long is the term of service?"

"About twenty standard years. Most people prefer to do more. Nothing compares to preventing an interstellar war, knowing billions of lives hang in the balance." The man grinned, wrinkling his nose. "It's a bit of a rush."

The spymaster felt his pulse rise and strained to hold it in check.

"We recruit only the best, and I'm afraid the offer is made only once. You do not get to say good-bye."

"So I must decide now?"

"Yes."

The spymaster drained his glass.

Below, someone screamed.

"And that's our cue." The dark-haired man smiled again. "Yes or no?"

"Yes."

"Great."

"My brother comes with me. I'd like to extend an offer of service to two others."

"We can arrange that. Of course, you realize that the decision is up to them. We do not compel. We only entice."

The spymaster shrugged. "I'm sure they'll join me." They were also bored.

The sound of feet thudding up the stairs rushed from the hallway.

"Very well. We should be off then." The man offered him his hand. "As corny as it sounds, please take my hand."

The spymaster held out his hand, and the dark-haired man clasped it in a firm handshake.

"Welcome to the service, George Camarine. My name is Klaus Demille. I will be your guide for this orientation."

The door burst open.

A pale glow coated George's eyes. The last thing he saw was guards lunging at him in a vain attempt to avenge the murder of their master.

"Rest in peace, Spider," he murmured before the light swallowed him whole.

CHAPTER ONE

One year later...

W hen visitors came to the fine state of Texas, they expected a dry, rolling plain studded with longhorn
cattle, oil derricks, and an occasional cowboy in a huge
hat. According to them, that plain had only one type of
weather: scorching. That wasn't true at all. In fact, we had
two types, drought and flood. This December, the town of
Red Deer was experiencing the latter kind of weather. The
rain poured and poured, turning the world gray, damp,
and dreary.

I looked outside the living room window and hugged
myself. The view offered a section of flooded street and,
past it, the Avalon subdivision hunkering down under the
cascade of cold water determined to wait it out. The inside
of Gertrude Hunt's Bed-and-Breakfast was warm and dry,
but the rain was getting to me all the same. After a week of
this downpour, I wanted a clear sky. Maybe it would let up
tomorrow. A girl could hope.

It was a perfect evening to snuggle up with a book, play
a video game, or watch TV. Except I wanted to do none of
those things. I'd been snuggling up with a book, playing
video games, or watching TV every night for the past six
months with only my dog, my inn, and its lone guest for
company, and I was a bit tired of it.

Caldenia exited the kitchen, carrying her cup of tea. She looked to be in her sixties, beautiful, elegant, and cloaked in the air of experience. If you saw her on the street in New York or London, you'd think she was a lady of high society whose days were filled with brunches with friends and charity auctions. Her Grace, Caldenia ka ret Magren, was indeed high society, except she preferred world domination to friendly brunches and mass murder to charity. Thankfully those days were behind her. Now she was just a guest at my inn, her past barely an issue, aside from an occasional bounty hunter stupid enough to try to collect on the enormous price on her head.

On this evening she wore a sweeping kimono the color of rose wine, with gold accents. It flared as she walked, giving her thin figure a suitably regal air. Her silver hair, usually artfully arranged into a flattering hairdo, drooped slightly. Her makeup looked smudged and short of her typical impeccable perfection. The rain was getting to her as well.

She cleared her throat.

What now? "Your Grace?"

"Dina, I'm bored," Caldenia announced.

Too bad. I guaranteed her safety, not entertainment. "What about your game?"

Her Grace gave me a shrug. "I've beaten it five times on the Deity setting. I've reduced Paris to ashes because Napoleon annoyed me. I've eradicated Gandhi. I've crushed George Washington. Empress Wu had potential, so I eliminated her before we even cleared the Bronze Age. The Egyptians are my pawns. I dominate the planet. Oddly, I find myself mildly fascinated by Genghis Khan. A shrewd and savage warrior, possessing a certain magnetism. I left him with a single city, and I periodically make ridiculous demands that I know he can't meet so I can watch him squirm."

She liked him, so she was torturing him. Her Grace in a nutshell. "What civilization did you choose?"

"Rome, of course. Any title other than Empress would be unacceptable. That's not the point. The point, my dear, is that our lives are beginning to feel dreadfully dull. The last guest we had was two months ago."

She was preaching to the converted. Gertrude Hunt required guests, for financial and other reasons. They were the lifeblood of the inn. Caldenia helped some, but for the inn to thrive, we needed guests—if not a steady stream, then a large party. Unfortunately, I had no idea how to get those guests. Once upon a time, Gertrude Hunt had sat on a crossroads of a busy road, but decades passed, the world changed, the roads shifted, and now Red Deer, Texas, was a small town in the middle of nowhere. We didn't get much traffic.

"Would you like me to pass out flyers on the corner, Your Grace?"

"Do you think it would help you drum up business?"

"Probably not."

"Well then, that answers your question. Don't get snippy, Dina. It really doesn't become you." She glided up the stairs, her kimono flowing behind her like a mantle.

I needed tea. Tea would make everything better.

I went to the kitchen and reached for a kettle. My left foot landed in something cold and wet. I looked down. A small yellow puddle greeted me. Well, doesn't that just take the cake?

"Beast!"

My tiny Shih Tzu dashed into the kitchen, her black and white fur waving like a battle flag. She saw my foot in the puddle. Her brain decided it was time to beat a hasty retreat, but her body kept going. She tripped over her own paws and smacked headfirst into the island.

"What is this?" I pointed to the puddle.

Beast flipped onto her feet, slunk behind the island, and poked her head out, looking guilty.

"You have a perfectly good doggie door. I don't care if it's raining, you go outside."

Beast slunk about some more and whined.

Magic chimed, a soft not-quite sound only I could hear—the inn letting me know we had guests.

Visitors!

Beast exploded into barks, zooming around the island in tight circles. I hopped on one foot to the kitchen sink, stuck my foot under the faucet, and washed my hands and my foot with soap. The floor under the puddle split, forming a narrow gap. Tile flowed, suddenly fluid, and the offending liquid disappeared. The floor resealed itself. I wiped my hands on the kitchen towel, ran to the front door, Beast bounding at my heels, and swung it open.

A white Ford Explorer was parked in the driveway. Through the screen door I saw a man in the driver's seat. A woman sat next to him. Behind them, two smaller heads moved back and forth—kids in the backseat, probably stir-crazy after a long trip. A nice family. I reached forward with my magic.

Oh.

I'd thought the chime didn't sound quite right.

The man got out and ran to the front door, shielding his glasses from the rain with his hand, and stopped under the porch roof. About thirty-five, he looked like a typical suburban dad: jeans, T-shirt, and the slightly desperate expression of someone who has been in a car with small children for several hours.

"Hi!" he said. "I'd like to rent a room."

This was exactly why Gertrude Hunt had a private phone number and no online listing. We weren't on any tourist brochures. How had they even found us? "I'm sorry, we have no vacancy."

He blinked. "What do you mean, you have no vacancy? It looks like a big house, and there are no cars in the driveway."

"I'm sorry, we have no vacancy."

The woman got out of the car and ran over. "What's the holdup?"

The man turned to her. "They have no vacancy."

The woman looked at me. "We drove six hours in this rain from Little Rock. We won't be any trouble. We just need a couple of rooms."

"There is a very nice Holiday Inn only two miles from here," I said.

The woman pointed at Avalon subdivision. "My sister lives in that subdivision. She said the only person who ever stays here is some old lady."

Ah. Mystery solved. The neighbors knew I ran a bed-and-breakfast because that was the only way I could explain the occasional guests.

"Is it because we have kids?" the woman asked.

"Not at all," I said. "Would you like directions to the Holiday Inn?"

The man grimaced. "No, thanks. Come on, Louise."

They turned and went to their car. The woman was mumbling something. "…outrageous."

I watched them get into the car, reverse down the driveway, and leave. The inn chimed softly, punctuating their departure.

"I thought we had guests!" Caldenia called from the stairs.

"Not the right kind," I said.

The inn creaked. I petted the doorframe. "Don't worry. It will get better."

Caldenia sighed. "Perhaps you should go on a date, dear. Men are so attentive when they think there is a chance you will let them into your bed. It does wonderful things to lift your spirits."

A date. Right.

"What about Sean Evans?"

"He isn't home," I said quietly.

"Too bad. It was so much fun when he and the other fellow were around." Caldenia shrugged and went up the stairs.

About five months ago, I watched Sean Evans open a door and step through it to the greater universe beyond. I hadn't heard from him since. Not that he owed me anything. Sharing a single kiss could hardly be called a relationship, no matter how memorable it was. I knew from experience that the universe was very large. It was difficult for a single woman to compete with all its wonders. Besides, I was an innkeeper. Guests left to have exciting adventures and our kind stayed behind. Such was the nature of our profession.

And telling myself all those things over and over didn't make me feel better. When I thought about Sean Evans, I felt the way business travelers from Canada might feel about an overnight trip to Miami in the middle of February. They would ride in a taxi, see the beach outside their window, knowing they wouldn't get a chance to visit it, and wonder what it would be like to walk on the sand and feel the waves on their feet. Sean and I might have been great if only we had more time, but now we would never know if that beach would've turned out to be paradise, or if we would find jellyfish in the water and sand in our food.

It was probably for the best. Werewolves were nothing but trouble anyway.

I was about to close the door when magic brushed against me like ripples from a stone cast into a calm pond. This had a completely different flavor. Someone had entered the inn's grounds. Someone powerful and dangerous.

I reached for my broom, which was resting in the corner by the door, and stepped out onto the front porch. A figure in a gray rain poncho stood by the hedges, just on the edge of the inn's grounds, politely waiting to be invited inside.

We had a visitor. Maybe even a guest, the right kind this time. I inclined my head, more of a very shallow bow than a nod.

The two doors behind me opened on their own. The figure approached slowly. The visitor was tall, almost a foot taller than me, which put him around six two, maybe six three. He walked into the inn. I followed him, and the door closed tight behind me.

The figure pulled the cord securing his hood and shrugged off his rain poncho. A man in his early thirties stood in front of me, muscular but lean, his shoulder-length blond hair pulled back into a haphazard ponytail at the nape of his neck. He wore a white shirt with flaring sleeves, dark gray trousers, and supple black boots that came midway up his calf. An embroidered vest hugged his frame, black accented with blue, emphasizing the contrast between his broad shoulders and flat stomach. A leather sword belt graced his narrow hips, supporting a long, slender scabbard with an elaborate basket hilt protruding from it. He probably owned a wide-brimmed hat with some fluffy white feathers and possibly a cloak or two.

His face was shocking. Masculine, well-cut but not at all brutish, with strong elegant lines people usually called aristocratic: high, broad forehead, straight nose, good cheekbones, square jaw, and a full mouth. He wasn't at all feminine, yet most people would describe him as beautiful rather than handsome.

The man smiled at me. Quiet humor tinted his pale blue eyes, as if he found the world a perpetually amusing place. They were the kind of eyes that shone with intelligence, confidence, and calculation. He didn't look—he watched, noticed, and evaluated—and I had a feeling that even when his mouth and his eyes smiled, his mind remained alert and razor-sharp.

I had seen him before. I remembered that face. But where?

"I'm looking for Dina Demille." His voice suited him well: warm and confident. He had a light accent, not really British, not really Southern U.S., but an odd, melodious meld of both.

"You found her," I said. "Welcome to Gertrude Hunt Inn. Your poncho?"

"Thank you." He handed me the poncho, and I hung it on the hook by the door.

"Will you be staying with us?"

"I'm afraid not." He offered me an apologetic smile.

Figured. "What can I do for you?"

He raised his hand and traced a pattern between us. The air in the wake of his finger glowed with pale blue. A stylized symbol of scales, two weights in the balance, flared between us, held for a second, and vanished. He was an Arbitrator. Oh crap. My heart sped up. Who could possibly be suing us? Gertrude Hunt didn't have the finances to fight an arbitration.

I leaned on my broom. "I've received no notice of arbitration."

He smiled. His face lit up. Wow.

"My apologies. I'm afraid I've given you the wrong impression. You're not a party to an arbitration. I came to you to discuss a business proposition."

Business was so much better than arbitration. I pointed at the couches in the front room. "Please sit down. May I get you something to drink, Arbitrator?"

"Hot tea would be fantastic," he said. "And please, call me George."

We sat in my comfortable chairs and sipped our tea. George frowned, obviously collecting his thoughts. He seemed so... pleasant. Cultured and genteel. But in my line of work, you quickly learned that appearances were often deceiving. I clicked my tongue, and Beast jumped on my lap and positioned herself so she could lunge off my knees in an instant. Being cautious never hurt.

"Have you heard of Nexus?" George asked.

"Yes." I had visited Nexus. It was one of those bizarre places in the galaxy where reality bent into a pretzel. "But please continue. I would rather have all the information I need than assume I know something I don't."

"Very well. Nexus is a colloquial name for Onetrikvasth IV, a star system with a single habitable planet."

He didn't stumble over the name. That must've taken some practice.

"Very well. Nexus is a colloquial name for Onetrikvasth IV, a star system with a single habitable planet."

He didn't stumble over the name. That must've taken some practice.

"Nexus is a temporal anomaly. Time flows faster there. A month on Earth is roughly equivalent to over three months on Nexus. However, biological aging proceeds at the same pace as on the planet of origin."

My brother, Klaus, had once explained the Nexus paradox to me, complete with formulas. We were trying to find our parents at the time, and the complex explanation had flown right over my head. I chalked it up to magic. The universe was full of wonders. Some of them would drive you insane if you thought about them too long.

"Nexus also contains large subterranean reserves of kuyo, a naturally occurring viscous liquid that, when refined, is used in production of what my background file calls 'pharmaceutical assets of significant strategic value.'"

"It's used to manufacture military stimulants," I said. "They affect a wide variety of species in slightly different ways, but typically they boost strength and speed while suppressing fatigue and fear. They turn humans into berserkers, for example."

George smiled. "I should probably speak plainly."

I smiled back. "It would save us some time."

"Very well." George sipped his tea. "Kuyo occurs throughout the galaxy but only in small quantities, which makes Nexus extremely valuable. Currently there are three factions fighting for control of the planet. Each claims the rights to the entirety of Nexus's mineral wealth, and none are willing to compromise. They're engaged in a bloody war. It's been going on for a little over seven Earth years and almost twenty years in Nexus's time. The war is brutal and has cost everyone involved a great deal. Cooler minds on all sides agree it can't continue. The matter has been referred for arbitration by one of the interested factions, the other two agreed, and here we are."

"I'm guessing one of the factions is the Merchants?" When we landed on Nexus, we'd ended up in a Merchant spaceport. Merchants facilitated interstellar trade through the known galaxy and its many dimensions. When you needed rare goods or a large quantity of goods, you went to see a Merchant. They were motivated by profit and prestige.

George nodded. "Yes. The war is cutting into their profits."

"Which family? The Ama?"

"The Nuan. The Ama family cut their losses and sold its holdings on Nexus to Nuan two years ago."

Suddenly his presence here made a lot of sense. "Is Nuan Cee involved?"

"Yes. In fact, he was the one who recommended your establishment."

Before my parents disappeared, they did a lot of business with Nuan Cee. Running an inn sometimes required exotic goods, and he procured the rarest items. Even I had done a deal with Nuan Cee. I'd bartered the world's rarest honey for the eggs of a deadly giant spider.

"Your tea is delicious," George said.

"Thank you. Which are the other two factions?"

"House Krahr of the Holy Cosmic Anocracy."

Six months ago I had sheltered a vampire of House Krahr after he was injured trying to apprehend an alien assassin. His nephew had come to rescue him. The nephew's name was Arland, he was the Marshal of his House, and he had flirted with me. At least flirted in vampire terms. He'd assured me that he would be ecstatic to be my shield, and I shouldn't hesitate to rely upon his warrior prowess. He'd also gotten drunk on coffee and run through my orchard naked.

Good God, who could hold the vampires of Krahr off for twenty years? They were one of the most ferocious sentient species in the galaxy. They were predators who lived to war. Their entire civilization was dedicated to it.

"And the final faction?"

George set his cup down. "The Otrokars."

I blinked.

Silence stretched.

"The Hope-Crushing Horde?"

George looked slightly uncomfortable. "That's the official name, yes."

The Otrokars were the scourge of the galaxy. They were huge and violent, and they lived to conquer. They'd started with one planet and grown their holdings to nine. Their name literally meant Hope-Crushing, because once you saw them, all your hopes died. The Holy Anocracy and the Horde had collided several times over the past three centuries, always with disastrous results. The two species hated each other so much their feud had become legendary. Half the jokes in the galaxy started with "a vampire and an otrokar walk into a bar...."

Having vampires and Otrokars together in close proximity was like mixing glycerin with nitric acid and then hitting it with a sledgehammer. They would explode. It would be a slaughter.

I leaned forward. "So you need a neutral venue to hold the arbitration?"

"Yes. An inn on Earth is ideal. It is defined as neutral ground, and we can rely on an innkeeper's power to keep the participants in check."

"Let me guess: you've tried other inns and everyone turned you down. Am I your last stop?"

George took a deep breath. "Yes."

"There was an attempt to broker peace between Otrokars and the Holy Cosmic Anocracy during their Ten-Year Conflict," I said. "About fifty years ago."

He braided his long, elegant fingers into a single fist. "Yes, I'm familiar with it."

"Then you also know how it ended."

"I believe the patriarch of House Jero lunged at the Otrokar Khan, and the Khan beheaded him."

"He ripped the patriarch's head off with his bare hands and then proceeded to beat the Marshal of House Jero to death with it."

"Well, the venture could be viewed as risky, when taking into account their history..."

"It's not risky, it's suicidal."

"Should I take that as a no?" George asked.

This was a really bad idea.

"How many people do you expect?"

"At least twelve from each party."

Thirty-six guests. My heart sped up. Thirty-six guests, each with robust magic. This would sustain the inn for years to come. Not to mention that if I managed to pull this impossible thing off, it would raise the inn's standing.

No. What was I thinking? It would be crazy. I would have to keep the peace between thirty-six individuals, each dying to kill the other. It would be terrible. The risk... The gamble was too great.

What did I have to lose?

George reached into his pocket, produced a small tablet about the size of a playing card and just as thin, and showed it to me. Two numbers: $500,000 and $1,000,000.

"The first is your payment in the event the arbitration fails. The second is payment if we succeed."

Five hundred thousand. We needed the money. I could finally upgrade my books. I could buy the additional building materials for the inn.

No. I might as well set Gertrude Hunt on fire.

My gaze fell on the portrait of my parents. They were looking at me. Demilles never backed down from a challenge. But then, we didn't take unnecessary risks either.

Nothing ventured, nothing gained. I could simply sit here and continue to wait for a chance traveler to happen my way...

"If I do this, I would need you to meet my conditions," I said.

"Absolutely."

"I want agreements of reimbursement to be drawn up and signed by all parties. I want a sum of money to be set aside in escrow from each faction and placed under your control. If they damage the inn, I want them to pay for the damages."

"I find that reasonable."

"I need each party to review and sign Earth's nondisclosure policy. Ordinary citizens of this planet can't know of their existence. For example, we may experience visits from local law enforcement, and I want it expressly understood that nobody will be crushing necks or ripping off heads."

"Also reasonable."

"I may think of some additional restrictions. Do you have any concerns?"

"A couple." George leaned forward. "The nature of the relationship between the inn and its guests isn't quite clear to me. Why does the inn require guests?"

"It's a symbiotic relationship," I explained. "The inn provides the guests with shelter and food. It sees to their every need. In return, it feeds on the natural energy all living beings emit. The more varied and powerful that energy, the more magic the inn is able to generate and the stronger it becomes."

George narrowed his eyes. "So is the inn empathic?"

"No, not exactly."

"Can it influence the mood of its guests?"

"Only in as much as we are all influenced by our surroundings."

George frowned. "I've read of some cases that suggested a link can be forged between an inn and its guests."

Oh. That's what he was getting at. "That's not exactly accurate. It's possible for the inn to forge a mental link between an innkeeper and a guest, but the inn can't influence the guest's mental state. The linking ritual has been done only a handful of times, in rare cases when the inn or guests were in danger, for example, when a murder had occurred and discovering the identity of the killer was paramount. The guest has to be a willing participant in the process and try to forge the link. So if you're asking me whether the inn can magically make the guests more agreeable and likely to sign the peace treaty, then no. I can make sure the peace delegates have the softest linens and the most tranquil of rooms, but I have no power to influence them. Even if I could, I wouldn't. The privacy of my guests is sacred, and I am meant to remain as a neutral party. It would be a breach of ethics."

"Oh well," he said. "It was a thought."

Considering the enormity of the task at hand, I could understand why he would reach for any possibility that could influence the outcome. "Anything else?"

"Yes." George turned and glanced at the modest room. "I mean no disrespect, but your establishment is considerably smaller than I was led to believe. I don't believe we have enough room."

I rose. "Have you stayed at many inns?"

"No. I've visited several in connection with this summit, but I haven't had the pleasure of being a guest. Yours is my first."

I pulled the magic to me. What I was about to do would likely drain most of the inn's resources and mine. If he walked away from our deal after I was done, it would take us a very long time to recover. But if we could get guests, it would all be worth it.

I picked up my broom. The magic vibrated within me, building and building, held so tight, like a giant spring compressed to its limit. George rose and stood next to me.

I raised the broom, bristles up, pictured the interior of the inn in my mind, and brought the broom down. Wood connected with floorboards with a dry knock.

Magic rolled through the inn like an avalanche, the wood and stone suddenly elastic and flowing. The interior of the inn opened like a blossoming flower. The walls moved apart. The ceiling soared. The magic kept streaming out of me, so fast I felt light-headed. Polished pink marble rolled over the floor, sheathed the walls, and surged up, forming stately columns.

Next to me, George stood very still.

Two-story-tall windows opened in the marble. I leaned on the broom for support. Vaulted ceilings turned pure white. Crystal chandeliers sprouted like bunches of exquisite blooms. Golden flourishes spiraled and curved on the floor. Lights flared among the crystal.

I cut off the magic. The power snapped inside me like a rubber band. I reeled from the impact.

The grand ballroom spread before us, grandiose, elegant, and glowing.

The Arbitrator closed his mouth with a click. "I stand corrected."

CHAPTER TWO

The enormous bolt of faux silk unrolled slowly at my feet, its end disappearing into the marble floor. Beast had barked at it on principle for about five minutes, until she finally decided it wasn't that exciting and went off to explore the vastness of the ballroom. She sniffed at the corners, found a quiet spot, and lay down.

I would've loved nothing more than to join her, except not on the floor but in my nice soft bed. Opening the ballroom had drained me. I felt like I had run several miles. Given the choice, I would've retired for a nap right after the Arbitrator left, but the time line for the peace summit was tight. George wanted to get started within forty-eight hours, which meant that instead of taking a nap, I had stolen a can of Caldenia's Mello Yello to stay awake, jumped into my car, and drove through the rain to rent a truck. Then I drove the truck two hours to Austin to the largest regional fabric distributor. There I bought an enormous roll of faux silk and another of cotton. That cost me a third of my emergency fund. Next I stopped at a stone and landscaping place and purchased bulk stone. They helped me load it, and when I came back, I dumped it in the backyard where the inn promptly ate it.

Now I was here, valiantly doing my best to stay on my feet as the inn continued to consume the faux silk inch by inch.

"Well. This is quite a development."

I turned to see Caldenia standing in the doorway. "Your Grace."

The older woman slowly stepped into the ballroom. Her gaze slid over the marble floor, the columns, and the soaring white ceiling with golden flourishes.

"What's the occasion?"

"We're hosting a diplomatic summit."

She turned on her foot and looked at me, her eyes sharp. "My dear, don't tease me."

"This roll of faux silk cost me six dollars per yard," I told her. "Once I purchase food, I will be destitute."

Caldenia blinked. "Who are the attending parties?"

"The Holy Anocracy, represented by House Krahr; the Hope-Crushing Horde; and the Merchants of Baha-char. They are coming here for the arbitration, and they will probably try to murder each other the moment they walk through the door."

Caldenia's eyes widened. "Do you really think so? This is absolutely marvelous!"

She would think so, wouldn't she?

"Tell me the plan."

I sighed and pointed at the eastern wall. I had formed a balcony along the east, west, and south sides of the room. Each balcony terminated far from its neighbors, too far for any of the species to clear in a jump and too high to safely jump down from.

"The otrokars' rooms will be up there. They give prayers to sunrise, so they require a view of the morning sun."

I turned and pointed at the opposite wall. "The vampires go there. Their time of reflection begins as sunset ends, so they're in the west."

I pointed at the North wall. "The Merchants will reside there. They're a forest species and prefer shady rooms and muted light. Everyone has their separate stairwell. Nobody can enter quarters other than their own. The inn won't permit it."

I pointed to the south, where long windows sliced the wall into sections. "I'm going to put a table there for the leaders to conduct their negotiations."

"That's a well-planned layout," Caldenia said. "But why pink marble?" She waved at the ceiling. "Pink marble, white ceiling, *golden* accents... With the electric lighting, it will turn into this ghastly orange."

"I had one chance to impress the Arbitrator, and I had to improvise."

Caldenia arched one eyebrow.

"I saw it in a movie once," I explained. "It was easy to visualize."

"Was it a movie for adults?"

"It had a talking candelabra who was friends with a grumpy clock."

"I see. What about a ballroom from your parents' inn?"

I shook my head. I remembered it in excruciating detail, but when I thought about recreating it, my heart squeezed itself into a painful clump. I sighed. "I can make it completely white if you would prefer."

Caldenia's eyes narrowed. "So the color can be altered?"

"Yes."

"In that case, not white. White is the safest of choices. Also, as memory serves, House Krahr builds their castles with gray stone, and you don't want to show favoritism."

"Otrokars favor vibrant colors and ornate decoration," I said. "They tend toward reds and greens."

"So we must strike a balance between the two. Blue is a soothing color most species find conducive to contemplation. Why don't we try turquoise?"

I concentrated. The marble columns obligingly changed hue.

"A little more gray. A little darker. Little more... Now, can we put lighter streaks through them? Can you fleck it with gold... Perfect."

I had to admit the columns did look beautiful.

"Let's take down the gold leaf," Caldenia said. "Elegance is never ostentatious, and there is nothing more bourgeois than covering everything in gold. It screams that one has too much money and too little taste, and it infuriates peasants. A palace should convey a sense of power and grandeur. One should enter and be awestruck. I've found the awe tends to cut down on revolts."

I seriously doubted I'd face any revolts, but if it cut down on the slaughter I would be quite happy.

"Gold has its uses, but always in moderation," Caldenia continued. "Did I ever tell you about Cai Pa? It's a water world. The entire planet is an ocean, and the population lives on giant artificial floating islands. It's amazing how many people you can stuff into a few square miles. Each of them is ruled by a noble grown rich on pharmaceutical trade and underwater mining. Space is at a premium, so of course the fools build elaborate palaces. I had cause to attend a meeting in one of those monstrosities. They have these underwater algae forests, quite beautiful, actually, if you are into that sort of thing. The entirety of the palace walls was covered in algae cast in gold. There was not a single clear spot on the walls or the ceiling that didn't have some sort of flourish or a flower in gold or some other garish color like scarlet. And between the algae there were portraits of the host and his family with jewels instead of eyes."

"Jewels?"

Caldenia paused and looked at me. "Jewels, Dina. It looked ghastly. After ten minutes in the place, I felt like my eyes were under assault by an interstellar dreadnought. It was making me physically ill."

"Some people simply live to prove to others that they have more."

"Indeed. I lasted a single day, and when I departed, the host had the audacity to claim I had insulted his family. I would've poisoned the lot, but I couldn't stand to be in the building for another moment."

Her Grace raised her arms. "This is your ballroom, dear. Your space. The heart of your small palace. The sky is the limit, as they say. Abandon conventions. Forget the palaces of your world. Forget your parents' inn or any other inn. Use your imagination and make it your own. Make it glorious."

The sky is the limit... I closed my eyes and opened my mind. The inn shifted around me, its magic responding. My power flowed from me, and I let it expand and grow, unfurl like a flower.

"Dina...," Caldenia murmured next to me, her voice stunned.

I opened my eyes. Gone was the pink marble, the gold leaf, and the crystal chandeliers. Only three windows, all in the north wall, remained. A glorious night sky spread across the dark walls and the ceiling, endless and beautiful, the light patina of lavender, green, and blue forming gossamer nebulae dotted with tiny flecks of stars. It was the kind of sky that called space pirates to their ships. Long vines spiraled around the turquoise columns that supported the balconies, and delicate glass flowers glowed with white and yellow. The floor was polished white marble, inlaid with a rich mosaic in a dozen shades from black and indigo to an electric blue and gold, stretching to the center where a stylized image of Gertrude Hunt decorated the floor, circled by a depiction of my broom.

I looked up. Above it all three enormous light fixtures came on, each a complex constellation of glowing orbs bathing the room in bright light. I smiled.

"Now that is what I call awe," Caldenia quietly said next to me.

The magic chimed in my head. I opened my eyes. Ten past midnight. A little early for the summit, which was supposed to start tomorrow evening.

I swung my feet out of the bed. I'd gotten an hour of sleep. My head felt too heavy for my neck. I couldn't remember the last time I worked so hard. I still wasn't sure if the pits in the otrokar rooms were low enough. There was some sort of sacred proportion between the central "pit" area and the height of the plush circular couches around it. I'd consulted my guides and made them to the exact specifications listed, but my gut told me the height was off. It just didn't look right, so I'd spent the last thirty minutes of my day lowering and raising the wooden makeshift couches before I had the inn make them in stone. It would all be worth it.

Another phantom tug, like ripples in a shallow pond. Someone stood at the end of my driveway, just inside the inn grounds, waiting politely to be invited in.

I got up and slipped on my innkeeper robe. A simple gray affair with a hood, it hid me from head to toe. Beast raised her head from her post by my bed and let out a quiet, sleepy bark. I checked the window. A dark figure stood by the front hedge, melding with the thick night shadow of an oak. It would be tall for a human. Probably a couple of inches taller than Sean.

Ugh.

I picked up my broom and left the bedroom, walking down the long hallway to the front staircase. Beast trotted next to me. The architecture of the inn had changed so much in the past few hours, my trek to the front door nearly doubled.

The floor was cool under my bare feet. The rain was still falling, and the inn and I agreed on a comfortable seventy degrees inside, but as in any house, some spots were warmer and some cooler, and I wished I had worn socks.

Why did I even think of Sean Evans?

Sean was an alpha-strain werewolf. His parents had escaped the destruction of their home planet and come to Earth where they built a life, had Sean, and raised him, all in secret. Earth served as a waypoint for many travelers from the Great Beyond. The universe, with all its planets, dimensions, and timelines, needed its central hub to be a neutral place to meet, do business, or sometimes simply stop over on the way to somewhere else. Earth had served this role for thousands of years while its native population lived in complete ignorance of the strange beings who sometimes visited the planet in twilight. That's why inns and innkeepers like me existed. We had only two concerns: keeping our guests safe and keeping them hidden. We stayed neutral and we didn't get involved. Sean Evans had entered my life when I'd chosen to throw caution to the wind and involved myself in something really dangerous.

In retrospect it was probably foolish, but I didn't regret it. Together, Sean, Arland, and I had saved my small town from an interstellar assassin. Arland got to avenge a murder as an added bonus, and Sean learned the truth: he wasn't an Earthborn mutation like his parents had told him, but a product of a military genetic breeding program from another planet. All werewolves were soldiers designed to repel a planetwide invasion by an overwhelming force, but Sean was an alpha-strain variant. Bigger, faster, stronger, a Special Forces kind of warrior. The genetic programming must've held true, because he became a soldier here on Earth, but he could never quite find the right place for himself.

Then we met, and I thought we had something.

No, that would be wishful thinking. We had the beginning of something, but once he glimpsed the universe beyond this planet, it was all over. The werewolves had destroyed their own planet rather than surrender it to their enemy, and he could never go "home," but the stars called him. Because of me he ended up owing an old werewolf a favor, and once the danger here had been dealt with, Sean left to repay his debt. I knew the pull of the stars. I'd answered it myself for a while. When he walked through a portal to the sun-drenched streets of Baha-char, some part of me knew he wouldn't be coming back anytime soon, but still I hoped he might be back in a month or two. It's been almost half a year now. Sean was gone.

I'd decided to put him out of my mind, and for the most part I completely succeeded, but sometimes he just popped into my head. I'd glance at the back patio, remember him jumping three feet in the air when I moved it, and smile. Or I'd recall his voice. Or how it felt to be kissed by him.

"I can't help it," I told Beast. "It will get better. It just needs time."

If Beast had an opinion about my occasional involuntary mooning, she kept it to herself.

I opened the front door and strode down the grass to the dark figure waiting for me by the oak. He stood swaddled in a cloak. He seemed tall when I looked at him from above, but on the same level he was towering, six five at least. I had to tilt my head. Beast growled low.

The dark figure raised his left hand, fingers up. "Winter sun." His voice was rough, but his diction was flawless. Whatever translator he was using worked perfectly.

An otrokar. "Winter sun to you as well." Winter sun was the kinder, gentler sun. "Welcome."

We walked back to the front door, and I let him in.

He shrugged off the cloak. I'd seen an otrokar before. They'd frequented my parents' inn. But having him here in my small front room was an entirely different experience.

His shoulders were broad, his stance light despite his size. A dark brown armor of braided leather strips clasped his body. Hard plates dappled with sprays of black and red in an organic pattern only a living creature could produce shielded his forearms, thighs, and shins. The same plates guarded his chest, the chitinous substance streaked through with complex swirls of golden metal that announced the presence of high-tech electronics. A belt with pockets sat on his waist, and small metal, bone, and wooden talismans hung from it. Otrokars were excellent spacers, and his was the kind of armor designed to protect while still letting one bend and flex when fighting within the confines of a space-craft. He carried no weapons except for a short sword or a long knife that rested in a sheath on his right thigh.

From the back he could almost pass for a really tall native, but his face made it clear—this was the same primary human seed that had given rise to us and vampires, but it had clearly grown on a different planet. Otrokars had evolved on a world with a scorching sun and endless plains. They hunted in packs and ran their prey to ground. The planes of his face were sharper than those of the Earthborn, as if he had been hacked with a knife from a piece of clay; the texture of his deep bronze skin rougher; the proportions of his features skewed slightly, giving him a dangerous, predatory air. His jaw was triangular, his nose narrow, and when he spoke, his lips showed a narrow flash of sharp teeth. His short hair, coarse like the mane of a horse, seemed black until it caught the light and shone with the deep, violent red of a pigeon's-blood ruby. His eyes, under thick eyebrows, were a startling light green.

We looked at each other. Beast growled low by my feet. She clearly didn't like his smell. The otrokar glanced at her, his eyes evaluating. He looked like a man who expects to be jumped at any moment, and he wanted there to be no doubt that he'd pull his knife out and slice his attacker to narrow ribbons.

"What can I do for you?" Stop sizing up my dog, please.

"My name is Dagorkun." The otrokar raised his hand. A golden medallion studded with jewels hung from a leather cord clasped in his fingers. A stylized sun with stabbing rays, the symbol of the Khan, the leader of the Horde.

I inclined my head. "I'm honored."

"I'm here on behalf of my people to inspect the rooms."

"Very well. Would you like some tea as we walk?"

He blinked. "Yes."

"It will only take a moment." I stepped into the kitchen. Some things were constant in the universe. Two and two didn't always equal four, but every water-based species at some point had heated water and thrown some plants into it.

Dagorkun followed me into the kitchen. I took two mugs from the cupboard, one with strawberries on it and the other with a small black cat, filled them with hot water from the Keurig, and put two bags of chai in to soak. Dagorkun watched me like a hawk. Clearly he expected to be poisoned.

"Is this your first time on Earth?"

He waited for a long moment, obviously deciding if it was wise to answer. "Yes."

"You are now a guest of my inn. Your safety is my utmost priority." I fished the tea bags out, opened a sugar canister made of thick blue glass, and put a spoonful of the sugar into my chai. "Neither my dog nor my inn will hurt you unless you attempt to harm another guest."

"The vampires recommend you," Dagorkun said.

I spooned sugar into his cup. One, two... "Yes, but that doesn't mean I'll treat them any differently than your people. I'm a neutral party."

Three... Four ought to do it. He looked like a northerner to me. The southern Otrokars had a greener undertone to their skin. I offered him the cup. He picked it up carefully.

"What if you stopped being neutral?"

"The rating of my inn would be downgraded. It would become known that this was an unsafe place to stay. No guests would visit, and without guests, the inn would wither, fall into hibernation, and die."

"And the witch?"

"Which witch?"

"The old witch who stays with you."

Most people would've taken "witch" as a slur, but for an otrokar a witch meant someone of great dark power. He was simply giving Her Grace the respect she had earned.

"Caldenia won't interfere with the peace talks. This inn and I are the only reason she is still alive. She'll do nothing to jeopardize that."

Dagorkun mulled it over, raised the cup to his lips, and sipped. His eyes lit up. "Good."

"Shall we see to the rooms?"

He nodded. I led him through the front room to a simple hallway. It matched the front of the house perfectly: wooden floor and plain beige walls. And the portrait of my parents in the dead center, in a small alcove just as you walk through the doorway. I'd moved it there just for this occasion. Dagorkun glanced at them. I scrutinized his face. No reaction.

One day someone would walk through this doorway, see my parents, and recognize them. When that happened, I would be ready. I just needed a faint trail, a crumb, some drop of information that told me where to start looking for them. I would not stop until I found them.

We turned right, walked a few feet to another plain doorway, and stepped through it. Dagorkun stopped. A curving stairway of dark wood led up, its rail decorated with carved, stylized animals: the long-legged three-horned stag; the kair, a wolflike predator; the massive armor-plated garuz that looked like a three-horned rhino on steroids... I'd gone right down the list of the otrokar heraldry in the traditional order. Light fixtures imitating torches glowed in their sconces on the dark walls streaked with red and gold. Colorful banners of the Hope-Crushing Horde hung between them.

"Does the stairway meet with your approval?" I asked.

"It will suffice," Dagorkun said carefully.

"Please." I pointed to the stairs.

He started up the steps. Here's hoping the pits were deep enough.

Twenty minutes later, we established that the pits were perfectly proportioned, the faux-silk pillows were sufficiently soft and in the correct array of colors, the arched windows were properly ornate, and the view of the orchard, which had required enough dimensional finagling to make an entire university of theoretical physicists beg for mercy, was stimulating enough. The orchard was visible from every new guest room I had built for the summit, which should've been impossible, but I never bothered too much with the laws of physics anyway. If they decided to jump out of their windows, they would end up in my orchard behind the house and out of sight of the main road and subdivision. Not that I had any intention of letting anyone exit the inn without my knowledge.

By the end of the tour, Dagorkun had relaxed enough to stop continuously checking corners for hidden assassins. We were almost back to my front room when the inn chimed. I glanced out the window just in time to catch the last glimpse of a familiar red flash. Oh no.

"We have company," I told Dagorkun. "Excuse me, please."

I walked to the front door and opened it. A massive figure filled the doorway, broad-shouldered and clad in black armor shot through with blood-red, which made him look enormous. His blond hair spilled onto his back like a lion's mane. His face, masculine with a heavy, square jaw, was handsome enough to make you pause.

"My lady Dina." His voice was rich and resonant, the kind of voice that would overpower the roar of battle, which was fitting since he was the Marshal of House Krahr and had to snarl orders in the middle of battle quite frequently.

"Lord Arland," I said. "Please enter."

Arland stepped through and saw Dagorkun. The two of them froze.

"Hello, Arland," Dagorkun said. No traditional sun greeting, huh?

"Hello, Dagorkun," Arland said.

The vampire and otrokar glared at each other. A moment passed. Another. If they kept this up, the floor between them would catch on fire.

I sighed. "Would the two of you like some tea?"

The vampire and the otrokar stared at each other over the rims of their cups. Arland was built like a saber-toothed tiger: huge, powerful, and strong. Dagorkun was taller than him by a couple of inches, and while his build was not quite as massive, he was corded with muscle. Neither of them seemed especially worried. They were just sitting there politely, drinking tea and trying to strangle each other with pure will.

"How is your father?" Arland asked, his voice nonchalant, each word precise.

"The Khan is well," Dagorkun answered. "How is Lady Ilemina?"

"She's well also."

"That's good to hear. Will she be joining us?"

Arland raised his thick eyebrows. "No, she must attend to matters elsewhere. Will the Khan grace us with his presence?"

"Likewise, the Khan has many responsibilities," Dagorkun answered. "He sends the Khanum in his stead."

So, Arland's mother wasn't coming but Dagorkun's was. The Guide to Major Powers, which I had purchased during the summer and which had cost me an arm and a leg, listed Lady Ilemina as the Preceptor of House Krahr together with two pages of her titles and decorations, some of which included words like "Slaughterer of" and "Supreme Predator of." The Khanum had an equally long list of titles studded with gems like "Spinebreaker" and "Gut Ripper." All things considered, I was glad only one of them was coming.

Having their sons sitting across from each other, sipping tea and wishing they could drop all pretense and just tear each other's head off was difficult enough. I finally realized the full extent of the mess I'd gotten into. When there were twelve or more individuals from each side, keeping them from violence was going to be almost impossible. This is exactly why Caldenia thought these peace talks were going to be great. My imagination painted a huge brawl in the ballroom and Her Grace quietly sneaking off with a bloody body.

"The Khanum?" Arland coughed. The last sip of tea must've gone down wrong.

"Are you unwell?" Dagorkun inquired.

"Healthy as a Krahr," Arland said.

"That's such a relief. I would hate for some illness to interfere and spoil the grand celebration I have planned for when I send you to your afterlife."

"Really?" Arland's eyes narrowed. "I'd think my succumbing to an illness would be a blessing, as that is the only way you could manage such a feat. I daresay, it would have to be a *severe* illness, and even then I fear the chances of your victory would be remote."

The otrokar clicked his tongue. "Such hubris, Marshal."

"I detest false modesty."

"Perhaps we can test this theory?" Dagorkun offered.

Okay, that's just enough of that. "I am glad the rooms were to your liking, Under-Khan. Unfortunately, I must ask you to depart, so the Marshal of House Krahr can inspect the quarters of his people."

Dagorkun's eyes narrowed. "And if I insisted on staying?"

Thin, brilliant blue cracks formed in the handle of my broom. The floor in front of Dagorkun shifted, fluid as the sea. "Then I'll seal your body in wood, so all you can do is breathe, and use you as a lawn ornament."

Dagorkun blinked.

"This summit is very important to me," I explained.

The wall behind me creaked as the inn bent toward Dagorkun, responding to the tone of my voice. The otrokar's hand went to his knife.

I waved my fingers and the wall snapped back to its normal state. "I won't let anyone or anything interfere with the peace talks in my domain."

Arland set his cup on the table. "You should test her, Dagorkun. She couldn't possibly be that powerful."

I pointed the handle of my broom at him. The vampire grinned, flashing his fangs, and chuckled.

"I see." Dagorkun rose. "Thank you for the tea, Innkeeper."

I solidified the floor and led him to the door. He pulled on his cloak and walked into the night. I waited until the inn announced his departure and turned to Arland.

"Ours is an old rivalry," he said. "You can't blame us. They are barbarians. Do you know how one becomes a Khan? One would expect a proper progression—a ruler's son, learning statecraft at his father's knee, studying with the best tutors, gaining experience under the guidance of talented generals on the battlefield, building alliances, until finally he takes his rightful place, supported by his power base. One would expect this, but no. They elect him. The army gathers and votes." He spread his arms. "It's ridiculous."

Of course hereditary aristocracy was much better. That never went wrong. How silly of them to try this thing called democracy. I wondered what he would say if I reminded him that the U.S. was a republic. "Shall we see to the rooms?"

"It would be my pleasure."

Arland rose, and I led him to the hallway. We turned left this time. The hallway brought us to the formal stairway of pale gray stone. Crimson banners of the Holy Cosmic Anocracy hung on the walls, illuminated by delicate glass ornaments that glowed with gentle, pale light.

Arland raised his thick eyebrows. "Just like home."

Perfect. We started up the stairway.

"Six months ago, House Krahr was going stale from the lack of war," I said. "Now suddenly you're involved in the Nexus Conflict? What happened?"

Arland grimaced. "House Meer happened. What is taking place on Nexus isn't a war; it's hell. It's been going on for almost a decade, and it's too much for any one House. About a year into this war, the Holy Anocracy divided the Houses into seven Orders to share the burden of the conflict. Each Order takes the responsibility for Nexus for a year. House Krahr is the House of the First Order. We already fought on Nexus five years ago. We didn't expect to return so soon."

Every time he said Nexus, he paused for a tiny second the way one would before saying *Hell* in the true sense of that word. Five standard years ago he would've been a seasoned knight. It must've been terrible, because the memories of it still haunted him.

The stairs ended in a stone arch. The walls there rose to a dizzying height and the bloodred banner of the Holy Anocracy hung from the ceiling with the Holy Fangs and the eight-point star emblazoned in silver on it. The star commemorating the vampire progress to interstellar flight wasn't above or below the stylized fangs but sat between them. The symbolism was clear: the Holy Anocracy would bite the galaxy with its fangs and swallow it. Without a word, Arland lowered himself on one knee and bowed his head. He closed his eyes for a moment, then rose, as if the heavy armor he wore was light as silk. We stepped through the arch.

"Two months ago the Sixth Order was scheduled to take over, but the two major Houses of the Sixth Order had been decimated, one by a war and the other by a planetwide natural disaster. They had neither the means nor the power to mount a suitable defense against the otrokar offensive. They were willing, but it was determined that we would lose our hold on Nexus if they bore the sole responsibility for it. The duty should've passed to the Seventh Order. The Seventh Order consists of four Houses, with House Meer being by far the most powerful. House Meer dishonored itself and refused to fight. Given that the other three houses in the Order are small, and two of them are also warring with each other at the moment, the responsibility for Nexus passed on to us."

I frowned. "House Meer can do that?"

"Not without repercussions. The Anocracy will excommunicate them and level economic sanctions, but they are willing to risk it. They've been eyeing our holdings for years. When we come off the Nexus rotation, our House will be exhausted. It will take us years to recover. House Meer will attack us when we're at our weakest, and the riches they rip from our corpse will more than offset any economic sanctions. The Anocracy embraces victory and shuns defeat. The Preceptor of Meer may sacrifice his eternal soul on the altar of betrayal, but his descendants will be welcomed back into the fold of the Holy Church."

Yes, they would be too powerful and too rich to remain ostracized. "On Earth we say that history is written by the winners."

Arland nodded. "I've spent the past two months on that cursed planet. I've lost men, I've lost family, and I don't intend to lose anyone else. If I have to make peace with the Horde, so be it. It would be infinitely easier if the Khan were coming himself instead of the Khanum. The Khan is a great warrior and a great leader; he understands diplomacy and he is the man the Horde wants to follow into the slaughter. The Khanum is a great general; she plans their wars and their battles, which the Khan then leads. I do not relish dealing with Dagorkun's mother."

He stopped. Bright rooms of pale stone spread before us, the lines elegant and powerful. Green vines drooped from the tall ledges, cascading to the floor of polished stone. Massive dark wood furniture, sturdy and simple, offered a place to rest, its upholstery and linens crimson and white. Floor-to-ceiling windows opened onto narrow stone balconies. It was a serene place, elegant and beautiful to behold the way a honed, functional blade was beautiful.

Arland turned around, his face puzzled. "This is Zamak, our House's coastal castle."

"It's a duplicate," I said. "Unfortunately, I couldn't reproduce the sea, but I was told the view of the orchard is soothing. Does it meet with your approval?"

"It's perfect."

Yes. Great. Wonderful. Fantastic.

"How will the meal orders be handled?"

My stomach tried to pirouette out of me. Somehow I made my lips move. "Should any of your party have special dietary needs, please list them for me, and I will do my best to meet them."

"Absolutely."

Ten minutes later, I watched Arland step into a bright red glow, turn into a star, and shoot up to the night sky. The inn chimed in my head, informing me of his departure, and I sagged against the doorframe.

The food. I had forgotten about the food.

What was I going to do?

CHAPTER THREE

Most successful inns had a staff. Some jobs required a dedicated person: usually there was a chef, a bookkeeper, sometimes a kennel master if the inn catered to guests with animal companions. Typically the innkeeper's family handled many of these tasks. In my parents' inn, I'd worked as a gardener. It was my responsibility to keep the vast flower gardens, service the ponds, and maintain the fruit trees. I loved the gardens. They were full of small secret places that were just mine. My memory served the delicate scent of apricots in bloom, their dark crooked branches bearing small white flowers; rows of strawberries; the two yellow cherry trees I used to climb… All of it was gone now, disappeared without a proverbial trace, together with the inn and my parents within it. One day the inn that used to be my home simply vanished. Nobody knew how or why.

A familiar pang pierced me, worry mixed with anxiety and a dash of mourning. I missed my parents so much. So much. It had been years, and still sometimes I woke up, and in those drowsy, half-asleep moments, I thought I heard Mom's voice calling me down for breakfast.

I was in a different inn now, my own inn. Up until this moment, Gertrude Hunt hadn't needed a staff. I cooked for Caldenia, myself, and whatever rare guest happened to stop by. Cooking for two people and cooking for a party of at least forty, counting the Arbitrator's staff, with at least four different species in attendance, was completely different. Not only that, but with otrokars and vampires in the same building, all my attention would be occupied with keeping them from killing each other. And they would expect a banquet. Of course they would. We didn't even have a definite date for the end of the summit. I might end up feeding them for weeks.

I couldn't do it. It wasn't feasible. I had to hire a cook, but a cook good enough to prepare a banquet for four different species would cost a fortune because he wouldn't be a cook, he would be a chef. I had set funds aside for the food, but somehow in all my preparations it never occurred to me that someone would have to be cooking it. I hadn't budgeted for a chef. Where could I even find a chef with less than twenty-four hours to go? It took weeks to find and hire one.

I could imagine the ad now. *Hi, my name is Dina. I run a small inn on Earth, two and a half stars, and I need you to drop everything and prepare meals for a party of otrokars, vampires, and spoiled Merchants. I have a shoestring budget and your pay would be a pittance.*

I groaned. Beast barked at me, puzzled.

I looked at the tiny Shih Tzu. "What am I going to do?"

My dog furiously wagged her tail.

I blew air out. Panicking never solved anything. I had to go about fixing the problem in a logical fashion. First hurdle, money. Where could I get some money to hire a chef?

The only money I had, besides the food fund, was the inn's six-month budget. Guests came and went, and an innkeeper's income was usually somewhat erratic. My parents had taught me to always budget six months ahead and to never touch that money. If I dipped into that budget, I wouldn't be able to cover utilities in the upcoming months, and nobody would visit an inn without running water or electricity. We had backup generators, but they were an emergency measure. If I used that money, I'd be breaking one of my parents' most fundamental rules.

Was there any way around it? Any way at all?

No.

No, there wasn't. I couldn't take out a business loan because my business didn't generate enough income to qualify me for one and because business loans and lines of credit took several days to process. Personal loans were out of the question too. Asking other innkeepers for financial assistance wasn't an option. It wasn't done. Besides, without a solid track record, and the inn only rated at two and a half stars, I was a bad business risk. All things considered, I wouldn't lend myself money.

There was simply no other money to be had. I had to feed the guests. Vampires required meat with fresh herbs, otrokars had to have spices and citrus with everything, and Nuan Cee's clan had a taste for poultry, and they were particular about how it was prepared. I had to hire someone, whatever it cost.

Realizing that was like dipping my head into a bucket of ice water. If there was no other way, then there was nothing I could do about it. I had to use that money and pray it would be enough to entice someone to work through the summit.

"One problem solved," I told Beast.

Now hurdle number two. The chef.

My parents knew many innkeepers, but were friends with only a few. Our kind were a solitary lot. Innkeepers operated in secrecy. Deals were done on a handshake, meetings usually took place face-to-face, and each inn was its own little island of strange in a sea of normal. When my parents' inn had vanished, even our former friends distanced themselves. What had happened was odd and unexpected; nobody had ever heard of an entire inn simply blinking out of existence. Odd and unexpected was dangerous, and for people who dealt with the universe's weirdness on a daily basis, most innkeepers were surprisingly risk averse.

I was on my own, but I did know one man who could help. His name was Brian Rodriguez. An innkeeper like me, he ran Casa Feliz in Dallas, one of the largest, busiest inns in the Southwest. Like others, he had been a friend of my parents. A few months ago, when I went to ask him for advice out of pure desperation, he helped me. Since then we'd corresponded a few times and he had given me his cell phone number, a huge sign of trust in our world. Begging him for money was out of the question, but asking for a loan of staff wasn't unheard of.

I dialed the number on my cell. He answered on the second ring. "Dina, how are you?"

"I'm fine," I lied. "How are you?"

"Surviving. What can I do for you?"

"I'm so sorry to ask this, but I need a cook on short notice." I really didn't want to say what I had to say next. The words stuck in my mouth, but I forced them out. "Could you lend me one?"

He didn't miss a beat. "What grade?"

"The highest I can get."

Mr. Rodriguez paused. "Are you hosting the Nexus summit?"

"Yes." News traveled fast.

"They asked me and I declined. The risk to my other guests would be too great."

I was well aware of the risks, but I had no choice.

"Unfortunately…"

My heart sank.

"...all of my kitchen staff is really busy. We're short-handed at the moment."

I fought hard to keep despair out of my voice. "Thank you anyway."

"So happens I know someone who might help," he said. "If you're desperate enough."

What? My hopes soared. "I'm very desperate."

"He was ranked as a Red Cleaver a few years ago."

My hopes plunged to the ground, hit hard, and exploded. "I can't afford a Red Cleaver chef."

Mr. Rodriguez probably couldn't afford a Red Cleaver. That was the second-highest ranking. I couldn't even afford a Gray Cleaver, which was the lowest rung. A Cleaver ranking meant certification by the Galactic Gastronomy Board, a diploma from the best cooking school in the galaxy, and a long apprenticeship in one of the most prestigious restaurants. Cleaver chefs were worth their weight in gold, literally.

"He was stripped of his certification."

I'd never heard of someone losing their Cleaver. "Why?"

Mr. Rodriguez hesitated. "He might have poisoned someone."

I put my hand over my face. This was just getting better and better. A poisoner chef. What could possibly go wrong?

"Dina, are you there?" Mr. Rodriguez asked.

"Yes. I'm just wrestling with it."

"I warned you that you would have to be desperate. I don't believe he was ever convicted of the crime, but somehow he was involved in the death of a diplomat. You would have to talk to him to get the whole story."

With my back against the wall, I didn't have options. The least I could do was talk to him. "Where can I find him?"

"He lives in a small hole-in-the-wall hovel on Baha-char. Just past the Gorivian gun merchant."

"I know where that is. Thank you."

"Oh, and Dina, he is a Quillonian. They can be touchy."

That was the understatement of the year. Quillonians were notoriously difficult.

"I hope it works out."

He hung up. I slumped against the wall. Tired or not, I needed to go and see this touchy, dishonored Quillonian chef who might or might not have poisoned someone, because the Arbitrator was due to arrive the following evening.

I had quite possibly bitten off more than I could chew. No, thinking like that would only get me into trouble. It was the fatigue talking. I would host this summit, and it would be successful. Gertrude Hunt needed the guests.

I got my boots out of the closet, put them on, and buckled a belt with a knife on it around my waist under my robe. Baha-char was the place where you went to find things. Sometimes things found you instead and tried to take your money. On the inn grounds, I ruled supreme. Outside them, my powers dropped off sharply. I could still take care of myself, but it never hurt to expect the worst and be prepared.

Beast barked once, excited. I took my broom, pulled the hood of my robe over my head, and headed down the hallway. The inn creaked in alarm.

"I'll be back soon," I murmured. "Don't worry."

The door at the end of the hallway swung open. Bright light spilled through the rectangular opening, and dry, overbearing heat washed over me. I blinked as my eyes adjusted to the light, and Beast and I stepped into the heat and sunshine of Baha-char.

❖ ❖ ❖

I strode through the heat-baked streets of the Galactic Bazaar, the hem of my robe sweeping the large yellow tiles of its roads. Around me the marketplace of the galaxy breathed and glittered, its heart beating fast, pulsing with life. Tall buildings of pale, sand-colored stone lined the streets, decorated with bright banners streaming from the balconies. Plants, some green, some blue, others red and magenta, spread their branches on the textured terraces, offering cascades of flowers to the sun in the light purple sky. Above me narrow stone arches of bridges spanned the space between the buildings. Merchant booths offering a bounty of goods from across the universe lined the through-way. Open doors marked by bright signs invited customers. Barkers hawked their wares, waving holographic projections of their merchandise at the crowd flowing past them.

Around me the bright, multicolored crocodile of shoppers crawled through the streets. Beings from dozens of planets and dimensions, clothed in leather, fabric, metal or plastic, tall and short, huge and small, each with their own odd scent, searched for their particular goods. A constant hum hung in the air, a cacophony of hundreds of voices mixing together into the kind of noise that could only be heard on Baha-char.

The last time I had come here, Sean was with me. I didn't even know if he was dead or alive. It had been so fun to watch him here. He had traveled while in the military, and he thought he was worldly, then I opened the door to these sun-drenched streets, and Sean turned into a child entering Disney World for the first time. Everything was new, strange, and wondrous.

Six months and no word. Either I'd imagined things and he wasn't at all interested, or something had happened to him. Thinking about Sean being dead somewhere out there among the stars made me angry. First my parents vanished. Now Sean was gone.

I caught myself. Yes, clearly this was all about me. Not exactly my proudest moment. As soon as I straightened out the chef situation, I needed to go back to bed before the lack of sleep made me weepy.

Ahead, the traffic slowed. I stood on my toes and glanced over the spindly shoulder of some insectoid being. A creature that resembled a Penske truck-sized maggot slowly crawled up the street. It was wearing a plastic harness along its back. Bright burgundy and gold umbrellas protruded from the harness at even intervals, shielding its wrinkled, pallid flesh from the sun. Several shopping bags hung from the hooks on the sides of the harness. One of the bags had Hello Kitty on it.

We were moving about half a mile an hour. I sighed and looked around. I'd been coming to Baha-char since I was a child, and most of the time I walked through on autopilot.

A familiar dark archway loomed to the right. I strained and heard a quiet, haunting melody playing. That shop belonged to Wilmos Gerwar, an old werewolf. Last time we were on Baha-char, Sean had stopped here. Wilmos had a nanoarmor on display, made especially for alpha-strain werewolves such as Sean. Sean saw the armor and became obsessed with it. It called to him somehow, and he had to have it. Wilmos offered him a deal: he would give Sean the armor, but Sean would owe him a favor. I thought it was a terrible idea and told him so, but Sean took the armor, and once we dealt with the assassin threatening the inn, he went to Baha-char to repay the favor. That was the last time I saw him.

If anybody knew where Sean was, it would be Wilmos.

People bumped me. The crowd was moving, and the current of beings tried to carry me with it. To go in or not to go in? What if Sean was in there, drinking tea from Auul, his now-shattered planet? That would be really awkward. *Hi, remember me? I threw you out of my house because you were an ass and later you kissed me?* He'd left for a reason, and I didn't want to be anyone's blast from the past. Still, not knowing was worse than any potential awkwardness.

I cut through the crowd and stepped through the arch. A meticulously arranged shop greeted me. Weapons with wicked curved blades hung on the walls. Knives lay displayed under glass. Strange armor adorned mannequins lined up like soldiers at a ceremony next to high-tech guns in metal racks.

A large animal padded into view, its paws bigger than my hands. Blue green, with a shaggy mane and ears that reached to my chest, it moved like a predator. Despite the size and the mane, there was something lupine about its build. He felt like a wolf, and if you saw him on Earth, you'd think he was the spirit of all wolves come to life.

"Hello, Gorvar," I said.

At my feet Beast opened her mouth and growled low.

"Who is it?" A man walked in from the other room. Tall, grizzled, and still fit, he moved like Sean, with natural, easy grace. His graying hair fell to his shoulders, and as his eyes caught the light from the doorway, pale gold rolled over his irises.

"Hello, Wilmos." I smiled.

"Ah yes. Dina, right?"

"Right."

"What can I do for you?"

"I happened to be in the neighborhood and thought I'd stop by to check on Sean. Haven't seen him for a while." There, that didn't sound too desperate.

"He's out on a cruise with a Solar Shipping freighter," Wilmos said. "He owed me a favor, and I owed a friend of mine. The friend has a shipping route and picks up credit vouchers from a couple of leisure planets, so he gets boarded a lot. He needed a good security person, so I gave him Sean for a year. It's good for him. He wanted to see the glory of the universe, and now he gets a tour."

Hmmm.

"You want me to get word to him?" Wilmos asked. "I can probably leave a message for him. I've got the codes for the freighter."

I gave him a nice, sweet smile. "Sure! That would be great."

Wilmos tapped the glass of the nearest counter. It turned dark, and a small circle with glowing symbols appeared in the corner. "Sorry, it will have to be text only. They're too far out for face-to-face." He tapped the circle, spinning it with his fingertips. An English keyboard ignited at the bottom of the rectangle. I was about to send an interstellar text.

"Go ahead," he said.

I had to send something that only Sean would know. At least I would find out if he was dead or alive. I typed. *It's Dina. The apple trees recovered.*

Wilmos touched a glowing symbol. The message flashed brighter and dimmed. Seconds ticked by. I kept my smile on.

A message flashed in response to mine. *I told you I wasn't poisonous.*

Sean was alive. Nobody else would know that I nearly brained him with my broom for marking his territory in my orchard.

"Anything else?" Wilmos asked. He was trying to be nonchalant, but he was watching me very carefully.

"No, that was it. Much appreciated."

"Anytime. I'm sure he'll visit when he gets shore leave."

"He's welcome anytime and you as well. Come on, Beast."

Beast gave Gorvar one last parting snarl, and we walked out of the shop, joined the crowd, and kept going down the street.

It made no sense. Wilmos built and sold weapons. Some of the gear in his shop looked too new to be antique. He must have a lot of connections in the soldier-for-hire world. When Wilmos recognized Sean, he'd come unglued. Sean was a natural biological child of two alpha-strain werewolves, who weren't supposed to have survived the destruction of their planet. A normal werewolf was bad news, but Sean was stronger, faster, and more deadly than ninety-nine percent of the werewolf refugees strewn across the galaxy. Wilmos had acted as if Sean was a miracle.

"You don't stick a miracle onto a freighter where he'll be a security guard," I told Beast. "There are more exciting ways to see the glory of the universe."

It was like finding the last-known Tasmanian tiger and selling him to some rich guy to be a pet in his backyard. It just didn't add up.

Wilmos didn't want me to know what Sean was doing. I didn't know why, and I really wanted to find out.

It took me almost half an hour to get to the Quillonian's place. The shop owners pointed the door out to me, but it was on the third floor, and I had to find the way up and then the right set of stone bridges to get to the terrace. Quillonians were a reclusive race, proud, prone to drama, and violent when cornered. A couple of them had stayed at my parents' inn, and as long as everything went their way, they were perfectly cordial, but the moment any small problem appeared, they would start putting exclamation marks at the end of all their sentences. My mother didn't like dealing with them. She was very practical. If you brought a problem to her, she'd take it apart and figure out how best to resolve it. From what I remembered, Quillonians didn't always want their problems resolved. They wanted a chance to shake their clawed fists at the sky, invoke their gods, and act as if the world was ending.

My father was brilliant at handling them. Before he became an innkeeper, he was a very good con man, excellent at reading his marks, and he finessed our more difficult guests. Before long, they were eating out of his hand. I tried to remember what he'd said to me about it. What was it? Something about plays...

I crossed the terrace to a stone bridge. The bridge, without a rail and barely two feet wide, terminated in a narrow balcony with a dark wooden door. Deep gouges scoured the wood as if something with superhuman strength and razor-sharp claws had attacked the door in a frenzy. I squinted. The scratches blended into a phrase repeated in several common languages. KEEP OUT. Wonderful.

I leaned and looked over the side. At least a fifty-foot drop to the street. If the Quillonian jumped out of his door and knocked me off the bridge, I would die for sure. I'd be a Dina pancake.

Beast whined.

I picked her up and started across the bridge, taking my time. I didn't mind heights, but I would've liked something to hold on to.

Step, another step. I stepped onto the balcony and knocked. Before I could get the second knock in, the door flew open. A dark shape filled the doorway. I saw two glowing white eyes and a mouth studded with sharp teeth.

The mouth gaped open, and a deep voice roared, "Go away!"

The door slammed shut inches from my face.

I blinked. Really now. I think he actually blew my hair back with that. I knocked again.

The door sprang open, jerked aside by a powerful hand, and teeth snapped in my face. "What? What is it? Do I owe you money? Is that it? There is no money! I have nothing!"

"I need a chef."

There was an outraged pause. "So that's it. You have come to mock me." The dark lips that hid the teeth rose, baring fangs the size of my pinkies. "Maybe I shall COOK YOU FOR DINNER!"

Beast's fur stood straight up. Wicked claws slid from her feet. Her mouth gaped open, unnaturally wide, displaying four rows of razor-sharp teeth. She snapped her teeth and let out a piercing howl. "Awwwreeerooo!"

The Quillonian leaned back, shocked, and roared.

Beast snapped her teeth, lightning fast, biting the air and struggling in my arms. If he slammed the door in our face now, she'd shred it like confetti.

"Stop it, both of you!" I barked.

Beast closed her mouth.

The Quillonian sagged against the doorway. "What is it you want?"

"I need a chef," I repeated.

"Holy Mother of Vengeance, fine. Come inside. You can bring your small demon as well."

I followed him through the doorway into a narrow hallway. The walls were filthy with grime baked into the plaster over the years. The hallway opened into an equally filthy living room. The glass in the windows had been shattered long ego, and a single dark shard stuck out from the top of the frame. Dirt lay in the corners, gathered against the wall like dunes in a desert. A ratty couch sat in the middle of the floor. Soiled high-tech foam stuck out through rips in its upholstery. A pile of wooden slivers filled a singed metal bucket in front of the couch. The Quillonian must make a fire in the bucket when he got cold.

The draft brought a sour, revolting stench. I glanced through the window as I followed my host. Below us stood huge concrete vats. One was filled with what had to be lime and the other with some dark substance. The other three vats held red, blue, and yellow dyes. Tall, birdlike beings waded through the dye vats, stirring something with their feet. It had to be a tannery, which probably meant the substance in the other vat was bird dung. The wind flung another dose of reek at me. I clamped my hand over my mouth and nose and squeezed through the next doorway.

A pristine kitchen lay before me. Its cheap wooden cabinets were so clean they glowed. The countertop, a single slab of simple stone, was polished to a near mirror shine. A butcher block carved out of a plain block of wood held three knives in the corner next to an ancient but clean stove. The contrast was so sudden I stole a glance at the living room to make sure we were still in the same place.

The Quillonian turned toward me, and I finally saw him in the light. Even slightly stooped, he was seven feet tall. Short chocolate-brown fur covered his muscled body in the front, flowing into a dense forest of foot-long spikes on his back. That's why the innkeepers called them Quillonians. Their real name was too difficult to pronounce.

He had a vaguely humanoid torso, but his thick, muscular neck was long and protruded forward. His head was triangular with a canine muzzle terminating in a sensitive black nose. His hands had four fingers and two thumbs, each digit long and elegant. Two-inch-long black claws tipped the fingers. Quillonians were a predatory species, my memory reminded me. They didn't hunt humans, but they wouldn't mind ripping one apart.

"What do you know?" The Quillonian fixed me with his stare. At the door his eyes had appeared completely white, but now I saw a pale turquoise iris with a narrow black pupil.

"You were a Red Cleaver, but you were stripped of your certification because you might have poisoned someone."

"I did *not* poison anyone." The Quillonian shook his head, his quills rustling. "I will explain, and then you can leave and slam the door behind you. I worked at the Blue Jewel on Buharpoor. I don't expect you to know what it is or where it is, so trust me when I say it was a glittering gem of a restaurant in a hotel of mind-boggling luxury."

I could believe it. The implant that let him speak English was clearly high quality.

"We were hosting a gala for the neighboring system. Three thousand beings. I was responsible for all of it. It was going splendidly until my sous chef took a bribe and served one of the princes a poisoned soup. The prince collapsed during the dinner and died."

"So you didn't actually poison anyone?" Why had they stripped him of his rank then?

"That is not the point!" The Quillonian threw his hands up. "I have two million taste buds. I can taste a drop of syrup in a pool of water the size of this building. I know thousands of poisons by taste. Had I sampled the dish before it left my kitchen, I would've detected the poison within it. But I did not taste it. I tasted the ingredients for freshness, I tasted the soup during the preparation, but Soo had worked with me for ten years, and we were serving a banquet to three thousand beings, and I let the soup go. The moment the poison's presence was detected, the entire galaxy knew that I let a dish go out of my kitchen without tasting it."

He slumped against the wall, defeated, one hand over his eyes.

"So let me get this straight. They took your Cleaver because you did not taste the soup?"

"Yes. I did it. I let it go. I waved it on." The Quillonian waved his hand. "Now you know my shame. Two decades of training, a decade of apprenticeship, two decades of being a chef. Accolades I received, dishes I created... I was a rising star, and I threw it all away. I hope you enjoyed tormenting me. The door is that way."

Now it made sense. He was punishing himself. He lived in this filthy hovel above a tannery because that was all he deserved. But his kitchen was still spotless. As much as he wanted to degrade himself, his professional pride wouldn't let him dishonor the kitchen.

"I still need a chef," I told him.

He bared his teeth at me. "Did you not hear? There is no chef here."

"I'm an innkeeper from Earth. I run a very small inn, and I'm hosting a peace summit. I'm desperate for a chef."

He pushed from the wall. The quills on his back stood straight up. "There. Is. No. Chef. Here."

I finally remembered what my father told me about the Quillonians. It just popped into my head. *Shakespeare said, All the world's a stage, and all the men and women merely players. They have their exits and their entrances. So, Dina, let them have their monologue.*

My future chef was an oversized, hysterical hedgehog with a martyr complex. He obviously loved what he did. I had to lure him with work, and I had to let him play his part and show him that it was time to let the martyr go. There was a new role to be played, that of an underdog winning the race.

"Three parties to the summit," I said. "At least twelve members each, probably more. The Holy Anocracy represented by House Krahr and others, with at least one Marshal in attendance. All of them are used to the finest cuisine available." That wasn't exactly true. Vampires were a carnivorous species. Their cuisine was sophisticated, but they were perfectly happy to bite through the neck of some random woodland creature, pop it on a stick, and scorch it over a fire.

The Quillonian looked at me. I had his attention.

"The second party to the summit is the Hope-Crushing Horde. The Khanum will be present."

The Quillonian blinked. "Herself?"

"Herself, and with some Under-Khans."

His eyes widened. He was thinking about it. Maybe...

The Quillonian slumped back against the wall and shook his head. "No. Just no. I am not who I once was."

That's okay. "Also, the Merchants of Baha-char. They are spoiled with wealth, and their palate is very refined."

"Which clan?"

"The Nuan Cee's family. In addition to them, the Arbitrator and his party."

I could almost feel the calculation taking place in his head. "For how long?"

"I'm not sure," I said honestly.

"What's the budget?"

"Ten thousand to start."

"Earth currency, the dollar?"

"Yes."

"Impossible!"

"Perhaps for an ordinary cook. But not for a Red Cleaver chef."

"I am no longer that." He rolled his eyes to sky. "Somewhere the gods are laughing at me."

Time to find out if I'd read him correctly. "It's not a joke. It's a challenge."

His eyes went completely white. He stared at me. Come on, take the bait.

"I can't." He closed his eyes and shook. "I just can't. The shame, it's too…"

"I understand. You're right, it is too much for anyone but a true master of his art."

He surged forward. "Are you implying I am anything less?"

"Are you?"

He sighed. "What happened to your previous chef?"

"Usually I cook. But this is beyond my abilities. I will be very busy trying to keep our esteemed guests from murdering each other."

"What about the front of the house?" he asked.

"We won't need it. The inn will serve the dinner following your commands."

He opened his mouth.

"I came here to find a chef," I said. "I'm not leaving without one."

"My spirit is broken."

I held my hands up. "This kitchen says otherwise."

He looked around as if seeing the kitchen for the first time.

"It may not be the Blue Jewel, but it is the kitchen of a chef who takes pride in his work. You can come with me and triumph against impossible odds, or you can reject the challenge of the gods and stay here. Would you rather be a hero in charge of your own destiny or a martyr wallowing in self-pity? What will it be?"

⚜ ⚜ ⚜

The Quillonian surveyed my kitchen. I wasn't familiar enough with Quillonian faces to identify his expression with one hundred percent accuracy, but if I had to guess, it would fall somewhere between shock, disgust, and despair.

The Quillonian heaved a deep sigh. "You expect me to cook *here?*"

"Yes."

He closed his eyes for a long moment. "Pantry?" he asked, his eyes still closed.

"Through there." I pointed at the door in the wall.

He opened his eyes, glanced at the doorway through which we'd come and which showed the wall to be about six inches wide, and stared at the door. "Is this a joke?"

"No."

His clawed hand closed over the handle, and he resolutely flung it open. A five-hundred-square-foot space stretched in front of him, its nine-foot-high walls lined with metal shelves supporting an assortments of pots, pans, dishes, and cooking utensils. Dry goods waited like soldiers on parade, each in a clear plastic container with a label. An industrial-size chest freezer sat against the wall next to two refrigerators.

The Quillonian closed the door, marched back to the doorway, examined the wall, came back, and opened the door again. He stared at the pantry for a long moment, shut the door quickly, and jerked it back open. The pantry was still there. Magic was a wonderful thing.

The Quillonian carefully extended his left leg and put his foot onto the floor of the pantry as if expecting it to grow teeth and gulp him down. Contrary to his expectations, the floor remained solid.

"Well?" I asked.

"It will suffice," he said. "Whom shall I expect to serve this morning?"

"Caldenia and me. Possibly the Arbitrator and his party as well. He mentioned three people."

"Caldenia?" His spikes stood up. "Caldenia ka ret Magren? *Letere Olivione?*"

"Yes. Will that be a problem?"

"I have never had the pleasure to serve her, but I certainly know of her. She's one of the most renowned gastronomes in the galaxy. Her palate is the definition of refinement."

I wondered what he would say if he knew the owner of that refined palate frequently indulged in bingeing on Mello Yello and Funyuns. "The inn will help you. If you need something, ask for it." I raised my voice. "I need a two-liter pot, please."

The correct pot slid to the front of the middle shelf.

"I'll need a gastronomical coagulator, please," the Quillonian said.

Nothing moved. The Quillonian glanced at me. "Nothing's happening."

"We don't have one." The only coagulator I knew about was used in surgeries.

"You expect me to serve vampires and Caldenia without a coagulator?"

"Yes."

"Immersion circulator?"

"No."

"A spherification device?"

"I don't even know what that is."

"It's a device that creates spheres by submerging drops of a liquid in a solution such as calcium chloride, causing the drops to form a solid skin over the liquid center. They pop in your mouth under the pressure of your teeth."

I shook my head.

"Do you at least possess an electromagnetic scale?"

"No."

He shook his hands. "Well, what do you have?"

"Pots, pans, knives, bowls, measuring cups, and silverware. Also some baking pans and molds."

The Quillonian rocked back and stared at the ceiling. "The gods are mocking me."

Not again. "It's a challenge."

He flexed his arms, his elbows bent, his clawed arms pointing to the sky. "Very well. Like a primitive savage who sets out to tame the wilderness armed with nothing but a knife and his indomitable will, I will persevere. I will wrestle victory from the greedy jaws of defeat. I shall rise like a bird of prey upon the current of the wind, my talons raised for the kill, and I shall strike true."

Oh wow. I hope the inn filmed that.

"When do you normally have your morning meal?"

The clock told me it was four in the morning. "In about three hours."

"Breakfast shall be served in three hours." He hung his head. "You may call me Orro. Good day."

"Good day, Chef."

I left the kitchen and went up the stairway. I was so tired I'd start to hallucinate if I didn't get some sleep.

Caldenia emerged from her side of the stairs. "Dina, there you are."

"Yes, Your Grace?"

A metal pot banged in the kitchen.

Caldenia frowned. "Wait, if you are here, who is in the kitchen?"

"Daniel Boone, cooking with his talons."

"I love your sense of humor. Who is it really?"

"A Quillonian former Red Cleaver chef. His name is Orro, and he'll be handling the food for the banquet."

Caldenia smiled. "A Quillonian chef. My dear, you shouldn't have. Well, you should have months ago, but one mustn't be petty. Finally. I shall be dining in a style to which I am suited. Fantastic. Does he have moral scruples? I am reasonably sure this summit will result in at least one murder, and I have never tasted an otrokar."

"Let me get back to you on that."

I walked to my room, took off my shoes, my robe, and my jeans, collapsed into my bed, and fell asleep.

CHAPTER FOUR

The inn woke me up fifteen minutes before six, and I crawled into the shower, which nicely banished my sleepiness but did nothing for my face. My skin was puffy, the bags under my sunken-in eyes certainly weren't Prada, and I generally looked like I'd had a weeklong drunken binge and was just now coming out of my stupor. There was no time to fix it, so I brushed some mascara on my eyelashes, dabbed some powder here and there, put on light workout pants and a loose T-shirt in case I had to move really fast, and grabbed my favorite robe. Dark blue, very elastic, and beautifully light, it was made from spider silk and had higher tensile strength than Kevlar. Wearing it was like wrapping yourself in silk armor. It wouldn't stop a bullet, but it would block a knife. My mother had given it to me for my eighteenth birthday.

Sadness gripped me, so intense I stopped, holding the robe in my hands. I wanted my mother back. I wanted her back right now, right this second, as if I had reverted to my childhood, and like a scared toddler, I wanted to hug her and let her make everything okay.

I exhaled, trying to get rid of the sudden ache in my chest. If I had any hope of getting my parents back, I had to get more guests into my inn. At least forty of them would arrive today, and I would scrutinize their faces as they passed by my parents' portrait. I slipped my robe on.

Robes were the traditional garb of an innkeeper. My father used to say they served dual purposes: they hid your body so people had a harder time targeting you, and they gave you "a certain air of mystery." I would need the air of mystery. The three parties to this summit would be bringing their best people. Each vampire was a fortress unto himself, each otrokar possessed overpowering strength, and Nuan Cee's clansmen were ruthless. It would help if they hesitated before they decided to do something unwise.

The inn chimed, announcing an influx of magic behind my orchard. I picked up my broom, left my bedroom, and crossed the hallway to the wall. Beast was curiously missing in action.

"Terminal, please."

The wall split and peeled back, revealing a large screen.

"Feed from the orchard cameras."

The screen ignited, showing the field behind my apple trees. A dense sphere formed a foot above the grass, as if some transparent liquid twisted into a nine-foot-tall bubble. The bubble popped, leaving three beings and a large wheeled platform filled with bags on the grass. First was the Arbitrator, tall and blond, wearing dark gray trousers, a dark gray shirt, a black vest with golden embroidery, and pirate boots.

The man to the right of him was about a foot shorter but had to be at least a hundred pounds heavier, with broad shoulders, a massive chest, and hard, defined arms. High-tech tactical armor shielded his torso, contoured to his flat stomach, and it had to be custom-made. He was simply too large for anything designed to fit average-sized people.

His black hair was pulled back from his face into a rough ponytail. His body radiated strength and power. He seemed immovable, like a stone colossus, but then he stepped forward, surprisingly light on his feet. There was something odd about his face. The proportions weren't quite right for a human.

"Zoom in, please."

The man's face filled the screen. His skin had an olive tint, but his eyes, deep set under thick black eyebrows, were a startling light gray, the kind of silver hue most people could only achieve with contact lenses. His jaw was too heavy and too well muscled, the kind of jaw I usually saw on old grizzled vampires, except he definitely wasn't a vampire. I'd seen all sorts of beings, but this was a new one for me.

The gray-eyed man grabbed the platform's handle, and the visitors started toward the house.

The third man was almost as tall as the Arbitrator, but where George was lean with the elegant, sophisticated grace of a trained swordsman, this man communicated tightly controlled aggression. He didn't walk, he stalked, deliberate, quiet, watchful. His hair, a deep russet shade, was tousled. He wore black, and while the dark pants and black doublet obscured the exact lines of his body, it was very clear that he was corded with hard muscle. A ragged scar crossed his left cheek like a small, pale starburst on his skin. He looked hard, the way veteran soldiers sometimes look hard without trying.

The scar looked so familiar... I definitely had seen him and the Arbitrator before. I just couldn't quite recall where.

"Showtime," I murmured and went downstairs.

As I walked down, the delicious scent of cooked bacon swirled around me, laced with some spices. Beast shot out of the kitchen, like black and white furry lightning, carrying a small strip of bacon in her teeth. There you are. Mystery solved.

I stuck my head into the kitchen. Orro stood by the stove, holding a spoon. Three different pans sizzled on the fire and various ingredients filled the island.

"The Arbitrator is here. Three extra guests, male, probably human."

He growled and went back to stirring whatever he was cooking. Okay then.

I went to the back door, waited until someone knocked, and swung it open. "Welcome."

George nodded. "Hello, Dina. I hope we're not too early."

"Not at all. Just in time for breakfast. Come in."

George walked inside. The auburn-haired man followed. The third man glanced at the platform, which was too wide to go through the door.

I smiled. "Please leave it. I'll take care of it."

The man turned back to me. Behind him, the platform sank soundlessly into the ground. The inn would move the bags into their quarters.

"It's heavy," he said, his voice deep. "I can just take the bags in one by one."

"It's okay," I assured him. Behind him the grass flowed closed, as if the platform had never existed.

He glanced back and did a double take.

"Gaston?" George called from inside.

The big man shrugged and entered the inn.

I led them to the front room. George took a chair to the left, Gaston landed on the couch, and the auburn-haired man leaned against the wall, inhaling deeply. Sean used to do that. This man was a shape-shifter. Not a werewolf or a werecat of the Sun Horde, but something else.

"Breakfast will be served at seven," I said.

"It smells divine," George said. "I'd hoped to take this opportunity to go over some of our strategy."

I sat in my favorite chair. Beast ran into the room, saw the auburn-haired man, and growled. He glanced at her. His upper lip rose slightly, betraying a flash of his teeth. Yes, definitely a shape-shifter.

"Please don't try to intimidate my dog," I said.

"I'm not," the russet-haired man said. "When I decide to intimidate…"

"I will know." I finished for him. "She isn't an ordinary dog. If she bites you, she will cause real damage."

The shape-shifter studied Beast. "Mm-hm."

George smiled. "This is my brother, Jack. That over there is Gaston, our cousin."

Interesting family. "You must realize that both the otrokars and the vampires will see Gaston as a challenge."

"I'm counting on it. To put it plainly, I'm the planner," George said. "Gaston is the muscle. His job is to attract attention and appear to be a threat. He is very good at it."

Gaston grinned, displaying serrated teeth.

"Jack is the killer," George continued. "He knows other killers, he understands them, and if necessary, he will remove a physical threat before it has a chance to cause any damage."

Something shattered in the kitchen.

The three men glanced at the kitchen doorway.

"I understand that people in your profession are familiar with the otrokars and the vampires," George said. "Perhaps we could compare notes?"

The archives of the Arbitrators were legendary. He likely knew everything it was humanly possible to know about all three factions participating in the summit. No, this was his way of trying to gauge the extent of my knowledge. Either he wasn't familiar with innkeepers, which I doubted given those archives, or he didn't trust me to already know all the relevant information, which was annoying. Maybe lack of sleep was just making me short-tempered. "I'd love to—"

The vicious snarl of a Quillonian in mortal danger cut through my voice. Now what?

"Excuse me." I got up and walked into the kitchen.

The door of the far cabinet stood wide open. Orro stood by it, all his spikes erect on his back. His hands clenched a plate. A thick wooden tendril clamped the other end of the plate, trying to pull it out of Orro's hands and back into the cabinet.

"What's going on?"

"I broke a plate, and it refuses to let me have another one!" Orro snarled. "How was I supposed to know the dishes were prehistorically breakable?"

"Let him have the plate, please."

The tendril let go and Orro stumbled back, the plate in his hands.

"Please help him," I said to the inn.

The kitchen creaked.

"I know," I said. "But you have to learn to work with him."

Orro waved the plate. "I will persevere."

"I'm sure you will."

I went back into the living room and sat back in my chair, pushing with my magic. "Terminal, split screen, files on vampire and otrokar, please."

A wide screen formed in the far wall, the left side showing a vampire and the right an otrokar.

George raised his eyebrows. "Thank you. On the surface, the vampires and otrokars seem like similar species. Both evolved from the same predatory humanoid strain. Both have a martial society centered on the ideas of conquest and land acquisition, valuing it over other forms of material wealth. They are both aggressive and quick to respond with violence. The art and religions of both civilizations show a strong veneration of a warrior's honor. Both cultures show almost no gender gap. That's where the similarities end."

A fair point.

"The vampires of the Holy Anocracy try to become perfect soldiers," George said.

"Vampire," I murmured. The left screen delivered a close-up of a vampire knight in battle armor, swinging a black-and-red battle mace.

"Each knight is a versatile killing machine, a warrior skilled in a variety of martial styles."

The vampire on the screen clashed with a lizard-like opponent. The purple lizard grasped the vampire's mace and ripped it out of his hands. The vampire pulled two short swords from the scabbards in his armor and spun, changing his stance.

"If fifty vampires are on the field, one of them will be a leader and two others will serve as sergeants," George said. "If the leader is killed, one of the sergeants will take his place, and the best of the soldiers under his command will become a sergeant. They go through stages of martial education. Everyone begins as a rank-and-file soldier and receives the same basic martial training. Those who so choose go on to study and train further, attaining the rank of knight and advancing within the knighthood. Specialization does occur, but overall each vampire is quite adaptable. The core of the Holy Anocracy, the noble Houses, consists of individuals who are hereditary soldiers. They are the warrior elite. The otrokars function differently."

"Otrokar," I whispered to the inn. The screen expanded to show an enormous male otrokar. He had to be over seven feet tall and at least three hundred and fifty pounds. Muscles bulged on his frame. The image faded and a new one slid into its place: another otrokar, but this one under six feet tall, lean, spinning two axes impossibly fast.

"You're probably wondering why there is such discrepancy in size," George told me.

Actually, no. I wasn't wondering. I sighed and pretended to look bored. "At puberty, otrokar bodies begin producing a certain hormone that has the ability to greatly reshape their bodies. If they begin lifting weights, the hormone bulks them up and makes them larger. If they train in gymnastics, it makes them more compact and lean. This hormone has evolved as a part of their evolutionary adaptation, allowing them to survive in a wide variety of climates. Children who mature during the times of drought are smaller, children who mature in cold climates are larger, and so on. Unfortunately for their health, the otrokars pushed it to the next level, and until they implemented strict monitoring of adolescents, some of them grew so large that their cartilage wore out under their own weight. This condition is called Veteran's Knees, and guests suffering from it require special accommodations."

The room fell silent.

Jack grinned. "He occasionally forgets that the rest of us are not idiots."

"No, I never expect people to be idiots," George said. "I do expect them to lack some of the necessary information, because experience has demonstrated to me that assuming someone in a key position knows everything you do leads to disaster. But we were talking about the high degree of specialization among the otrokars. The hormone production stops after they reach maturity, and they are locked into the choices they made in adolescence. They learn to do one profession, but they do it exceedingly well."

"So if you need someone to blow up a bridge in enemy territory…," Gaston said.

"Vampires would send a team of five," Jack said. "All five will know how to arm and disarm the bomb."

"Otrokars will send a group of twenty," George continued. "Five will know how to operate the bomb, and the rest will keep them alive until they get there. Otrokars have large families and outnumber vampires roughly three to one. Individually, vampires are better soldiers, which is why otrokars prefer to conquer in a horde. Vampires are led by hereditary aristocracy, while promotion within the otrokar ranks is a meritocracy influenced by a popularity contest. The differences between their ideologies are vast; the two civilizations have great contempt for each other, not to mention they are currently engaged in a bloody war. If members of the two delegations come in direct contact, we can expect fireworks."

"They won't have a lot of opportunities for unsupervised contact," I said. "They will be housed in separate sets of rooms with individual access to the common dining room and ballroom. If they attempt to get at each other, they will be strongly discouraged."

"Exactly how are you planning on doing that?" Jack asked. "We really need to discuss the security measures with your team."

Really? "I'm an innkeeper. I don't require a security team."

His eyes narrowed. "So you're planning on keeping them apart all by yourself?"

"Yes."

Gaston rubbed his chin.

"You do realize they are professional soldiers," Jack said.

"Yes."

Jack looked at his brother. George smiled.

Jack wouldn't stop. I recognized his type. He might not have been part of the Sun Horde, but he was a shapeshifter, and he was likely a cat. Cats trusted in themselves and chafed at any authority. Sean had at least given me the benefit of the doubt, but Jack wouldn't. Not until I swatted him on the nose.

"Are you a professional soldier?" I asked.

"I was for a while," Jack said.

Aha. "And I assume you're fast and deadly?"

Jack furrowed his eyebrows. "Sure."

I glanced at Gaston. "Are you also a professional soldier? He grinned. "I'm more of a gentleman of adventure."

George laughed under his breath.

"I save these two from themselves," Gaston continued. "Occasionally I do a bit of skulduggery."

What? "Skulduggery?"

"Scale a ten-foot wall, jump out of the shadows, break a diplomat's neck, plant false documents on his body, and prevent an international incident type of thing to keep the war from breaking out," Gaston said helpfully. "Dreadful stuff, but quite necessary."

That was a really specific description of skullduggery. I smiled at the two of them. "Since you're both men of action, this should be an easy challenge. Take my broom away from me."

The two men measured the distance between me and them.

Jack glanced at his brother. "Are you going to say anything?"

George shook his head. "No, I'm just going to let you walk into this noose. You're doing a fine job."

Jack shrugged.

Gaston leaped into the air. It was an incredibly powerful jump. He shot off the floor as if he'd been fired out of a cannon, flying through the air and straight for me. The inn's wall split. Thick, flexible roots, smooth with wood grain but agile like whips, exploded from the wall, jerking Gaston out of the air and wrapping him in a cocoon.

Jack dashed underneath Gaston. The inn's tendrils snapped at him, but he dodged, gliding out of their reach as if his joints were liquid. It was a beautiful thing to watch. I let him get within three feet of me and tapped the broom on the floor. The broom's handle split, fracturing. Brilliant electric blue shot out and hit Jack's skin. He convulsed and crashed down like a log.

George threw something. The hand movement was so fast it was a blur. The tendrils shot out to block and a four-inch dart fell harmlessly to the floor.

The floor of the inn parted, and Jack sank into it up to his neck. Around me the room stretched slightly, waiting. The broom reformed in my hand. I flicked my fingers and the floor surged up, twisting with elastic flexibility to raise Jack to my eye level. Above him Gaston hung, suspended upside down. Only his face was visible.

The gray-eyed man unhinged his massive jaws. "Well. This is a bit of a predicament."

I faced the far wall and pushed with my magic. The wood disintegrated. A vast, shallow sea, pale orange, stretched before us under amethyst sky. In the distance jagged peaks tore through the water. The wind bathed me, bringing with it the scent of salt and algae. Yes, this would do nicely.

Ripples troubled the surface. An enormous triangular fin with long spikes carved the water like a knife, speeding toward us.

"The inn is my domain," I said. "Here, I am supreme. If you keep making yourself into a nuisance, I'll banish you to that ocean and leave you in there overnight."

The fin was barely twenty-five yards away.

Twenty.

Fifteen. A glistening blue hide rose out of the water.

The wall rebuilt itself just before an enormous mouth studded with dagger teeth thrust out of the ocean.

Caldenia descended the stairs. "Ooh. Bondage so early in the morning, dear?"

If only. "May I present Caldenia ka ret Magren," I said. "Her Grace is a permanent guest of the inn."

George got off the couch and executed a flawless bow with a flourish. I let the tendrils unravel around Gaston, and he dropped to the floor softly and bowed as well.

"Are you going to let me go?" Jack asked quietly.

"I'm thinking about it."

"So Gaston gets let go, but I don't?"

"I like him more than I like you."

Jack looked at me and grinned. "Fair enough. I've got what I asked for."

I dissolved the floor and let Jack go make his introductions.

George drifted over to me. "I didn't know you can open dimensional gates."

"I can't, but Gertrude Hunt can."

A cough made me turn. Orro stood in the doorway of the small dining room.

"I think breakfast is ready," I announced.

The three men, Caldenia, and I walked into the dining room and sat around the heavy old table. Tendrils slipped from the wall, gently sliding a plate in place in front of me. I blinked. An egg, cooked paper-thin like a crepe and folded into an elaborate purse, was filled with small chips of potatoes fried to golden perfection, crumbled sausage, and tiny pieces of mushrooms. A thin green stalk sprouted from the center of the mix, bearing delicate pink flowers carved from a strawberry. A small basket woven of narrow strips of bacon sat next to the egg purse, holding a sunny-side up egg sprinkled with spices and next to it a flower of cucumber petals blooming with a center of creamed egg yolk that had been piped onto it with a surgical precision. It was so pretty I didn't know whether to eat it or to frame it. The aroma alone made my mouth water.

"Eggs three ways!" Orro announced and retreated into the kitchen.

Eggs three ways was unbelievably delicious. Watching Caldenia sample them was an experience in itself. Her Grace daintily tried the filling of the egg purse, swiped the tines of her fork across the piped egg yolk, picked up the tiny bacon basket and delicately slurped the entire thing into her mouth. Sharp carnivore teeth flashed, bacon crunched, and she dabbed her lips with a napkin.

My seat let me glimpse a narrow slice of the kitchen from the doorway. Inside it, Orro paused at the island, a kitchen towel in his hand.

Her Grace put down her napkin. "Exquisite."

All of Orro's needles stood on end. For a second he looked like one of those neon-colored spikey balls you can buy in the toy section of Target. A moment later his needles lowered back into place and he continued to wipe down the island.

Lunch was served at twelve and featured something called "simple crème fraiche chicken and vegetables," which turned out to be roasted chicken with crispy skin and meat so tender it fell apart under the pressure of my fork, served with fresh spinach, citrus, almonds and some sort of heavenly dressing. I couldn't possibly keep Orro. He was sure to be too expensive, but I'd be a fool not to enjoy it while it lasted.

By six thirty everything was ready and I waited on the back porch, wearing my robe. The designated point of entry was in the field behind my orchard, out of the way of the front road, and the brush and trees would block most of the flashy side effects of the guests' arrival. I had gently encouraged six apples trees to move a few yards to the side, so we had a clear path through the orchard, and from where I stood I could see the field, its grass freshly mowed. The sky was overcast, promising an early, gloomy evening followed by a dreary night. A cold breeze came, swirling through the trees.

Almost forty guests, most of them high-ranking. One misstep and my reputation and the inn's ranking wouldn't recover. My mind kept cycling through the preparations: quarters, ballroom, instructions to Orro... At the last minute I had reactivated the stables. The Merchants of Baha-char sometimes traveled with animals. They didn't do it all the time, but when my parents hosted them all those years ago, they occasionally showed up with a beast of burden or a pet. The inn had already formed the stables once, many decades ago, so all I had to do was move it out of the inn's underground storage. Unearthing them strained the inn and me both, but it was better to have the stables and not need them than let someone's prized racing dinosaur soak in the cold rain while you made them available.

I'd thought of everything. I went down my checklist and crossed off every item. Still, I felt keyed up. If I were an engine, I would be idling too high. I could handle forty guests. I had handled more than that at my parents' inn but only for a short time, and none of them had been actively at war with each other.

It would be fine. This was my inn, and no amount of guests could change that.

I reached out and touched the post supporting the roof over the back porch. The magic of the inn connected with mine, restless. The inn was nervous too.

The posts and the roof were a new addition the inn had grown on its own. I hadn't realized it, but I had developed a habit of walking out onto the back patio, which used to be a concrete slab, and watching the trees. Sometimes I would bring a folding chair out and read. The Texas sun knew no mercy, and after I burned for the second time by staying out a minute or two too long, the inn took the matters into its own hands and sprouted stone and wood porch posts and a roof. It also replaced the concrete slab with pretty flagstone, and I wasn't sure where the inn had gotten it.

"It will be fine," I murmured to the house, stroking the wood with the tips of my fingers. The inn's magic leaned against me, reassured.

"It will," George said. He stood next to me wearing the same outfit as this morning, but now he also held a cane with an ornate top, a dark wood inlaid with twisted swirls of silver. I wouldn't be surprised if there was a knife in it. He'd also developed a mysterious limp. It appeared the Arbitrator liked to be underestimated.

Behind us Gaston and Orro carried on a quiet conversation. The window was open and the sound of their voices carried to us.

"So if it was your first meal, why eggs?" Gaston asked. "Why not caviar or truffles or something complicated?"

"Consider coq au vin," Orro answered. "Even the simplest recipe for this dish requires a long process. One has to have a mature bird and marinate it in burgundy for two days. Once marinated, thick slices of bacon must be sautéed in a pan. Then the chicken must be browned, smothered in Cognac, which is then to be set on fire."

That was definitely an Earth recipe, specifically French. Where in the world did he learn it?

"Then the chicken must be seasoned. Salt, pepper, bay leaf, and thyme. Onion must be added, chicken must simmer, flour is to be sprinkled onto the whole endeavor, and then it will be simmered again. More ingredients are added—bacon, garlic, chicken stock, mushrooms—until it all blends into a delicious harmonized whole."

"You're making me hungry," Gaston said, "But I still don't see the point."

"No single ingredient is the star of that dish," Orro said. "It is a whole. I could cook it in a dozen ways, altering amounts of ingredients and spices and creating new variations. How is the stock made? What vintage is the wine? A second-year cooking student can make this dish, and it would be edible. The very complexity of its preparations makes the recipe flexible. Now consider the humble egg. It is possibly the oldest food known throughout the universe. The egg is just an egg. Cook it too long, it becomes hard. Cook it too little, and it turns into a jellied mess. Break the yolk because of your carelessness and the dish is ruined. Gouge the gentle skin as you peel the shell and no culinary expertise can repair it. The egg allows no room for error. That's where true mastery shines."

Jack slipped into the kitchen and walked out onto the porch. "There is a police car parked down the street, two houses over. The male cop inside is watching the inn."

I sighed. "That would be Officer Marais." Like clockwork.

"Should we be concerned?" George said.

"Officer Marais and I have a history."

All people had magic. Most of them didn't know how to use it because they never tried, but magic still found ways to seep through. For Officer Marais, it manifested as intuition. Every gut feeling he had was telling him there was something not quite right with me and Gertrude Hunt. He couldn't prove it, but it nagged at him all the same. Officer Marais was both conscientious and hardworking, and tonight a hyper hunch had warned him that something "not quite right" was about to happen, so he must've driven to the Avalon subdivision and settled down to watch the inn.

"He has an overdeveloped sense of intuition," I explained. "That's why I've made sure everyone knows to enter through the orchard. As long as he doesn't see anything, we'll be fine."

"Did you confirm with the delegates?" George asked.

Jack nodded. "Otrokar at seven, the Merchants at seven thirty, and vampires at eight. I heard something interesting from the home office. They said we're in for some rough waters with the vampires."

George raised one eyebrow. "House Vorga."

Jack sighed. "This thing when you know things before I tell them to you is really annoying."

"So you've said." George turned to me. "The delegation includes knights from every House immediately engaged in combat on Nexus. There are three major Houses and two minor. All major Houses initially were receptive to the peace talks; however, in the past few days, House Vorga began to lean in favor of continuing the conflict."

"So what does that mean?" Gaston asked from the kitchen.

"Your guess is as good as mine." George grimaced. "It could mean House Vorga made a secret alliance with House Meer to bring down the other Houses. It could mean someone in House Vorga has been offended by someone from House Krahr stepping on their shadow or wearing the wrong color or not pausing long enough before a sacred altar. It could mean someone saw a bird fly the wrong way over the steeple of the local cathedral. It's vampire politics. It's like sticking your hand into a barrel filled with forty cobras and trying to find one garden snake among them by touch."

The best thing about vampire politics was that they were the Arbitrator's problem. I just had to keep the vampires safe.

George was looking at the orchard, his face distant.

"Say, George?" Gaston asked. I glanced at him and he winked at me. "Why forty?"

"Because it's a sufficiently large number to make the odds of finding a garden snake improbable," George said, his voice flat.

"Yes, but why not fifty or a hundred? Why such an odd number? Forty? Snakes aren't commonly measured in forties."

George pivoted on his foot and looked at Gaston. The big man flashed a grin.

Jack chuckled to himself.

"When he concentrates like that," Gaston told me, "if you're really quiet, you can hear the gears in his head turning. Sometimes you catch a faint puff of smoke coming out of his ears..."

The air above the grass tore like a transparent plastic curtain, showing a deep purple void for a fraction of a second. The void blinked its purple eye, and a group of otrokars appeared on the grass. One, two, three... twelve. As expected.

The otrokar in the front started toward us. Huge, at least six five, and muscular, judging by the powerful arms and legs, he was wrapped in the traditional otrokar half cloak, which was more of a really wide, long scarf designed to shield your arms and face from the sun. While worn, it covered the head, shoulder, and torso to midthigh. The handle of a giant sword wrapped in leather rose above the otrokar's shoulder. The second otrokar followed the first's footsteps. He was slender and shorter than the leader by about four inches. The difference between the two was so pronounced they almost didn't look like they belonged to the same species.

The others followed.

The leader reached the porch and pulled the cloak off in a single fluid move. An enormous otrokar woman stood before me, clad in leather and wearing the traditional half kilt. Her skin was a deep, rich bronze with a hint of orange. Muscles corded her frame. Her hair was french-braided at her temples, the braids running toward the back of her head. The remaining wealth of hair was brushed back into a long mane, so dark at the root it seemed black. The mane gradually lightened, and at the tips the color turned to deep ruby, as if her hair had been carefully dipped in fresh blood. Her dark violet eyes under black eyebrows examined us, assessing. Her posture shifted slightly. In the split second she glanced at us, she had seen everything: Jack, George, me, Gaston in the doorway and Orro in the kitchen, and she'd formulated a battle plan.

George bowed. "Greetings, Khanum. I'm sorry we have to keep our voices down. Local law enforcement is nearby. I trust the trip went well?"

"We survived." Her voice was deep for a woman. The kind of voice that could roar. "I hate void travel. It feels like my stomach is turned inside out." Khanum grimaced. "I suppose we'll have to do the formal entrance once everyone is here."

"That is the custom," George said.

The otrokar at her side pulled off his cloak. He didn't wear armor, only the kilt, and his torso was exposed. He was lean and hard, his muscles light but crisply defined under bronze skin tinted with green, as if life had chiseled all softness off him. If he were human, I would put him in his thirties, but with the otrokar age was difficult to tell. His hair, long and so black it shone with purple highlights, fell down his back. Thin leather belts and chains wrapped his waist, and dozens of charms, pouches, and bottles hung from them. The Khanum looked like a powerful predatory cat. Next to her he looked like a weathered tree, or perhaps a serpent: nothing but dry muscle. His face matched him: harsh, chiseled with rough strokes, with green eyes so light they seemed to glow with some eerie radiance. If he wasn't a shaman, I'd eat my broom.

He surveyed the inn. "Is there a fire pit?"

"There is a room set out specifically for spirits," I told him. "With the fire ring."

His eyes widened a fraction. "Good. I will ask the spirits to show me the omens for these peace talks."

"The omens better be good," Khanum said quietly, her voice laced with steel.

The shaman didn't even blink. "The omens will be what the omens will be."

The Khanum took a deep breath. "I suppose I have to get on with it." She raised her voice slightly. "Greetings, Arbitrator. Greetings, Innkeeper."

"Gertrude Hunt welcomes you, Khanum." I bowed my head. "Winter sun to you and your warriors. My water is your water. My fire is your fire. My beds are soft and my knives are sharp. Spit on my hospitality and I'll slit your throat." There. Nice and traditional.

Next to me Jack became very still. He didn't tense; he just became utterly at peace.

Khanum smiled. "I feel at home already. Winter sun to you. We will honor this house and those who own it. Our knives are sharp and our sleep is light. Betray the honor of your fire, and I'll carve out your heart."

The door swung open, obeying the push of my magic. I stepped through. "Please follow me, Khanum."

Ten minutes later I was back at my post on the porch. The inn had sealed the entrance behind the last otrokar. The only way they could exit would be through the main ballroom.

At seven thirty the area above the field shimmered as if a ring of hot air suddenly rose above the grass. The shimmer solidified into a giant ship with sleek, curving lines that made you think of a manta ray gliding through the water. The elegant craft sank to the ground, landing like a feather, a hatch opened, and Nuan Cee stepped out. Four feet tall, he resembled a fox with the eyes of a cat and ears of a lynx. Soft, luxurious fur, silver blue and perfectly combed, sheathed him from head to toe, turning white on his stomach and darkening to an almost turquoise dappled with golden rosettes on his back. He wore a beautiful, silky apron and a necklace studded with blue jewels.

Nuan Cee saw me, waved, and called over his shoulder. "This is the right place. Bring all the things."

He started toward me. Four foxes emerged, carrying a palanquin with rose curtains. Behind them five other foxes, their fur ranging from white to deepest blue, walked, hopping lightly over the grass, all five adorned with silks and jewelry. A low braying sound came out of the belly of the ship. A moment later and a small fox emerged, tugging on the reins of what looked like a furry cross between a camel and a donkey. A precarious stack of bags, packs, and chests sat on top of the beast, piled almost twice as tall as the creature itself. The fox tugged on the reins again, and the donkey-camel stepped into the grass. Behind him another beast appeared, led by a different fox.

"So let me get this straight," Jack murmured. "They fly around on spaceships, but they load donkeys in them?"

"They like donkeys," George told him.

The fifth donkey made its way out of the ship, loaded like all the others. My parents had hosted Nuan Cee before. I mentally patted myself on the back for assigning them enough rooms to house a party three times their number and for pulling the stables out of storage.

"How long do they expect this to last?" Gaston whistled. "A year?"

"They love their luxuries," I explained. "The worst thing you can do to one of them is to force them to go without. Once we get them all inside, would you mind showing them to their rooms?" I would follow behind to make sure nobody wandered off the beaten path, and then I'd settle all the donkeys into the stables.

"No problem," Gaston said.

Nuan Cee finally reached us. Jack studied the tufts on the little fox's ears with more than just curiosity. Maybe he turned into a lynx.

"Diiina!" The Merchant stretched the word.

"Shhh," I whispered. "Honorable Nuan Cee, we have a policeman watching the house outside."

"Oh." Nuan Cee lowered his voice. "Right. I am so happy to visit your inn, so happy. Allow me to present to you my family." He waved his hand-paw, and the foxes lined up, with the palanquin in the lead. "My grandmother, Nuan Re." The palanquin passed by us. "My sister, Nuan Kuo. My sister's cousin by marriage, Nuan Oler. My second brother-in-law ..."

Five minutes later, the final fox finally stepped onto my porch. "Nuan Couki, my thrice-removed cousin's seventh son!" Nuan Cee triumphantly announced. "This is his first trip."

The seventh son looked at us. He was barely three and a half feet tall, with pale, sandy fur and huge blue eyes. He waved his paw at us, squeaked "Hi!" in a tiny voice, and dashed after the procession of Nuan Cee's relatives and into the inn.

"Phew." Nuan Cee wiped imaginary sweat off his brow. "I work too hard. Let us see our rooms."

He disappeared into the inn, and I followed him.

"Cookie?" Jack said behind me.

"Just go with it," George told him.

I made it back to the porch right at eight o'clock. Dealing with Nuan Cee's clan had taken longer than expected. I barely had a minute to spare. At least they didn't make that much noise. If all went well with the vampires, we'd dodge the bullet.

We waited in silence.

A minute passed.

Another.

"It's very unusual for them to be late." George frowned.

My magic chimed in my mind. Oh no.

"In front!" I dashed through the house. The men chased me. "They're coming through the front!"

I burst out of the front door.

"Get down on the ground!" a male voice barked.

In the middle of the street, twelve knights of the Holy Cosmic Anocracy in full blood armor brandished their weapons. Officer Marais stood by his vehicle, pointing a Taser at the leading knight.

"I said get down on the ground!" Officer Marais roared.

The vampire nearest to him gripped his enormous axe. Streaks of bright red shot through the weapon. He'd just primed it.

"No!" I sprinted into the street.

Officer Marais fired the Taser. The electrode darts snapped at the vampire's blood armor, sparking with blue.

The vampire roared. The huge axe swung in an arc and sliced the hood of the police cruiser in half like it was an empty Coke can. For a second Officer Marais stared at it in stunned silence. His hand went to his gun.

I couldn't let him fire.

Magic shot from my hand into my broom. The handle split into dozens of long filaments and shot at Officer Marais like some face-hugging monster from a horror movie. The filaments wrapped around him, binding his body into a cocoon. He spun in place and toppled onto the asphalt.

The vampires roared in triumph.

CHAPTER FIVE

I turned to the vampires. I was so furious I couldn't even speak.

The knight with the axe saw my face. A second later he also realized I was wearing an innkeeper's robe and that he had done something really, really bad.

I marched over to him. He took a few steps back toward the inn, moving away from the car like a toddler who'd broken something and was now trying to distance himself from it. His foot touched the inn's boundary. A root whipped out of the gloom, grasped the vampire, and yanked him into the ground as if he weighed nothing. One second he was there, the next he vanished.

I glared at the other vampires. "Pick up this car and this man," I said, forcing the words through my teeth. "Bring them into my driveway undamaged, or I'll reduce you to bloody spots on this pavement. Now."

To the right, two points of light announced an approaching vehicle.

"Move!" Arland snarled from somewhere behind the hulking vampires.

Lord Soren, Arland's uncle, grabbed Officer Marais and sprinted to the inn as fast as his enormous armor would allow. Two vampires grasped the cruiser, lifted it, and carried it onto the driveway. The moment the wheels touched the ground, the cruiser sank into the driveway. The ground gulped it and the car vanished. The vampires streamed into the house.

The lights were almost on us.

I stepped behind the oak. The house shifted, hiding the weapons. George crouched behind a hedge.

At the door Arland barked a short command. The three vampires still outside dropped flat.

A white truck thundered by.

I waited a couple of seconds and nodded to Arland. The knights rose and ducked into the house. George followed. I paused and surveyed the street. It lay empty.

I waited, straining to hear any stray noises.

Nothing.

No sirens, no outraged neighbors racing out of their houses to see what was happening, no shots fired. The dreary weather and the cold night on a regular old Tuesday kept the inhabitants of Avalon subdivision indoors.

Could we have dodged a bullet?

As an innkeeper, I had only two official duties: to safeguard my guests and to keep their existence hidden from the rest of the planet. The vampires knew this. Arland and his uncle, in particular, knew and understood this extremely well. How could they have put the inn in jeopardy?

Cold drizzle sifted from the night sky.

The subdivision remained silent. Somewhere in the distance a dog barked in short plaintive yips, asking to be let inside. It might have been my imagination, but I thought I heard a door swing open. The barking stopped.

I exhaled slowly and went into the inn.

The vampire delegation crowded in my front room.

A huge knight, his hair jet-black, stood chest to chest with Arland, their armor almost touching. Both had their shoulders back, legs planted, their powerful muscles flexed, ready to grip and tear at each other. Their mouths gaped open, fangs on display, their faces contorted with rage. They radiated aggression like two space heaters emitting heat. Everyone else had backed away, giving them room. They were a second away from direct violence, and they were almost exactly the same size and height. It would be bloody and terrible.

No, uh-uh. They would *not* be having it out in my front room. I snapped my fingers. I didn't really have to, but I wanted to underscore the point for the rest of the audience. The two vampires sank into the floor up to their waists. I touched my index fingers and moved them apart. The vampires slid away from each other, leaving about five feet of space between them. George walked into this space, leaning on his cane.

"Marshal of House Krahr." He nodded at Arland. "Marshal of House Vorga." He nodded at the dark-haired knight. His voice was light and cheerful. "Whose idea was it to come through the front door?"

"Where is my knight?" the Marshal of House Vorga snarled.

I sank him another six inches into the floor.

"I demand…"

Another six inches. He was almost up to his armpits.

The Marshal of House Vorga opened his mouth and clicked it shut.

George turned on his heel. "Marshal of House Sabla, perhaps you would like to clear the air?"

A female knight stepped forward. Long, straight chestnut hair framed her face. "Coordinates were presented to us by the Marshal of Krahr. The Marshal of House Vorga entered them personally."

"Might I trouble you for those coordinates?" George asked.

She raised her hand. A small display ignited on the inside of her wrist. Alien marks dashed across it in pale red.

"Thank you, Lady Isur," George said. "Let the record show that Arland of Krahr presented the correct set of coordinates to the Houses. Lord Robart, did you enter incorrect coordinates by mistake?"

"We are the knights of the Holy Anocracy," Lord Robart answered. "We do not slink through the back door. We do not follow the otrokar."

"I see," George said. "And you made that decision on your own?"

"I am a Marshal of a Vampire House," Lord Robart snarled. "I don't answer to the likes of you."

George smiled. "Fair enough, although you have already answered my first question, so the impact of your gesture is somewhat diluted. Very well then." He raised his hand. A scroll appeared in it as if by magic. He let it unroll. A brilliant red symbol of the Holy Pyramid blazed in the middle of it. The vampires knelt as one and I saw Caldenia sitting in a chair at the back wall, sipping her cup of tea, a small amused smile bending her lips.

"This is a holy writ granted to me by Her Brilliance, the Hierophant," George said.

He had a holy writ from the religious leader of the Holy Cosmic Anocracy. Wow. He'd just unleashed the equivalent of a nuclear bomb.

"This writ grants me the power of life and death over every single one of you," George said. "I may kill any of you at any time without reason or fear of retribution. To defy me is to defy the Hierophant. Should you choose to do so, you will be excommunicated. Upon your death, your soul will be turned away from Paradise, forced to wander the lifeless, icy plains of Nothing, where no sun shines upon you, no animal crosses your path, and no sound interrupts the silence. Have I made myself clear?"

"Crystal clear," Lady Isur said, her head still bowed.

George rolled up the scroll and slid it into his sleeve. "Rise."

The vampires rose.

George looked at me. "Dina, you may release the Marshals."

I let the floor push both vampires out and to their feet. Neither of them spoke. The room was absolutely silent. You could hear a pin drop. George had their complete attention.

"This galaxy's interactions with Earth are governed by a treaty of the Cosmic Senate," George said. "Lady Dina, what is the most important provision in it?"

"The existence of other intelligent life in the galaxy must remain secret," I answered.

"What is the punishment for breaking this provision?"

"Banishment," I said.

Lord Robart locked his teeth.

"Would House Vorga suffer consequences if Lord Robart's transgression became public?"

"Yes. His House would be dishonored and banned from Earth."

A couple of vampires winced. Earth was a vital waypoint. Losing access to it meant House Vorga would be severely impaired in their travel. Other Houses would happily take advantage of that.

"Lord Robart of House Vorga," George said. "I don't believe in starting peace negotiations with blood. Nor do I feel House Vorga should suffer penalties for what was likely a transgression resulting from pride rather than malice.

However, your actions nearly compromised this summit, and atonement must be made for us to proceed. Lady Dina, do you recall the demonstration you provided earlier? If you could open that door one more time, please."

Making George angry was a really, really bad idea. I faced the far wall and pushed with my magic. The wood fell apart, melting into nothing, revealing the endless amber sea under the purple sky. In the distance ragged, dark crags pierced the water under the broken necklace of red planets. The salty breeze washed over us, and the planet exhaled in my face.

A body sliced through the orange water, thick, scaly, and crowned with a long ridged fin. Its coils kept going and going, sliding and bulging under the surface.

George looked at Lord Robart. "One hour, Marshal. We will postpone formal introductions until your return."

The vampire raised his head.

If he stepped into that water, his armor would be too heavy. He would be too slow. He would drown. To go into that water at all was suicide.

Lord Robart bared his fangs.

They wore their armor as if it were their second skin. He would never...

Lord Robart unsheathed a short, brutal axe and clasped the House crest on his armor. The black metal fractured, falling off him, leaving him standing in a plain black bodysuit. He stepped out of his boots, primed his axe with a flick of his wrist, and jumped into the water. It came up to his waist.

"Seal the doorway, please," George said.

I let the wood flow back, hiding the vampire knight from view. We'd need a countdown. I murmured to the inn, and a large digital clock appeared on the wall, counting the seconds down from sixty minutes.

George turned to me. "We still have the problem of the car and the police officer." He gave me a brilliant smile. "This is your area of expertise. The delegation of the Holy Anocracy, my people, and I are at your disposal, my lady. How would you like to handle that?"

I turned to Arland. "Marshal, I'll need your best engineer. The rest of you must go to your quarters."

"Hardwir, with me," Arland commanded.

An older, dark-haired vampire shouldered his way to the front of the group.

"I'm coming as well," Lady Isur announced.

"Rest of you, through the hallway on the left. Go. Do not attempt to leave. The inn won't permit it."

The majority of the knights left the room, but five of them remained behind. "We cannot abandon our Marshal," a female knight said.

Lady Isur glanced at me. "Innkeeper?"

"You may choose two of your number," I told them. "You can keep watch here. If you attempt to move from this room, you will be detained."

The female knight and an older, grizzled vampire took up a post by the wall. The rest went to their quarters. Caldenia still sipped her tea, looking perfectly satisfied.

Now I had to fix this nightmare.

"Follow me." I started down the long hallway.

The stables occupied the northeastern corner of the house, opening into the orchard. From the outside, they would look just like a screened-in porch.

Beast darted back and forth in front of me, scampering in pure excitement. Well, at least someone was having fun.

"I could kill him," Lady Isur offered.

"That would only make more problems," Jack said.

"Law enforcement here is very well organized," Arland said. "If one falls, the rest converge on the area. It would make everything exceptionally difficult."

The door flew open in front of me and I entered the stables. My hands shook slightly. Too much adrenaline and too much magic expended too quickly. With the guests within the inn, I would rebound, but right now I felt jittery, as if I'd drunk three cups of strong coffee on an empty stomach.

Officer Marais lay on the floor next to his ruined squad car, flanked on both sides by the stalls. A female from Nuan Cee's clan was quietly distributing feed to the buckets. She saw us and stopped. As I approached, the filaments slid off Marais's body, leaving the inn's hard roots anchoring him to the floor. The filaments streamed to me, smoothly reforming into the broom in my hand. The roots gagged Officer Marais's mouth, but his eyes told me everything I needed to know. He was furious. If he could've gotten loose, he would fight all of us for his life.

I glanced at the car. It was even worse than I thought. The axe had gone straight through the hood, slicing through the engine like it was made of Jell-O. I could see the floor through the gap.

The stables were quiet save for the rhythmic chewing coming from the donkey-camels in their stalls.

"I can make it painless," Lady Isur murmured. "He won't feel a thing."

I held up my hand. "Give me the Last Resort."

The wall of the stables spat out a small syringe. I crouched by Officer Marais and injected the contents into his arm. He glared at me as if he was wishing with every fiber of his being that my head would explode. His face softened. His breathing deepened. His body went slack, his eyes closed, and he slipped into a deep sleep.

"What did you give him?" George asked.

"A tranquilizer."

"But he will still remember what happened," Jack said.

"It doesn't matter," I told him. "To be believed he will need evidence. We're going to remove the evidence."

"This is it?" Lady Isur frowned. "This is the plan?"

"Yes," I told her. "It has worked many times for many different innkeepers. Sometimes simple plans are the best." I turned to Arland's engineer. "Please fix it."

Hardwir stared at the cruiser. "You want *me* to fix *that?*"

"Yes. It must be restored to its original condition, exactly as it was before the blow."

The dark-haired knight frowned, approached the cruiser, glanced through the gap, and wrenched the hood up. "This is an internal combustion engine."

"Yes," I agreed.

"This is an abomination against nature." Hardwir let go of the mangled hood. It fell, broke off, and crashed to the ground. "I won't do it."

Arland's eyes blazed. He gathered himself, somehow turning larger. "What do you mean, you won't do it?"

"I won't do it! I swore an engineer's oath. I owe obligations to my profession, obligations which bind me to practice my craft with integrity and to preserve the precious nature of the universe." Hardwir stabbed his gauntleted finger in the direction of the engine. "It poisons the environment, it's horribly inefficient, and it runs on *fossil fuels*. It requires a finite, high-pollutant resource to function. What idiot would build an engine based on a nonrenewable resource?"

"I don't care," Arland snarled. "You will fix it."

Hardwir raised his chin. "No, I will not. You're asking me to repair something that makes toxins and releases them into the environment. If this was an engine of war, it would be outlawed."

"You swore fealty to me personally. You swore fealty to our House."

"I am an engineer. I won't betray myself."

Arland opened his mouth and said one word. "Ryona."

Hardwir snarled, baring his teeth.

Arland's face showed no mercy. "If we don't fix this, we will be discovered, which means this peace summit will fail. All the sacrifices of your sister on the battlefield will be for nothing."

Hardwir spun away from him, glared at the exposed engine, and turned back. "No."

Arland touched his crest. "Odalon? I'm sorry to interrupt your vigil. We need you. It's an emergency."

A single word emanated from the crest.

A moment later the inn chimed, announcing a visitor at the back of the orchard. I opened the gates of the stables. A single vampire knight walked through the trees. He was of average vampire height, just over six feet, and lean, almost slender. His skin was the darkest of the vampire genotype, a gray with a blue tint, like the contour feathers of a mature blue heron. His hair fell on his shoulders in a cascade of long thin braids. It must've been black at some point, but now it was shot through with gray. Vampires didn't go gray until well into their seventies, but he didn't look anywhere close to that. He wore long crimson and silver vestments over his armor, but unlike the single robe of a Catholic priest, his vestments were cut into long ribbons, eight inches wide. They flowed as he moved, streaming from his shoulders like an otherworldly mantle. Watching him approach was surreal.

Arland had called on his Battle Chaplain. They must have a spacecraft in orbit.

The chaplain strode into the stables. His face was completely serene, his eyes calm as he surveyed the cruiser, Officer Marais, and finally us.

Arland stepped closer to him and spoke quietly, his voice barely above a whisper.

Odalon nodded and turned to Hardwir. "Your concerns do you credit." His voice was soothing and even, a kind of voice that made you relax almost in spite of yourself.

"I won't do it," Hardwir said.

"Walk with me," Odalon said, his voice an invitation.

The engineer followed him out into the orchard. They stopped by one of the apple trees and spoke quietly.

Arland sighed. "All of this could've been avoided."

Lady Isur shrugged. "If not this, then something else. Robart is going to make the negotiations as painful as possible. You knew that going in."

Hardwir and the Battle Chaplain walked back.

"Even if I agreed to do this, it wouldn't work," Hardwir said. "I would need a molecular synthesizer to repair the parts…"

"They are standard issue on most military vessels," Lady Isur said.

"I wasn't finished, Marshal," Hardwir said. "We have a molecular synthesizer on board, but the repairs must match the wear and tear of the engine. For that I must determine the age and the degradation of the current engine, which means I need an age sequencer and specialized software. We don't have that. We're a military vessel, not an archaeological exploration ship."

The female member of Nuan Cee's clan cleared her throat. We all looked at her.

"Uncle Nuan Cee has one," she said. "It's very complicated. Very expensive. Far beyond my understanding."

George smiled. "Perhaps I can prevail on esteemed Nuan Cee to let us use it."

"I'm sure he would," she said. "For the right price."

"The right price?" Arland growled. "More like a lung and half a heart. I've dealt with him before. He'll squeeze the last—"

"I'll take care of it," I told him.

George and I found the esteemed Nuan Cee in his quarters. He was lounging on the plush furniture by a small indoor fountain. George sketched out the situation.

Nuan Cee leaned forward, the glint in his eyes clearly predatory. "The age sequencer is a very delicate piece of equipment. Very expensive. I carry one because people sometimes try to sell me objects and I must ascertain their authenticity. Can you imagine if I sold something that might be a reproduction?" He chortled.

This was going to cost us, I could feel it. "We are in awe of your wisdom," I said.

"And we count on your generosity," George said.

"Generosity is a terrible vice," Nuan Cee said. "But of course, even I am not infallible." He had us by the throat and he knew it.

I smiled. "You have a vested interest in this summit succeeding. After all, if the war continues, your spaceport on Nexus will be overrun."

Nuan Cee waved his paws. "We have Turan Adin. Even if the Holy Anocracy and the Hope-Crushing Horde united, we would have nothing to fear."

Who or what was Turan Adin?

"Still, the war is bad for business. I find myself being inclined to do you this favor."

I braced myself. There was a but coming.

"But I require a favor in return."

"Name it," George said.

"Not from you. From Dina."

Of course. "How may I help the great Nuan Cee?"

Nuan Cee grinned, showing me small sharp teeth. "I do not know yet. I shall think about it. Normally I would ask for three favors, but out of respect for your parents and the friendship between us, I restrained myself. Do not tell anyone. I do not want to lose face."

An unspecified favor to Nuan Cee. I would have to be insane to take it. There was no telling what he would ask.

The peace summit had to proceed at all costs. I had no choice. I held out my hand. "Done."

Nuan Cee laughed, grasped my fingers, and shook. "Delightful. I do so love this Earth custom. Talk to Nuan Sama in the stables. She's an expert in operating it."

Of course she was.

We thanked Nuan Cee and made our exit.

"I take it you can't trust anything they say," George said.

"It depends. All is fair while they are bargaining, but once they make a deal, they will honor it." And I had just managed to get myself into a bigger mess.

Five minutes later Hardwir and Nuan Sama walked off toward Nuan's camouflaged craft in the field. I reached into the car and pulled the SD card out of the dashboard camera.

"The Eye." I held my hand out. A silver sphere about the size of a lemon rolled out of the new hole in the wall and fell into my palm. I squeezed its sides gently. The sphere clicked, revealing an SD card slot. I slid the card into it and opened my hand. The sphere streaked outside through the open stable door and vanished behind the house.

"What did you tell Hardwir?" Arland asked Odalon.

The Battle Chaplain sighed. "I reminded him that an engineer's oath also obligated him to give freely of his skill and knowledge for the public good if so required. I cannot think of a greater public good than ending a war that devours lives but brings neither honor, nor glory, nor land. This misery must end, whatever the cost."

A soft beep echoed through the stables.

"The Marshal of House Vorga has three minutes left." I hurried back to the front room. The vampires and George chased me. All this running around would be comical if lives and the Gertrude Hunt weren't at stake.

I walked into the front room. The timer was down to fifteen seconds. The two vampires stood completely still, watching it.

I hoped he was still alive.

The numbers ran down to zero and flashed once. I melted the wall.

The Marshal of House Vorga walked into my front room. He was soaked. Blood dripped from a dozen cuts on his body suit. His right hand gripped his axe. His left carried a three-foot-long monstrous head. It was pale orange, covered with shimmering scales, and looked like something that would be drawn on an antique map with a caption "Here be monsters" underneath.

With a grimace, the Marshal dropped the head and the five-foot-long stump of the neck in the middle of the floor, stepped over it, and looked at George.

"The Office of Arbitration is satisfied," George said.

Lord Robart turned toward the hallway. The two vampires picked up his armor and followed him without a word.

"What do you want us to do with the head?" Orro asked from the kitchen doorway.

The Marshal paused. "Do whatever you will."

They turned into the hallway leading to the vampire quarters.

"I think it's time I retired as well," Lady Isur said. "Arbitrator, Innkeeper, Marshal, Your Grace, please excuse me. I must make myself presentable before the opening ceremony."

"Of course," George said.

Arland grimaced. "I suppose it's best I go as well. By your leave."

The two Marshals departed.

Orro stalked out of the kitchen and grabbed the head with his long claws.

"Please don't tell me you're going to cook that," I said.

"Of course I'm going to cook it." He waved the head around for emphasis. "Might I remind you that you're on a limited budget?"

"What if it's poisonous?" Jack asked.

"Preposterous!" Orro growled. "This is clearly a Morean water drake."

He tucked the severed head under his arm and walked into the kitchen, dragging the neck across the floor behind him.

"I shall have to make some preparations as well," George said. He and Jack left the room.

My legs gave out and I collapsed into a chair. Beast leaped into my lap.

Caldenia looked at me across the room. "So much excitement, and the peace talks haven't even started."

I groaned and put my hands over my face.

George wore soft charcoal trousers. Supple boots made of dark gray leather with a hint of blue hugged his feet and lower calves. His shirt was pale cream, and his dark blue vest was embroidered with a dazzling silver pattern too complicated to untangle at first glance. His long golden blond hair was brushed back from his face and caught at the nape of his neck in a ponytail. He leaned on his walking stick and his limp was back, but as he stood at the rear of the grand ballroom, he looked like an ageless prince from some hopelessly romantic fairy tale.

His brother stood on his right, wrapped in layers of brown leather. I could see no weapons, although he must've had some stashed somewhere. His auburn hair was slightly disheveled. George emanated an almost fragile elegance, but Jack was completely relaxed, his posture lazy and his face distant, as if he had absolutely no interest in what was about to happen and couldn't be bothered to pay attention.

They looked nothing alike, but I was absolutely sure they were brothers. I'd never seen two people so skilled at pretending to be the exact opposite of themselves.

Gaston had parked himself on Jack's right. Of the three, he seemed to be the only one being himself, which meant he stood there like a short but immovable mountain and scowled. I chose a place to the left of George and off to the side. I wasn't really part of the ceremonies, but I was the host of this insane gathering, and the members of the delegations would need to know my face. I'd opted for a simple robe. I'd also turned my broom into a staff for the occasion. The staff could become a spear on very short notice. Not that I would need it, but you never knew.

Behind us a long table waited, ready for the heads of the delegations to discuss the possibility of peace. Right now the

prospect seemed rather remote, but the peace talks themselves weren't my problem. Keeping the peace was.

I glanced up. At the opposite wall Caldenia sat in a royal
box, about thirty feet up. Her Grace wore a copper-colored
gown with an elaborate lace pattern and sipped wine from
a glass. Beast sat next to her. Until I had a better idea of
the participants in the summit, I wanted Caldenia off the
main floor. Her Grace could take care of herself, but I'd
told Beast to stay with her as an extra precaution.

George glanced at the electronic clock in the wall above
the door. "We may begin."

I nodded and murmured, "Lights."

Bright light bathed the ballroom floor.

"Release the Holy Anocracy."

The doors on the left side of the grand ballroom swung
open. A huge vampire stepped out, dressed in blood armor.
Enormous even by vampire standards, he carried the standard of the Holy Anocracy, black fangs on a red banner. He
faced us and planted the banner into the floor, holding it
with his left hand. Music blasted from hidden speakers, an
epic march, relentless, unhurried, and unstoppable. Images
slid along the walls of the ballroom: an armored vampire
tearing into a centipede-like creature five times her size; two
vampires locked in mortal combat, fangs bared; a vampire
with a House standard atop a mountain of corpses, bellow-
ing in rage. This was the Holy Anocracy's "We Are Scary
Badasses" reel. The same images were being streamed to the
otrokar and Merchant quarters.

The terrifying footage kept coming. A citadel of the
Crimson Cathedral, unbelievable in its size; endless rows
of vampires poised before boarding a spacecraft; a vampire
woman in the flowing robes of a Hierophant dashing up the

spine of an enormous creature, leaping straight up and slicing into its neck. An image of a small group of vampires in bloodstained armor appeared on the wall, calmly, methodically cutting their way through ranks of maddened otrokars. The Horde crashed against them again and again like an enraged sea against rocks, and fell back, bloodied and helpless. The message couldn't be clearer. The otrokar were wild undisciplined savages and hundreds of them were no match for the six vampires.

Nice. How to ruin the peace talks in two minutes or less. That had to be some sort of record.

George sighed quietly.

The images stopped and blossomed into one enormous picture that took up all three walls: the seven planets of the Holy Anocracy. As the image came into focus, the rest of the vampire knights marched out in three distinct groups, one for each house. They reached the standard-bearer and froze.

Three faces appeared against the starry expanse of space, one per each wall: the severe face of the Warlord, a middle-aged vampire with jet-black hair on the right; the serene face of the female Hierophant on the left; and an old vampire in the middle. His hair was pure white, his skin wrinkled, and his eyes probing. He looked ancient, like the space behind him. It had to be Justice, the chief judge of the Holy Anocracy's highest court.

The vampires roared in unison. The tiny hairs on the back of my neck stood on end.

The vampire delegation turned as one and formed a line on the left side of the grand ballroom, the three Marshals and the standard-bearer closest to us.

"We're ready for the otrokars," George murmured to me.

"Release the Horde," I whispered.

The heavy door clanged open on the right and the otrokars emerged, Khanum in the lead and her son close behind. Three giant otrokars followed, each bigger than anything the vampires could throw at them, the rest of the delegation at their heels. They didn't walk, they stalked like great predatory cats, emerald, sapphire, and ruby highlights playing on their chitin armor, their ceremonial kilts falling in long plaits on one side. An ear-piercing whistle rang through the grand ballroom and broke into a wild melody, full of pipes and a quick drumbeat. The walls ignited again, now bright with the endless plains of Otroka, the Horde's home planet. A group of otrokars rode through yellow grass on odd mounts with reddish fur, hoofed feet, and canid heads. The image fractured and exploded into a mountain landscape filled with crags and fissures. The hard ground bristled with metal spikes, each supporting a severed vampire head.

The faces of the knights to my left were completely blank.

The puddles of vampire blood at the bases of the metal spikes trembled. The ground shuddered. A dull roar, like the sound of a distant waterfall, filled the air. The camera panned upward, showing a glimpse of a valley beyond the heads. An ocean of otrokars filled it, too many to count, a horde running at full speed, howling like wolves, the impact of their steps shaking the ground. They swept past the camera, bodies flashing by it. A muscular otrokar appeared on the screen, his face savage with fury. He swung a long sword, the muscles on his forearm flexing as he slashed, and the image turned black.

Okay. They weren't called the Hope-Crushing Horde for nothing.

The music kept going. The image on the wall transformed into the shield of the Horde backlit by flames. The Khanum moved aside, the otrokars parted, and one of them stepped forward. He was of average height and slight build, small enough to pass for a human. His black hair was cut short. The otrokar shrugged off his armor, letting it fall to the floor. Every muscle on his torso stood out. He wasn't beefy like a bodybuilder, but he was cut with superhuman precision. His stomach looked hard enough to shatter a staff if someone hit him with one. The otrokar pulled two long dark blades from the sheaths on his hips.

The Khanum clapped in rhythm with the music, and the otrokars followed her lead. The swordsman in the center spun in place, warming up. We were about to be treated to show-and-tell.

Another otrokar brought a basket filled with small green apple-like fruit to the Khanum. She picked one and hurled it at the swordsman. He moved at the last second, catching the fruit on the flat of his left blade, tossed it to his right then back again with superhuman dexterity. The otrokars kept clapping. The swordsman tossed the fruit up. His sword flashed and the fruit fell to the floor, cut in half.

"Nothing we can't handle," Jack said quietly.

The Khanum took a handful of fruit and passed the basket to her left. Dagorkun grabbed several and handed the basket to the next person. The Khanum gave a short whistle and the otrokars pelted the swordsman with apples. He spun like a dervish, dancing across the floor and slicing. The apples dropped to the ground, cut. Not a single fruit hit him.

"He might be a challenge," George said. His lips barely moved. If I weren't standing next to him, I wouldn't know he had spoken. "One on one, I can take care of it."

The swordsman spun, faster and faster, lithe, flexible, strong. A faint orange luminescence coated his blades. They began to glow.

George's eyes narrowed.

The swordsman stopped, swords raised at his sides like wings of a bird about to take flight.

The otrokars parted, revealing a female otrokar holding what looked like a machine gun. Oh no you don't.

She put the gun to her shoulder and fired.

I jerked my magic. Transparent walls shot out of the floor, shielding the vampires and us.

The stream of bullets hit the swordsman. He swung his blades, too fast to see, so fast they turned into arcs of orange light. Breath caught in my throat.

The gun clicked empty. A staccato of light knocks echoed through the grand ballroom—the last of the bullets clattering to the floor. The swordsman stopped moving. Sweat sheathed his torso. No wounds marked his body. The bullets, each sliced in half, lay in a horseshoe around him.

Unbelievable.

The otrokars bellowed in approval. The Khanum smiled broadly, winked at the vampires, and led her people to the right side of the grand ballroom, forming an identical line.

I exhaled and let the floor swallow the bullets and the mutilated fruit.

"We're going to need help," Jack said, his face grim.

George didn't answer. "The Merchants, please."

I opened the front doors. The Nuan Cee clan had to come from the front, because their quarters opened in the back wall, so I had made another hallway just for that purpose. The doors swung open, revealing Cookie. He was wearing a bright turquoise apron and carrying a basket. A fast, intricate melody filled the room. Cookie skipped forward in time with the music, like a human child on the last day of school, dipped his hand into the basket, and tossed a handful of gold and jewels into the air. Behind him four foxes in diaphanous blue veils embroidered with gold danced forward, gold bracelets and hoops tinkling on their wrists and ears. Then came the older members of the clan, swaying in step to the music: three steps forward, one step back, turn, and repeat. One carried a glittering cage with a beautiful blue bird in it. The second brandished a jeweled sword as big as himself. The third spun around, revealing spiderweb-thin layers of glowing fabric.

Cookie threw more gold, hopping back and forth between the lines of otrokar and vampires. One of the otrokars reached for a bright red jewel the size of a walnut by his foot. The older warrior next to him growled and the younger man stopped.

"To take their gold is to become their slave," the vampire next to me said softly.

The foxes kept coming, each display of wealth more ostentatious than the last. The palanquin with Nuan Cee's grandmother followed, floating in midair all by itself, and finally Nuan Cee himself, sitting cross-legged on his own palanquin, which was covered in shimmering silk dotted with piles of gems and plush pillows, and showing his sharp, even teeth in a bright smile.

The procession ended and the Merchants formed the third line, closing the square. The music died.

George's voice rang in the sudden quiet. "Welcome! The summit is now in session."

He stepped aside, inviting the gathering to the table with an elegant sweep of his hand.

The leaders of the three factions moved to the long table. George and Jack followed. Everyone took their seats.

I raised a transparent soundproof wall, sealing the table and its occupants from the rest of the guests. They were still plainly visible, but not a single sound escaped.

The otrokars, vampires, and the Merchants looked at me expectantly.

I raised my hand. The floor opened and Orro and three large tables, already set, rose into the room from below. Each table offered beautifully cut fruit on large white plates, baskets of bread, rice, sliced meat, bowls of soup, and as a centerpiece, a delicate, translucent flower the size of a watermelon, made of tiny individual slices of some pale meat.

The soup smelled heavenly.

"Evening's refreshments!" Orro called out. "Morean water drake sashimi with fruit and grains!"

CHAPTER SIX

The first session of the peace summit took three hours. The leaders of the three factions sat stone-faced behind the transparent wall the inn and I had made, while their subordinates formed three distinct groups in the ballroom. The Merchants chattered with each other while the otrokars and the vampires proceeded to flex their muscles, lounge about, and give each other the stink eye. There was no point in having them in the ballroom, but as long as their leaders were in each other's company, nobody would leave on the chance a fight might break out. I would have to figure out some entertainment for them if the summit went on for more than a few days.

I had to split my attention between the ballroom and the stables. The repair of the police cruiser was proceeding well, but keeping an eye on both areas at once tired me out. I would have to practice more. My father could track five or six areas of the inn at once. It was a learned skill that got better with practice, and I had been slacking off these past few months.

Finally Khanum slammed her fist on the table—which looked surprisingly comical without any sound coming through—and George waved the wall down.

I unsealed the side doors that led to the sleeping quarters. The otrokars exited first and the door melted into the wall behind them as if it had never been there. The Merchants were next. Nuan Cee paused by me.

I nodded at him. "How did the negotiations go, great Nuan Cee?"

"It is too early to tell." He pointed to Cookie, who began picking up the gold off the floor, carefully depositing it into a large satchel, and smiled. "My thrice-removed cousin's seventh son is working so hard. Such diligence. The blood always shows true in our family."

"I can have the inn gather the gold and jewels for him," I offered.

Nuan Cee waved his paw-hands. "Menial labor is good for the soul. I have done it for my family when I was his age, his father has done it, and his mother has done it for her family... It is a fine lesson to learn. When one starts at the bottom, there is no place to go but up. He is responsible for the riches; let him gather them."

"It will take him a while," I said. "I may have to lock him in the ballroom until he is done for his own safety." Having a tiny fox running around the inn carrying millions in jewels and gold in a canvas sack wasn't a good idea.

"I take no insult." Nuan Cee waved his hand again. "Keep him under lock as long as you wish."

The Merchants filed out. The vampires followed, all except Arland and Robart, who both made a beeline for me. Almost instantly both of them realized they were going to the same place. Arland glowered at Robart and sped up. The Marshal of House Vorga glowered back, matched Arland's pace, and then went faster. Arland accelerated to keep up. The sight of them rapidly marching in full armor was like standing on train tracks and watching a locomotive barrel toward me at full speed.

I wondered if they would sprint if the distance was great enough.

I brushed the floor with the bristles of my broom. I had turned it into a staff at the beginning of the ceremonies, but an hour into the session, I let it flow back into the broom shape. The past couple of days and the lack of sleep had taken their toll, and the broom felt comfortable and familiar. The floor stretched slightly, then more and more, rising at a slight incline and flowing toward the vampires like one of those moving sidewalks that transports people at airports. Except my sidewalk was moving in the opposite direction.

Neither vampire noticed that they were now going uphill and sliding backward with each step. They were still neck and neck and not getting any closer.

I bit my lip to keep from laughing.

At the wall Jack chuckled into his fist.

I put a little more speed into the floor. They had to notice now.

The Marshals redoubled their efforts. They were almost running now. If I didn't stop this now, they might crash into each other and I would have blood on my hands.

"My lords! I'm not a castle. You don't have to storm me."

Both vampires stopped in their tracks. The floor stopped as well. Normal people would have lost their balance, stumbled, and possibly landed on their faces. The two vampires leapt up simultaneously, like two great jungle cats, and landed on their respective sides of what was once a moving sidewalk. The floor thudded, accepting the full weight of their armor.

Jack dissolved into a coughing fit.

Don't laugh, don't laugh, don't laugh...

The two vampires strode toward me and said in one voice, "Lady Dina..."

Oh no.

The Marshals clamped their mouths shut and tried to kill each other with their stares.

I squeezed my left hand into a fist. If I guffawed in their faces, I could kiss any further business from the Holy Anocracy good-bye.

"Lord Robart, how may I help you?"

Robart shot a triumphant look at Arland. "I've paid the Arbitrator's price for the car."

"Yes, you have. Thank you, the giant water serpent was delicious."

Robart blinked, momentarily thrown off track, but recovered. "I will have my knight returned to me."

Knight? What knight? Oh shoot. I had completely forgotten about the vampire who'd almost chopped the police car in half. I'd left him in the basement holding cell for almost four hours. I concentrated. The knight was alive and well. He was sitting on the floor meditating. I gave the floor a little push and felt it slide up, carrying the knight with it.

"You will find your knight in your quarters."

Robart nodded. His gaze narrowed. "Perhaps if you were less heavy-handed in your treatment of the guests you claim to honor and protect, your inn would have a higher rating."

He did not. Oh yes, yes he did. "Perhaps if you trained the knights under your command to follow simple orders, your House would've reached greater prominence within your empire."

Robart locked his jaw.

If my smile were any sweeter, you could pour it on pancakes and call it syrup. "Good night, Marshal. Lord Arland, how may I assist you?"

Robart turned and stalked off to the vampire entrance.

Arland nodded at me, his face grave. "I've come to check on the progress of the car."

"Of course. Give me a moment to set things in order."

"Take all the time you require," Arland said.

I watched Robart exit and dissolved the door behind him. Caldenia rose in her box, waved at me, and retired, Beast following her. I'd have to pick her brain tomorrow for any insights. Only Arland, Cookie, Jack, and I remained. I turned to Jack. "Did you need anything?"

He shook his head. "Just making sure everyone goes to bed like good boys and girls. See you in the morning."

Jack went out the front entrance.

I exhaled quietly and walked over to Cookie, who was crawling around on his hands and knees. "Hey there. I have to leave for a couple of minutes, but I'll be back soon. I'm going to lock the doors so you'll be safe in here. But if something goes wrong, call me and I'll be right over."

Cookie nodded and dropped a sapphire the size of a gummy bear into his bag.

I led Arland back to the stables, sealing the ballroom with Cookie inside it as we left. Beast caught up with me and hopped into my arms, gazing at me in canine adoration. That's the wonderful thing about dogs. If you're gone for a day or for an hour, they're just as ecstatic when you come back.

The engineer knight and Nuan Cee's niece were quietly chatting. Officer Marais still lay on the tarp on the floor where we'd left him. His chest rose up and down in a measured rhythm. A small smile spread over his lips. He must've been dreaming about something fun. For a moment I envied him the sleep. I was so tired.

The cruiser sat in the middle of the stables. It looked intact.

Hardwir opened the hood and showed me the engine. "Behold."

I beheld. It looked just like a normal, somewhat grimy, engine.

"No modifications?" Arland asked.

"None," Hardwir said.

Arland peered at him. "Are you sure? I know you. You didn't improve on it at all? In any way?"

"No improvements." Hardwir spat to the side. "Just as ugly and poisonous as it came to me."

I checked the hood, the inside, and the trunk. Everything seemed to be in order. The car looked exactly as it had before it was hit with a blood axe.

I turned to Arland. "Would you mind helping me? I have to leave the inn grounds and position Officer Marais in the car and he's heavy."

Arland nodded at me, his face grave. "It would be my honor."

Something was wrong. He normally wasn't this somber. "I need you to change clothes."

He didn't miss a beat. "Of course."

I stepped out and returned with a pair of jeans, a T-shirt, and size-fourteen athletic shoes. Arland arched his thick eyebrows. He had worn this outfit during his last visit when he pretended to be human. He took the clothes and went to change behind the cruiser.

I turned to Hardwir and Nuan Cee's niece. "Please don't leave the stables."

"You have my word," Hardwir said. "We will stay put. I was never a good swimmer. Besides, I will watch over the Marshal's armor."

"I will stay as well," Nuan Cee's niece said. "I'm weak and helpless, and I don't want to be punished."

Weak and helpless, sure. Next thing she would try to sell me a lovely coastal villa in Kansas.

Arland emerged, camouflaged as a very large human. The camouflage wasn't exactly working. Dressing Arland in Earth clothes was like putting bunny ears on a tiger. The ears were cute, but the tiger was still scary. The T-shirt stretched on his shoulders, too small for his arms. He was built like a bear: broad shoulders, carved arms, a wide chest, and a flat, hard stomach. It was the kind of frame that could effortlessly support the weight of vampire armor and let him swing a heavy weapon for hours without slowing down. If an NFL linebacker ran full speed at Arland, the football player would just bounce off.

The Marshal picked up Officer Marais as if the fully grown man was a child, put him in the backseat, and slid into the passenger seat. I started the engine, put the car in reverse, and drove backward slowly. The walls slipped out of the way. A moment later and we slid into my driveway, the rear of the car facing the street. I killed the engine and sat quietly, listening. This plan hinged on having no witnesses.

It was ten past midnight, and the subdivision lay silent. I eased the cruiser into neutral and let the slight incline of the driveway do the rest. Whisper-quiet, the police car rolled out of the driveway, across the street, and down Camelot Road. I gently steered it back to the spot where Marais had parked before the whole affair started and pulled with my magic. I only had a fraction of my power outside the inn's boundaries, but a fraction would be enough.

The air next to the driver's window shimmered, and the Eye materialized out of thin air behind and a little to the right of the car, its outer shell, once silver, now swirling with the perfect reflection of the road. I was off by three feet.

"Stop recording," I told it. "Erase last ten minutes. Project position."

The Eye emitted a pale beam of greenish light that snapped into a holographic projection of the dashboard camera. I slowly slid the car in place, trying to match it. It took me three tries. Officer Marais liked to park very close to the curb. Finally the real dashboard camera and the holographic projection matched.

"Home," I told the Eye. It landed in my hand and ejected the SD card. I slid it back into the dashboard cam.

The neighborhood was still empty. Great. Nobody had noticed my late-night maneuvering. I stepped out of the car and nodded to Arland. He exited the vehicle, picked up Officer Marais, and sat him in the driver's seat. I locked his seat belt in place, reached through the open window, careful to stay away from any mirrors, and pushed Record on the camera. We quietly moved to the side and went deeper into the subdivision.

"What are we doing?" Arland murmured, looming next to me.

"We're going to make a big circle and come into the inn through the back so the camera doesn't see us."

"Won't there be a break in recording?"

I shook my head. "The Eye recorded over four hours of video and then looped it into seven hours of footage, using a random algorithm complete with a false time stamp. It overwrote your arrival completely. Right now the real dashboard camera is recording over that video. By the time he wakes up, the tail end of the looped footage will be overwritten with the real video as well. When Officer Marais watches it, he will see hours and hours of the inn sitting there with no activity."

The only indication of foul play might be the slight jump in the view of the camera. The Eye had analyzed the footage on the SD card and had positioned itself to match the view precisely, but it was very difficult to match the position of the car. Given more time, I probably could've gotten closer, but sooner or later someone would notice me inside the police cruiser.

"Clever," Arland said.

Yes, clever and very expensive. The remote camera had cost me a lot of money and a favor that had been difficult to repay.

We turned right on Bedivere Road.

"Dina," Arland said. His voice had a slightly rough quality to it. Not Lady Dina, but Dina. He was up to something. That wasn't good.

"Yes?"

"I'm but a humble soldier."

Here we go. He had given me a version of this speech before. This definitely wasn't good.

"You and I, we have a history."

Okay, what could he possibly be upset about?

"We were comrades-in-arms, fighting at each other's side for the common goal. We have broken bread together."

Was this about the food? Was he upset that we didn't serve red meat at dinner? But we'd told them not to expect a big meal the first day because separate meals would be served in their quarters. We wouldn't set up the big dinner until tomorrow.

"That kind of connection, it stays with you."

Was he offended because I let the otrokars fire a weapon? Was it because the otrokars were scheduled to be the first to arrive to the inn and the vampires were last? But we had compensated the Holy Anocracy by inviting them to be the first to officially enter the ballroom.

"Dina…"

He dipped his head and looked into my eyes. A small shiver ran down my spine. Arland had focused completely on me. His face was handsome, but his eyes were breathtaking. Deep, intense blue, they usually communicated power or aggression, but right then they were warm, softened by emotion until they seemed almost velvet. He reached over and took my hand into his, the calluses on his strong fingers scraping against my skin.

I realized we had stopped under an oak by some house. The night was suddenly very small, and Arland had filled it completely.

I had left my broom at the inn. It was just me, the darkness, and the vampire knight.

He held my hand, running his thumb over my fingers. "I want to know what I have done to offend you. Whatever blunder I committed, I will strive to remedy it."

It would help so much if I knew what he was talking about. The way he looked at me made it difficult to concentrate.

"Tell me." He was standing too close. His voice was too intimate. And he was still looking at me with that warmth, as if I were someone special. "What may I do to get back into your good graces?"

He stroked my hand. For some reason it felt more intimate than a kiss. My pulse sped up. This was ridiculous. If I didn't put some distance between us, I might do something I would regret. If you said yes to a vampire, he heard "I surrender," and I had no intention of surrendering.

"You've done nothing to offend me."

"Then why did you acknowledge Robart before me?"

What?

"You addressed him before you addressed me."

I cleared my throat. "Just to be clear, you're upset because I spoke to Robart before I spoke to you? In the ballroom just before we went to check on the car?"

"I understand that the circumstances of the summit prevent frank exchanges," Arland said. "An appearance of propriety must be maintained and any hint of favoritism is to be avoided at all costs. But when one travels so far, one looks for the small things. A chance glance. A brief kindness, freely offered and gone unnoticed by all except its intended recipient. Some hint, some indication that he has not been forgotten. One might take an acknowledgment of a bitter rival before him, in public, as an indication of certain things."

It dawned on me. His feelings were actually hurt.

"You haven't been forgotten," I told him and meant it. "I looked forward to seeing you. I spoke to Robart before I spoke to you so I could get him to leave. If I hadn't, he would still be in the ballroom waiting for me to return."

Arland smiled at me.

Wow.

When they said a smile could launch a thousand ships, they had Arland in mind. Except in his case, that thousand ships would be an armada carrying an army of some of the best humanoid predators the galaxy had managed to spawn, ready to slaughter their enemy on the battlefield.

I wanted to exhale and back away slowly. But he was still holding my hand.

I pulled whatever will I could scrape together and made my voice sound casual. "Arland? Can I have my hand back?"

"My apologies." He opened his fingers and let my hand slip back through. "It was quite forward of me."

Judging by his self-satisfied smile, he didn't have any regrets. He had wanted a reaction and he'd gotten one.

I'd made a mistake. I'd dealt with plenty of vampires before. A few months ago, when he helped Sean and me destroy the dahaka assassin, he'd all but said he was interested in me. I hadn't heard from him in months, but that changed nothing. Vampires tended to be infuriatingly single-minded.

I should've never invited him to come with me. I should've never left the inn with him. I kept making these rookie blunders because I was too tired to see straight. I had to get some sleep. It was a necessity at this point.

I began walking. The sooner we got to the inn, the better.

The street turned. The last house had no fence. It had fallen down about three weeks ago, and the owners hadn't gotten around to replacing it. We quietly slipped through the yard, crossed the main road to the wooded area, and started down the narrow trail that would open to the back of the inn.

"I'm glad you relied on me for assistance," Arland said. "I once told you to call on me. I meant it. Anytime you require it, I will be your shield."

"Thank you. It's very kind of you."

I stepped onto the inn grounds. The magic flowed through me, and I let out a quiet breath.

Ten minutes later I let Arland, Hardwir, and Nuan Cee's niece into the ballroom. The inn had dimmed the lights and a soothing warm glow filled the big room. I opened the doorways and closed them after they passed through.

The floor of the ballroom was clean. No hint of gold and jewels remained. Where was Cookie?

I closed my eyes, concentrating. There he was, slumped in the corner. I walked over. The small fox was curled into a ball on the floor, his bag under his head like a pillow. I nudged him gently.

"Cookie? Cookie?"

He opened his turquoise eyes and blinked, his face drowsy.

"Come on, let's get you to bed."

"I can't," he yawned. "I have to find the emerald."

"What kind of emerald?"

"A big one. The Green Eye. Very expensive." His nose drooped. He looked exhausted. "If I don't find it, I'll be in trouble."

I nudged the inn to check the floor. Nothing. The emerald wasn't here.

"We'll find it in the morning." I took him by the hand and carefully helped him to his feet. "Come on. Off to bed."

I led him to the door and watched him go up the stairs. He knocked on the upstairs door. Someone opened it and another fox ushered him inside.

I sealed the ballroom and dragged myself upstairs. I needed to take a shower, but the bed looked so comfortable.

Gertrude Hunt and I had survived the first day. We dealt with a major crisis, we got through a big ceremony, and we managed to get everyone to bed without bloodshed. I patted the inn's wall. "I'm so proud of you."

The inn creaked slightly, the wood warm under my fingers.

I meant to sit down on my bed, but my legs must've been tired, because they decided to stop supporting my weight. I fell onto the covers, yawned, and passed out.

The inn woke me up at six thirty. I dreamed that Sean Evans came back. We were having a barbecue, and he kept fighting with Orro over how to season the ribs. I lay in bed with my eyes open and looked at the wooden beams crossing over my ceiling, taking a mental tally of all my guests. Everyone was where they were supposed to be, except for George who was in the kitchen with Orro. The Arbitrator and his people had freedom of movement in the inn, with the exception of the guests' private quarters. Each faction was secured by two doors. The outer doors opened to the ballroom. I had sealed those, but they would open at George's request. The inner doors were controlled by the guests. George and his people would have to knock and ask permission to enter. Even though he was the Arbitrator and paid my bills, I wouldn't let him have complete access. The privacy of my guests was sacred.

I closed my eyes. The barbecue dream had been so vivid. In the few seconds it took me to wake up, I was almost convinced that it was real.

This strange obsession with Sean Evans had to stop. It would've made sense if there was a relationship there, but even if I tried to lie to myself and say there was one, he had left. They all left. That was the basic truth of the life of an innkeeper: guests arrived, walked into your life, and departed, while you stayed behind, never knowing if you would see them again. I had plenty of conversations with my neighbors and Caldenia, but I had few friends. Sean had learned who I was and accepted it. I didn't have to pretend to be someone else.

I tapped the covers with my palm. Beast jumped up and scooted toward me, caught in the complete ecstasy of being invited on the bed. I hugged her to me and petted her fur.

I needed to get my emotions in order. Yesterday was the first day, but today the real work would begin.

"Reiki music," I murmured.

A quiet, soothing melody of flutes and drums filled the room, floating against the sounds of a distant thunderstorm. I had found the soundtrack on sale in a bargain bin, and it proved surprisingly relaxing. I sat quietly on my bed with my eyes closed. Just let it go. Sink into the music, listen to the soothing sound, and let things go...

The inn's magic tugged on me.

I opened my eyes. A screen formed in the wall. On the screen Officer Marais jumped out of his car. Red welts marked his face—the remindermuds of falling on the pavement last night. Beast saw him and barked once, baring her teeth.

This was going to be interesting.

Officer Marais ran to the front of the vehicle and stared at it in shock. The Reiki soundtrack kept playing. Trilling bird cries added a pleasant high note to the sound of flutes.

Officer Marais dashed back to the driver's seat, popped the release on the hood, ran back, and jerked the hood open.

"Who do you think I am, an amateur?" I murmured.

Officer Marais stumbled back from the hood, his face pale, and began to pace back and forth in front of the cruiser, glancing at the hood once in a while.

I felt guilty. I'd met some bad cops before. Sometimes when a person got a little bit of power, especially if the rest of their life made them feel powerless, they went to a dark place with it. Marais wasn't one of those cops. He calmly followed the rules and was dedicated to his job. He wasn't on a power trip, nor did he get off on screaming at people and bullying them. He was an Andy Griffith kind of cop, one who relied on his authority more than his gun. He probably wanted to be respected rather than feared. His sense told him that something about Gertrude Hunt was off, and he genuinely wanted to get to the bottom of it. If I were running a meth lab or a ring of car thieves, he would've dealt with me in no time, but the inn was so far outside his frame of reference he couldn't even begin to guess at the truth, and if he somehow managed it, he wouldn't believe it.

Marais pivoted and stared at the house.

"That's right. You've been beaten."

Officer Marais clenched his teeth, making the muscles on his jaw bulge, marched to the car, and got in.

"Zoom closer," I asked.

The inn zoomed in. Officer Marais was looking at his dashcam. His face was grim.

"No, there's nothing on there either. You lost. Go home."

Now he would start his cruiser and drive away, and I would get on with my day.

Officer Marais stepped out of the car, slapped the door closed, and marched to the inn.

Oh crap.

I jumped off the bed and pulled on a fresh pair of sweatpants. I needed a bra. Where the hell had I put my laundry? I yanked the laundry basket out of the closet and dug through it. If only I would put away my laundry after I washed it, I wouldn't be in this mess... Got it.

I slipped the bra on, threw a white T-shirt over it, and dashed out of my bedroom and down a long hallway. The Reiki music followed me. "Turn it off," I breathed. The music died. Beast shot ahead of me, barking her head off. I ran down the staircase two steps at the time and burst into the front room just as the doorbell rang.

I ran into the kitchen, past Orro and George, grabbed a cup from the cabinet, stuck it under the coffeemaker, and popped the first pod I touched into the Keurig.

The bell rang again. Beast barked in the other room.

I grabbed the coffee, dumped a whole bunch of creamer into it to cool it enough to drink, and went to the door.

The bell rang, insistent.

I swung the door open and stared at Officer Marais's furious face.

"Officer Marais! Good morning. What can I do for you? What's happened now? Has a chupacabra been spotted in the neighborhood? Or was it a Bigfoot? Maybe someone saw a UFO? I can't wait to hear how it's all my fault."

I sipped my coffee to appear extra casual.

"You…" Officer Marais pulled himself together through an obviously huge effort of will. "I know what happened."

"What happened when? Where?"

"Here." He stabbed his finger toward the floor.

I glanced at the floor. "I don't follow…"

"I saw a group of men appear on the road."

"What do you mean, appear?" George said behind me.

I glanced over my shoulder. He was wearing loose gray slacks and a fisherman's sweater of natural beige wool.

Officer Marais looked at him for a long moment, no doubt committing his face to memory. "When I attempted to question them, a large male suspect swung a bladed weapon and cut through the hood of my vehicle. Then you used an unknown device to restrain me. I was dragged through a tunnel to the stables, where I lay on the floor while you and the others discussed what to do with me. Then you gave me an injection and I lost consciousness."

I sighed and sipped my coffee. "If everything happened the way you say it did, there should be evidence. There must be damage to your car, and your dashcam would show a record of these events. Do you have any evidence, Officer Marais?"

His face turned red. "You repaired it."

"I repaired your vehicle? Setting aside that I'm not a mechanic and wouldn't know the first thing about repairing a car, if I had tampered with your vehicle, there would some indication of it. Are there any signs of repair?"

Officer Marais clenched his teeth together again.

"I think that you work very long hours," I said. "I saw you this morning sleeping in your cruiser. I think you had a very vivid dream. Your dreams do not give you the right to come here and harass me and my business. I don't know what I have done to make you dislike me, but this isn't right and it's not fair. You are now interfering with my ability to make a living. I didn't break any laws. I'm not a criminal. Does it seem okay to you that you are continuously coming here and accusing me of random things just because you don't like me?"

He looked taken aback.

"Go home, Officer. I'm sure you must have a family who probably misses you. I am not going to file a complaint, but I do wish you would stop coming here every time something odd happens or doesn't happen."

I closed the door and leaned against it.

A moment later the magic of the inn chimed in my head, letting me know Officer Marais had left the grounds. George stepped to the window. "He's leaving. Nicely done."

"If I argued with him, he would continue to attack. Instead I acted like a victim, and Officer Marais has been trained to be considerate of victims." I still felt bad for manipulating him.

"The summit is set to begin in two hours," George said. "I'm afraid I have to ask you for a favor. I need your help."

I looked at my cup of coffee. I didn't want to do anyone any favors. I wanted fifteen minutes of uninterrupted time with my refrigerator. I'd barely eaten last night, and I had just downed a whole cup of coffee on an empty stomach. But I had a job to do. Maybe it would be something simple.

I smiled at the Arbitrator. "How can I help you?"

"If I give you coordinates to a particular world, could you open a door to it?" George asked.

"Which world?"

He raised his cane. A set of numbers ignited in midair, written in crimson. The first two digits told me everything I needed to know.

"No," I said.

"But I've seen you open doors," he said.

"It's not that simple." It never was. "Why don't we sit down?"

We walked back into the kitchen and sat at the table. Orro swept by me like a silent blur of brown, and suddenly a plate holding two tiny crepes filled with cream and sliced strawberries materialized in front of me. I didn't even see him slide it there. Our kitchen was staffed by a ninja.

"Thank you," I said.

Orro nodded and went to the stove.

George quietly waited.

"The inns are not well understood." I cut a small piece of crepe and tried it. It practically melted on my tongue. "Orro, this is heavenly."

Orro's needles quivered slightly.

"We live within them, we use them, but even we, the inn-keepers, are unsure about why they function the way they do."

Jack and Gaston walked into the kitchen.

"It's easiest to imagine them as trees. An inn, like Gertrude Hunt, begins with a seed. The seed is weak and fragile, but if properly tended, it sprouts. It sends roots deep into the ground. What we see"—I made a small circle with my fork, encompassing the kitchen—"is but a small fraction of the inn's form. As it grows, it begins to spread branches through the universe. These branches don't obey our physics. Some puncture our reality. Some transform and evolve beyond our understanding. A single inn of some age, like Gertrude Hunt, may reach into other worlds."

"Like Yggdrasil," George said.

"Yes, like that."

"What's Yggdrasil?" Jack asked.

"A holy tree of the ancient Norse," George said. "It extends into all nine realms of their mythology."

"The problem is that innkeepers have no control over the direction of the branches," I said. "We know when the inn extends into a particular world, and after a while we can access it, but we can't make the inn grow a branch to the place of our choosing. Most inns instinctively seek out Baha-char. That's usually the first world that opens to us. We don't know why. People sometimes say that the seed of the very first inn was brought to us from Baha-char and that all its descendants instinctively seek the connection to their homeland the way salmon travel hundreds of miles to reach their spawning grounds. I can tell you that I know every world this inn has reached so far, and your coordinates are not among them. Furthermore, you are asking for a portal to a world that is very similar to ours. That world is another Earth that exists in its own tiny reality, splintered from the majority of the cosmos. It's like reaching into a pocket on the universe's coat. I don't know the capabilities of every inn on Earth, but I can tell you that my father always told me that creating a door to an alternative dimension like that could not be done. It would collapse the inn."

George leaned back in his chair. I ate my crepes, enjoying every single bite.

"But you can open a portal to Baha-char?"

"Yes."

"If you get caught, there will be hell to pay," Gaston said.

"I'll have to take the risk." George rose smoothly. "In that case, I would still be grateful for your assistance. I would like you to escort me to that world and back. I can find a way to it from Baha-char, but I will need you to lead me back to the inn."

I rubbed my face. "You're asking me to leave the inn while it's full of guests."

"Yes. I take full responsibility for it."

"I don't understand. You're an Arbitrator. You possess the technology to find the inn from Baha-char."

"I don't want to use the technology at my disposal for personal reasons," George said.

"There is something you're not telling me."

"He wants to go to a world that's forbidden to us," Jack said. "Our home world. If he uses any of the gadgets provided to us by the Arbitrator Office, he can be tracked. They'll have his ass."

I took a moment to mourn my empty plate and to think about what I was going to say next without completely alienating the man in charge of signing the check. "So you want me to endanger my guests by leaving the inn and escort you on a mission that could potentially cause you to be sanctioned, derailing the peace talks and my payment and ruining the reputation of this inn. Could you help me understand why I should do that?"

Gaston laughed under his breath.

George sighed. "I'm just as invested in the success of the peace summit as you are. As matters stand now, I do not believe the peace talks will succeed. The problem is Ruah, the bulletproof swordsman."

Aha. Was he implying that Gertrude Hunt couldn't handle one otrokar? "Do you doubt my ability to suppress him?"

George grimaced. "That's not the issue. I know that you can subdue Ruah. The problem is the otrokar mindset. The otrokars acknowledge that a single vampire is a more rounded warrior; however, they have an unshakable faith in their own supremacy through the use of genetic specialization. Ruah is the pinnacle of that process. They believe he is unbeatable with a sword. As long as he reigns supreme, he makes them feel invincible. I have to shatter that faith. I have to prove to them that he and the Horde are not infallible, and I have to do it in terms they will understand."

"Why not use the vampires?" I asked.

"Because that would simply flip the coin." Caldenia strode into the kitchen. Her hair was meticulously styled, her pale green gown flattered her complexion, and her makeup was flawless. Her eyes were sharp and her bearing had a slightly regal and dangerous air to it. Her Grace was back.

The three men bowed. She nodded at them and accepted a cup of tea from Orro.

"If he uses a knight to defeat an undefeatable otrokar, the same immunity the otrokars now feel will be transferred to the Holy Anocracy. To get them to cooperate and work together, both sides must be humbled. He has to shake their very worldview."

"I'm willing to put my career at risk," George said, "because I believe it to be completely necessary. This isn't a spur-of-the-moment decision."

I had a feeling that nothing George ever did was spur-of-the-moment. If he ever had a one-night stand, it would probably be meticulously researched and organized.

The ball was in my court. Leaving so many guests unattended was crazy. But George had a point. The longer the peace talks dragged on, the more rejuvenated the inn became, but also the more money their presence cost us. The summit had to end in a reasonable time frame, and it had to end with peace, not war. If the summit failed, there would be plenty of blame to go around, and Gertrude Hunt would earn a big black eye.

What to do? We'd be gone over an hour at least. A lot of things could happen in an hour. Officer Marais could return with backup. The otrokars could try to bust through the walls and go on a rampage. The vampires could set fire to the inn…

Okay, I had to stop. Wild theories got me nowhere.

My mother would not approve of this harebrained scheme. But my dad would think it was an adventure. Even my parents were no help.

"Escort me to Baha-char," George said. "I promise you, I can take things from there."

If we got caught, George would be in trouble and I would be in trouble with him.

"Breakfast is due to be served to the guests in their quarters in half an hour," I said. "According to the schedule, the summit is to begin an hour after breakfast. That gives us about an hour and a half. Your people have to uphold the peace until then."

"Won't be an issue," Jack said.

I rose. "We have to hurry."

⚜ ⚜ ⚜

I crouched on the floor of a small shop. Beautiful pale carpets lined the walls and the floor, providing a backdrop for hundreds of elaborate pieces of lacquerware painted with meticulous patterns of vivid turquoise, cheerful gold, and bright scarlet. Jugs shaped like exotic birds, plates where strange monsters clashed in battle with each other, platters showcasing foreign blooms, all filled the shelves and waited in every corner. It was good that I'd brought very little money with me, or I would have walked out of here with something.

George, wearing a plain brown cloak, crouched next to me, deep in negotiations with the owner of the shop. The shopkeeper was so swaddled in layers of blue and white tattered cloth that nothing except his eyes and a narrow strip of olive skin around them was visible. He waved his hands as he haggled with George in an unfamiliar language. His hands looked human enough, but each had only three fingers and a thumb.

It had taken us about twenty minutes to find the shop, and we had been crouching here for so long my legs were beginning to ache. I could feel time dripping away, one drop at a time. Part of me really wanted to be back at the inn. A smaller part wanted to find Wilmos again and ask him about Sean Evans.

The trader rose off his haunches. George stood up and dropped a small pouch into the trader's hand. The shopkeeper handed a ball of blue yarn to George, tied the end of it to a shelf, walked to the back of the store, and pulled a carpet aside. Morning daylight filled the shop. The shopkeeper waved at us.

Great. Here's a magic thread. Hold on to it so you don't get lost and hope there isn't a minotaur waiting to meet you.

George stepped to the light, letting the yarn pull from the ball as he walked. I got up and followed him. A vast garden spread before us, rows and rows of roses, surrounded by a forty-foot wall of burgundy-colored stone. Here and there towers punctuated the wall.

"Where are we?" I asked.

"This is Ganer College," George said. "In my world it's a place of healing."

A woman walked among the roses. She was about my height. Her very dark brown hair coiled on her head in a conservative but elegant bun. A gray gown hugged her figure, falling down in straight lines, its hem brushing the pebbles of the path as she walked. A gossamer-thin length of matching gray fabric wrapped the gown from the left, draped in an asymmetric swag over the woman's left shoulder. She seemed about my age and not particularly tall, strong, or very imposing.

I glanced at George. For a moment his cool mask slipped and I saw an intense, all-consuming longing reflected in his features. My father loved my mother completely. He also mistrusted the modern world. He understood it, but it moved too fast and all its dangers seemed magnified to him. He viewed each drive to the store as a failed suicide attempt and each major city as a den of cutthroats and thieves lying in wait for their victim. He would never dream of keeping my mother from doing something she wanted to do. But sometimes when my mother was about to leave on an errand, especially if she had to drive into the city, he would look at her just like that, as if he wanted more than anything in the world to wrap his arms around her and keep her safe with him.

The expression flickered and vanished off George's face, but it was too late. I'd seen it. The cosmic Arbitrator was not infallible.

George started down the path and I followed him. When we were about thirty feet from the woman, she stopped. "That's far enough."

George stopped.

"I'm angry with you." She spoke with an unfamiliar but cultured accent. "I don't like to be angry, George. I work very diligently to avoid that emotion. You should leave."

"I need your help," he said.

She turned around. I almost never got envious of other women. When I did, it was usually because I had gone grocery shopping. I'd stand in a checkout line, bored, and *People* magazine or some tabloid would catch my eye and I'd buy it, because I felt too guilty about putting it back after flipping through it. I would look at the actresses and models while drinking my tea and sometimes wish my eyes were bigger or my lips were fuller. But actresses and models were abstract people, half reality, half airbrushed perfection. This woman was real, she was my age, slightly taller, and she was incredibly, shockingly beautiful without any Photoshop assistance. Her skin was a light, golden bronze, her mouth was full and perfect, her cheekbones high, and her eyes, huge under nearly black eyebrows, were dark like bitter chocolate. When you saw her, you wanted to keep looking at her.

Right now she was looking at George, and the way her eyebrows bent, George was clearly not her favorite person.

"You didn't tell them," she said. "You had dinner with the family at Camarine manor. You helped little William catch fireflies in a jar, you brought presents for the girls, and you sat on the balcony and drank wine with Declan and your sister. A week later you were simply gone."

"I left a note," George said.

"A note that said you were going on a secret mission off-world and taking Jack and Gaston with you and that you would be back in twenty years. That is all you left by way of explanation. Do you have any idea how worried your sister is? Your nieces? Your nephew? You play with people's lives like they are toys, George. We are all chess pieces to you. You move us around the board as you please. I could understand if you were oblivious to human emotions, but you fully comprehend our feelings. You simply choose to ignore them. I don't understand it. You used to be so compassionate when we were children. Now we don't matter to you at all."

"It's part of a job," he said.

She simply looked at him.

"I was not permitted to say good-bye. The note was the best I could do."

"But here you are." Her eyes narrowed. "Didn't you tell me that once you accepted this job, you could not come back? Are you breaking the rules again?"

"Of course I am."

"So you have no problems breaking the rules when it suits you. Are you telling me that you couldn't find any way to personally soften that blow for your family?"

"I'm a selfish bastard," George said. "I didn't want the pain of saying good-bye, so I avoided it."

The woman sighed. "What is it you want?"

"I need your help."

"You already asked me. The answer was no then. It's still no. I'm not going on your mad adventure. My home is here."

George brushed his cane with his thumb. An image of Ruah appeared in thin air. We watched him spin his swords and slice through bullets. The woman tilted her head, tapping her bottom lip with her index finger. The recording stopped with the otrokar paused in midstrike, graceful like a dancer.

"Cute," she said. "He's good."

"Is he better than you?" George asked.

She pondered the still image. "I don't know."

"Don't you want to find out?"

A predatory spark flashed in her eyes and died. "No."

"Come with me," George said. "Please."

"George, I worked for years to put aside what the world outside these walls made me. Out there I am an abomination. I'm a killer. No, I belong here."

He shook his head. "Lark…"

"The name is Sophie," she corrected.

"What is here? This?" He turned, waving his hands to encompass the flowers.

"Here I'm not a monster." She raised her head. "Here I do not kill anyone. I'm at peace here."

"Your peace is a lie."

She glared at him, and I fought an urge to step back. "You have no right to tell me how to live my life. Let me be. Leave me alone, George. I want to be at peace!"

"You are not meant to be at peace. We, the human beings, are meant to live life to its fullest. We are meant to experience it all—sadness, disappointment, rage, kindness, joy, love. We are meant to test ourselves. It is painful and frightening, but this is what it means to be alive. You are hiding from life here. This isn't peace. This is a slow, deliberate suicide."

He stabbed his cane into the pathway. Images exploded: a vast, roiling nebula, spaceships, planets, ancient ruins, strange buildings, terrible and beautiful beings… They spun around us, vivid, bright, loud… Sophie looked at them and stars reflected in her eyes.

"Look at it!" George's voice shuddered with barely contained awe. "*Look* at it! Don't you want to experience it? Don't you want to be brave? You are not a gentle flower who spends its whole life in a greenhouse. You are a wildfire, Lark. A wildfire."

A sun burst on the images, its violent fury drowning the cosmos.

"Dare to take that step and I will show you wonders beyond your imagination. I will give you a chance to make a difference. Come with me." George offered his hand to her. "Live. Join me or not, but live, gods damn you, because I cannot stand the thought of you slowly aging here like some dusty fossil under glass. Take my hand and bring your sword. The universe is waiting."

CHAPTER SEVEN

We entered the inn twenty minutes before the start of the summit. Jack greeted us in the front room. A wide grin split his face.

He looked Sophie up and down, scrutinizing her gown and the two swords she carried in her hands. "What is it you're wearing? Are you trying to be mistaken for a girl?"

Sophie arched her eyebrows and punched him in the arm.

"What was that for?"

"That was for leaving without telling anyone good-bye."

I turned to George, who was carrying Sophie's large canvas bag. "You can set that down."

He carefully placed the bag on the floor and it sank into the wood. Sophie's eyes widened.

"Come with me, please," I told her. "I will show you to your room."

I led her down the east hallway. The best place would be near Caldenia, in the neutral wing. I had already explained the inn and the rules of being a guest. "I'm going to put you next to a permanent guest of the inn."

"You're irritated with George," Sophie said. "Why?"

I blinked.

"Don't feel bad. You hid it very well, but I've been trained to read body language."

I sighed. "I have to be there when the summit starts, so I have less than fifteen minutes with you. Welcoming a guest to the inn is a duty innkeepers hold sacred. It must be done properly, but George left me no time. I hate to rush."

Caldenia stepped out of her room. "Another guest? How delightful."

"Her Grace, Caldenia ka ret Magren," I said.

Sophie dropped into an elegant curtsy and rose.

Caldenia's eyes sparkled. "And what is your name, my dear?"

"Sophie."

"Just Sophie?"

Sophie smiled. "For now."

"Are you going to view the summit?" Caldenia asked.

"I was considering it."

"You absolutely must visit me. I have an entire balcony to myself."

"I would be delighted," Sophie said.

"It is settled then." Her Grace smiled and proceeded down the hallway, her gown flaring behind her with regal majesty.

I paused before the door. Normally I would have offered Sophie some refreshments and spoken with her in the front room, slowly building her room based on her responses. There was no time. I had to guess. Argh. What would Sophie like? She held herself with a kind of measured poise that seemed natural but was probably the result of years of etiquette training and education. Caldenia had picked up on it immediately. They were from different worlds, but they likely moved in similar circles, those of aristocratic, educated women. When I looked at her, I pictured her in a Southern mansion, all white colonnades and plush furniture, but something didn't feel quite right. So, clean and elegantly muted furnishings in a traditional style or the tastefully elaborate pattern medley of English countryside?

"She isn't human, is she?" Sophie asked.

"No."

"Her teeth are sharp and pointed."

"She is very dangerous," I said. There was something about Sophie behind all that polish and refinement, a kind of hidden fragility. Perhaps fragility was the wrong word. Brittleness, like a blade that was too sharp. No, neither clean and elegant nor elaborate. Damn it, George. I had to commit to something. I couldn't just stand there before the door.

Go with your gut feeling. That's what Mom always said.

"Caldenia will do nothing to harm you because the inn is her refuge and she knows that attacking another guest, unless it was done in self-defense, would violate our agreement. She is very manipulative, however."

"I'll keep that in mind," Sophie said.

I opened the door. Golden pine floors stretched to the wooden walls painted a gentle beige. I'd left the wall framing exposed, as if all the insulation had been stripped out. A simple but comfortable bed, built with rough Louisiana cypress, offered a thick mattress in a sturdy frame, plush white covers, and plump pillows. A beige woven rug, none too new, shielded the floor. Pale green curtains framed two wide windows, offering a view of the orchard. Between them a door permitted access to a long wooden balcony. A rough-hewn bookshelf in the corner held several paperbacks. A weapon rack waited next to the bookshelf, ready to receive swords.

Rustic modern. I had no idea why I went that way, but it felt right.

I turned to Sophie and almost stepped back. She looked shocked.

Damn it, she hated it. What was I thinking? Mixing pine and cypress, it didn't even make sense...

"Would you like a different room?"

"No," Sophie said quietly. "No, this is perfect."

The floor parted and her bag surfaced.

"As part of the Arbitrator's personnel, you have access to most of the inn," I said. "If you would like to join us on the main floor, turn right and go down two flights of stairs. If you would prefer to join Her Grace, turn left, make another left at the next hallway, and keep walking until you reach a large gray door."

"Thank you."

"If you need any information, just ask the inn. Gertrude Hunt will extend you every possible courtesy."

Five minutes until summit. I badly needed to go to the bathroom before I got down there.

Sophie brushed the wood of the sword stand with her fingertips. "It all comes full circle, doesn't it?"

I had no idea what she meant by that, so I listened.

"I shouldn't have come," Sophie said. "Do you believe in destiny, Dina?"

"No."

"Why not?"

"Because six years ago something took my parents. It ripped them out of my life and made them disappear. I can't believe that after everything they've gone through and everything they have done, that would be their destiny. I refuse to let their existence be erased. We make our own choices in life. Our actions shape our lives, and we alone are responsible for them."

"When I was younger, my mother was taken from me by our enemies," Sophie said.

"Did you find her?"

"My sister did, but by that time she was no longer my mother." A shadow of old grief clouded her eyes, blunted, but still raw and furious. "There is nothing that hurts more when you're a child. I hope you find your parents, Dina. I really sincerely do."

"Thank you."

A wallop of magic resonated through the inn and my head. I turned to the wall. "Outer perimeter."

A container the size of a house sat in the field on the edge of my orchard. A stylized symbol of the Office of Arbitration, the scales with two weights in the balance glowing gently with white, marked it. What now?

"Excuse me," I said.

"Of course."

I left Sophie to her own devices and went downstairs.

George met me at the foot of the stairs.

"What are you planning?" I asked as we turned toward the grand ballroom.

"Just a small demonstration for the public good," he said. "I'm so sorry."

"You're apologizing in advance."

"Yes."

Never a good sign.

I had expected George to open the negotiations with whatever wonderful surprise he left in the orchard, but he began the session just as he had yesterday, by escorting the leaders to their table. Almost three hours had passed, and nothing out of the ordinary took place.

The vampires looked mercilessly bored. The Merchants gathered in a circle around one of the older foxes, who was explaining something that required waving of paws and twitching of ears. Some of the otrokars abandoned all pretense at politeness and stretched out on the floor. One of the larger, older otrokar warriors was snoring. A couple of younger ones watched him, exchanging speculative glances. If they pulled out the interstellar equivalent of a magic marker and started drawing a penis on his forehead, I would have to step in.

I should've brought a book, except I wouldn't be able to read it. I had to watch the lot of them. I glanced up to the balcony where Caldenia and Sophie seemed engaged in some entertaining discussion. I wished I could be up there. Anything was better than this boredom.

Magic wailed in my head, emanating from the far side of the orchard. Here we go.

The opaque partition separating the leaders of the factions slid down, and George stepped out, his face concerned, the top of his cane glowing. "My sincerest apologies!"

Everyone dropped what they were doing and turned to him.

"Would you care to explain this?" I asked.

"Yes, Arbitrator," Nuan Cee said.

"I'm afraid one of our Sentinel guard units is malfunctioning." George's face was the definition of apologetic regret.

"You brought a Sentinel unit here?" Khanum's eyebrows crept up.

"Only for emergencies, I assure you." George turned to me. "Could I trouble you for a visual?"

I turned to the left wall. "Visual of the orchard, please."

The wall glowed, presenting the image of the orchard. The Arbitrator's container lay shattered. A wide strip of plowed earth cut through the field, veering to the brush where trees lay snapped. The sound of wood snapping echoed through the ballroom. A dark blur dashed behind the trees, dirt flew, and a huge metal contraption shot into the open. It looked like three complex frames of black metal, each a foot thick and bearing armored panels revolving over each other, all anchored by a glowing blue ball in the center, about six feet wide. The Sentinel hovered in place for a brief second. Bladed chains shot out of it. The Sentinel spun like a dervish, the blades barely three feet from the nearest apple trees.

No. He wouldn't dare.

Two feet. George gave me an apologetic smile.

The blade chipped the bark. *No, no, no...*

The Sentinel veered left. The blade passed cleanly through the apple trunk.

He didn't.

The tree collapsed with an ear-splitting crack.

He was out of his mind. "Lord Camarine," I growled.

"This is simply dreadful," George said. "My deepest, sincerest apologies."

The second tree fell. I raised my broom. Demonstration or not, he would regret this.

"No, no, please. We'll take care of it. I insist." He glanced up to the balcony. "Sophie, would you mind?"

Sophie rose and left the balcony.

He chopped down my apple trees. He would pay for this.

"A human?" Arland asked. "You are sending a human against that?"

Robart pointed at the Sentinel, which had veered away from the orchard and was spinning in the field. "That is a Class 6 mass-casualty guard unit. This thing is designed to be nearly indestructible. It will take concentrated laser fire or KPSM to take it down."

"KPSM?" I was too mad to keep the fury out of my voice.

"Kinetic Projectile of Significant Mass," Robart said.

"He means a giant chunk of metal launched from the cannon of a spaceship in orbit," Lady Isur told me.

Sophie appeared on the screen, walking through the orchard, still wearing her gray gown and carrying a sword in a sheath in her left hand. Her expression was resigned, her eyes sad. The Sentinel was a full twenty feet in diameter, bigger with chains and blades out. She was barely five and a half feet tall. Even if she was the best swordswoman in the history of the universe, it was like trying to stop a semi barreling down the highway with a toothpick.

"This is suicide." Dagorkun glanced at his mother. "I can take a squad right now. Give us twenty minutes, we'll turn it into scrap metal."

Khanum's eyes narrowed. She raised her hand and Dagorkun fell silent.

"We are in a residential neighborhood," I ground out. "There is a limit to how long I can hide this. I'm going to take care of it."

George shot me a warning glance. "Please. It's my mess. Let me clean it up."

I stared at him, wishing I could shoot laser beams out of my eyes.

Sophie bent down, picked up the hem of her gown, and ripped the fabric to midthigh.

The Sentinel sighted her. Its metal frames slid against each other. Spikes sprang up, shielding the panels. The blue glow pulsed and the Sentinel shot toward Sophie, an enormous, furious multiton tornado of razor-sharp metal.

Sophie leaned forward slightly on her toes.

She was going to get run over. The Sentinel would splatter her on what was left of my apple trees. I squeezed my broom.

George was watching Sophie with an odd look on his face.

The Sentinel barreled toward her. A chain shot out with a foot-wide black blade on the end.

Sophie *moved*.

It happened so fast I didn't actually see it. One moment she was standing still and the next the chain and the blade hurtled to the side, severed, and crashed into the brush, while Sophie was running at the Sentinel. Her sword sparked with pure white, as if someone had taken a hair-thin lightning bolt and bound it to the metal edge.

The Sentinel whirled, swinging to the side, its colossal frames rotating as the machine feverishly tried to process new data. Chains, spikes, and spears shot at Sophie. She dodged them, barely moving out of the way, graceful, beautiful, and she struck again. Her sword moved so fast it was a blur, a ghost of a movement, barely perceptible, like a puff of shimmering air shooting up from hot pavement. The Sentinel's weapons fell apart as if they were made of brittle glass.

The Sentinel's blue light pulsed. The colossal machine charged Sophie. It was a no-holds-barred direct assault. It meant to crush her.

She smiled. The melancholy in her eyes vanished. They shone with pure, unbridled joy. These eyes, they belonged to someone else, someone merciless and cruel and predatory. Someone who lived for a chance to take another being's life and reveled in doing it.

The Sentinel rolled straight at her.

She struck. Her sword flashed with white, so bright it was blinding.

The machine kept rolling. Sophie had vanished. Oh no, it must've rolled over her...

The Sentinel fell apart. The armored frames slid apart from each other, carved into pieces, the edges of the cuts perfectly smooth. The blue sphere turned dull and drained down in a heap of loose blue powder, revealing Sophie. She grinned at the remnants of the machine, and the expression on her face sent cold shivers down my spine. Sophie had enjoyed it. She'd enjoyed every moment of it.

George, who did you bring into my inn...

Sophie sheathed her sword.

"As I said, we will make all necessary reparations...," George started.

"This is enough diplomacy for today," Khanum said, her voice snapping like a whip. She turned and marched out of the ballroom, her otrokars at her heels.

I watched the vampires file out of the grand ballroom. The Merchants followed.

Someone tugged on my robe. I turned. Cookie stood next to me, his big blue eyes filled with sadness. The corners of his lynx ears drooped. He looked so pitiful I almost reached out to pet his fluffy head.

"Mistress Innkeeper?" Even his voice was tiny.

"Yes?" He was so *fluffy*.

"You didn't find the emerald, did you?"

"Not yet."

His ears drooped more. He was killing me with cuteness. "Oh."

"Is Nuan Cee giving you trouble?" I asked.

"It's a very expensive emerald. I'm responsible to my family."

Since the otrokars had taken their ball, no doubt made of skulls and wrapped in the skin of their enemies, and stomped off in a huff to their quarters, the peace summit had effectively ground to a halt. That meant my afternoon was free.

"I tell you what, I'll look for it today."

Cookie's eyes brightened. "Thank you!"

He scampered off, caught up with the Merchant procession, and followed them out.

Nuan Cee lingered in the ballroom and approached me. "What did Nuan Couki want?"

I raised my eyebrows. "That is between Cookie and me."

"Humph." Nuan Cee peered at the retreating form of his thrice-removed cousin's seventh son.

"Rough day?" I asked.

"I do not hold much hope for these negotiations," he said.

"It's only day two."

Nuan Cee glanced at me. "Trade is the oldest and most noble profession in the galaxy, and making deals is its currency. It is a rite as ancient as the cosmos and the very foundation of mathematics. Something is always equal to something else and an exchange can be made. You desire something and so you surrender something to obtain the desired result. Life is trade; we trade our labor for its fruit, we trade hours of study for knowledge, we trade pleasure for pleasure or sometimes for wealth, security, or offspring. I have made thousands of deals. I cannot deal with these people. I have nothing they want. I offer them peace, but they don't want it. They only want war."

He shook his head.

"Give them a chance," I said.

"I will. But I will take steps." He sounded ominous. "Also, we have some requests. I shall send my people to you with them."

Oh goodie. "I look forward to it."

I sealed everyone's doors and went into the orchard. Beast ran ahead of me and sniffed at the mangled trees.

The remnants of the Sentinel were still scattered on the ground. Four of my twenty trees lay broken. I clenched my teeth. The trees were an extension of the inn, as much as everything on the inn's grounds was a part of Gertrude Hunt. Seeing them broken like this physically hurt. I wanted to hug them and put them back together.

George would pay for this. One way or another.

I kicked a chunk of the Sentinel's frame. Ow.

"I'm so sorry," I said.

The remaining trees rustled.

I nodded at the Sentinel. "Take this thing. Absorb what you can." The inn could use all that metal and advanced circuitry. George wasn't getting any of it back.

The Sentinel sank into the ground. I reached down and petted the severed trunks. Their stems might be gone, but their roots were still there, still alive. Maybe they would return. Only time would tell. I wanted to punch George right in the face.

I went back inside, got a cup of tea, and sat down in the living room in my favorite chair. Beast hopped into her dog bed, turned around three times, and flopped.

The inn recorded every minute of the summit. It should be easy enough to find out who had taken Cookie's emerald. I just had to watch the some five hours of recordings and figure out where it went.

"I need a screen and the recording of the first night of the summit."

A screen descended from the ceiling, growing on a thin stalk. The recording began. I flicked through it, fast forwarding to Cookie's entrance... The problem was he was throwing gems by the pawful. It was hard to say which specific emerald he was referring to.

I became aware of someone looming at my side and paused the recording.

"Yes?"

"Mint." Orro shook a sprig of mint at me.

"Okay?"

He stuck the sprig under my nose. "It's wilted! I cannot be expected to cook with wilted mint."

"I'll go out later today and buy more mint."

"Good!" He thrust a piece of paper in front of me. Pictures of herbs, meat, rice, milk, and eggs filled it in two neat columns with the prices in big black numbers next to them.

"What is this?"

"Other things I need."

"Where did you get this?"

"Your markets send out lists of groceries printed on this obsolete paper."

"You took these from an HEB flyer?"

Orro waved his claws at me. "I don't know what it's called. Of all the grocery-market lists, that one was best. I need these things. We have to serve a banquet."

I opened my mouth to argue and clamped it shut. He had a point. We hadn't served a formal sit-down meal.

"Things!" Orro shook the paper at me.

"I will buy them." I took the paper. "Thank you."

He dropped a thin slice of lemon into my tea and disappeared into the kitchen.

I restarted the recording. Handfuls of gems scattering on the floor...

A soft chime announced an incoming request from a guest. I paused the recording and flicked the screen. It split, showing one of the members of Clan Nuan standing by the door leading to the ballroom. The demands Nuan Cee mentioned. I opened the door, sealed it again behind the guest, and rose when he walked into the living room. A gray fox flecked with spots of beautiful blue, he wore two gold hoops in his left ear and an apron. He was older than Cookie but younger than Nuan Cee.

"I'm Nuan Ara, Nuan Cee's blood sister's youngest son."

"It is a pleasure to meet you." I invited him to sit in a chair across from me and moved the screen to the left, out of the way. "What can I do to make your stay more comfortable?"

Nuan Ara folded his paws on his lap. "It is Nuan Re, the esteemed grandmother, she of great wisdom, the root from which we grow."

"May her feet never touch the ground." It wasn't my first rodeo. I knew the customs. The Merchant clans revered their elders. If Grandmother wanted something, the entire clan would turn themselves inside out to get it. I had to honor this request or the Nuans would hate me forever. What could she possibly want?

"She wishes to obtain a small predator."

"A small predator?"

"Yes." Nuan Ara nodded. "The silent, stealthy, vicious killer that prowls by night and mercilessly murders its victims for food and pleasure."

Um... What? "And she believes she can find this predator here?"

Nuan Ara nodded. "She has seen the images. They have glowing eyes and razor claws and are renowned for their cruelty."

"Aha." What was she talking about?

"She is in particular interested in the Ennui predator. She very much likes its demeanor and coloring in the
images. She understands she may not get that particular
one, but perhaps one that resembles it? A young one?"

The Ennui predator. "Where did she find these images?"

"On your planet's holonet," Nuan Ara said helpfully.

We didn't have holonet. We had Internet... Oh. "So, the
esteemed grandmother would like a kitten that looks like
Grumpy Cat?" I picked up my laptop, typed in the image
search for Grumpy Cat, and showed him the picture.

"Yes!"

"I will see what I can do."

"Wonderful!" Nuan Ara rose. "Many thanks. You have
the promise of our generosity."

I waited until he returned to his quarters and shut the
door behind him. I would have to stop at a local shelter and
possibly PetSmart. They had silent, stealthy, vicious predators available for adoption.

Sophie walked down the stairs and came to sit across
from me. She wore soft black pants that flared at the bottom
and a bright green tunic that was a cross between a hooded
sweatshirt and a blouse. Her feet were bare. She was carrying her sword, and her dark hair, previously arranged into a
complicated knot, was pulled back into a ponytail.

"I like your floors," she said, making small fists with her
toes on the wooden boards.

"Thank you. Would you care for some tea?"

"Certainly."

I went into the kitchen and fetched her a cup of green
tea.

"Thank you."

"You're welcome."

I restarted the recording. "Stop. Zoom." There it was, an emerald the size of a strawberry, the most beautiful, intense green you could imagine. If spring could cry, that would be its tear. That had to be the right emerald. "One-quarter speed."

"Did I scare you?" Sophie asked.

The emerald bounced off the floor in slow motion.

"You alarmed me. The safety of my guests is my first priority."

"I'm not a psychopath," Sophie said. "Nor am I psychotic."

The emerald landed in the path of the other Nuan Merchants.

"What's the difference?" I asked.

"A psychotic suffers a break from reality, often accompanied by hallucinations and delusions. They are not aware of their own illness. I'm quite aware of my reality."

One of the foxes kicked the emerald in passing, and the big jewel slid across the floor, spinning.

"A psychopath is unable to experience empathy. He can murder without remorse. His existence is free of guilt. His victim has no more significance to him than a used tissue he has discarded into a wastebasket. I'm able to empathize. I feel guilt and sadness, and I'm capable of acts of genuine kindness."

She described it so clinically, almost as if talking about someone else.

"However, I'm a serial killer."

"Pause."

I nudged the screen to the side and looked at her. She sat in my chair, her legs tucked under her. Her sword rested on the floor next to her.

"When I was younger, I experienced some of the worst things adults could do to a child," she said. "It caused damage, and I realize now that this damage is irreversible."

"I'm sorry," I said and meant it.

"When I was an adolescent, my uncle married a woman who became my second mother. She recognized that something was wrong with me, and she took me to Ganer College where the best mind-healers of my world tried to mend my scars. I made an honest effort to get better, but then an opportunity appeared to do what I do best in the interests of my country, and so I indulged. I returned to Ganer when I spilled too much blood, then left again, then came back and finally stayed for almost three years. I've read countless books. I've undergone many therapies and meditations. Yet here we are." She smiled. "There comes a point where you have to stop trying to repair yourself and accept the fact that you're broken. George is right. I hate him for it, but he is right. Today was the first time I truly lived in months, if only for a few moments. I've decided that I would rather live for a few moments every few weeks than try to deny my nature."

As long as her nature didn't interfere with the safety of my guests, we would be just fine.

"I don't want you to be afraid of me, Dina. Murder doesn't interest me. I'm addicted to winning fights. I love it, the thrill of it, the rush of testing my skill against my opponent, the sharp finality of it, but I control my sword. My sword doesn't control me."

"I'm not afraid of you," I told her. "But if you attack a guest in my inn, I will contain you."

"We understand each other then."

"Yes, we do."

"That makes me happy." She smiled and drank her tea.

My screen chimed. I reached to my left and flicked it. George's face appeared on the screen. His damp blond hair fell to his shoulders, framing his elegant face. He was wearing some sort of light white robe... The man was ridiculously handsome. That's all there was to it.

I still wanted to punch him.

Something in Sophie's cup must've been incredibly interesting, because she was studying it with cool detachment.

"What can I do for you, Arbitrator?" I asked.

"George, please. There is no hot water in my bathroom."

"Oh really?" You don't say.

"Yes. In fact, it's ice-cold." He raised a half-filled glass. Thin slivers of ice floated on its surface. "I drew this from the tap in my sink."

"How unfortunate. When did this happen?"

"About two minutes ago."

"While you were in the shower?"

"Yes."

"My apologies. I'll get right on that."

George squinted at me, his face thoughtful, and waved the call off.

Sophie leaned back and laughed. "You really love those trees."

I restarted the recording. "When I came here, Gertrude Hunt lay dormant. The inn hadn't been active for years. Without visitors, it slowly starved and fell into a deep, death-like sleep. I was told it would be so, but I didn't realize what that actually meant."

The memories of that day surfaced and took over, bringing with them a sharp, intense dread.

"It was an overcast spring day. The yard was an overgrown tangle of brush that hadn't been looked after for years, all old leaves and dead grass, and in the middle of this mess sat a ruin of a house with rotting siding and dark windows. I felt no magic. No presence. There are not many dormant inns left, and this was my only chance at becoming an innkeeper. If I couldn't awaken Gertrude Hunt, I would have to grow a new inn from the seed, and that takes years. I was so terrified the inn was dead that I couldn't bring myself to go inside the house, so I picked my way around the building to the back, and then I saw the trees. There were twenty of them, and all of them were blooming with these delicate white flowers with a gentle touch of pink. That's when I realized that the inn was still alive."

Sophie nodded. "I understand. George understands as well."

"I doubt it."

"Do you know what George did before he became an Arbitrator?"

"No." And I didn't care.

"He was the head of intelligence for our country. Every spy and counterspy answered to him. Among dozens who have held this position, he was the best. The most cunning and the most ruthless. When we were growing up, he was the kindest, gentlest person I knew. Now he has the blood of hundreds on his hands. I know it came at a great personal cost to him."

"Then why did he do it?"

"Duty," Sophie said. "George will do everything in his power to fulfill his obligations, even if he has to sacrifice a piece of his soul for it."

My screen chimed again. What is it? What? I flicked at it. Arland's face came into view.

"My lady."

Oh spare me. "How may I assist you?"

"I do apologize. My knights are warriors. They are creatures of the battlefield. They came here anticipating a fight…"

"Lord Arland, it would help if you spoke plainly."

"They are bored," he said. "Completely bored. I was hoping to prevail on you for some form of entertainment."

"I will make sure to provide you with something by tonight."

"Thank you."

I looked at Sophie. She grinned at me.

I dismissed the screen, letting it retract into the ceiling. The emerald would have to wait. I had to purchase enough groceries for a small army, review the kittens at the shelter, and find some sort of entertainment to occupy a detachment of trained killers, or they would never leave me alone. Piece of cake.

CHAPTER EIGHT

I bought mint first. I didn't even mess around with grocery stores. I took a pair of dog biscuits from the pantry and drove straight to Mindy's Mud and Weeds. Mindy raised English springer spaniels and ran the town's most successful nursery. The woman could plant a wooden skewer into the ground and it would grow into a gorgeous orchid in two weeks. Beak, Mindy's latest prizewinning dog, greeted me at the door with a look of canine despair. Mindy swore that in private Beak was an accomplished thief of socks and spoons who knew no shame, but whenever I saw her, the black-and-white spaniel looked like she was the saddest, most long-suffering canine in the whole wide world. I gave her two dog biscuits—one just didn't seem enough to snap her out of world-weary despair—chatted with Mindy, bought four big buckets of living mint and basil, loaded them into the back of the car, and headed for the grocery store.

Orro's list burned through five hundred dollars' worth of groceries and forty-five minutes of my time. I probably could've gotten at least some of it cheaper and faster at Costco, but last time I went there, I was attacked by some alien monsters. Unfortunately a woman saw me and even helped me. When she went to report it, I hid the evidence and it took all my power to do it. I escaped before she came back with a manager, but it probably made her look like a crazy person. I had no wish to run into her, so I only went to Costco during dinner hours. I'd met her in the morning, and she seemed like she might have a family, so I thought dinnertime would be least likely for her to be out.

GameStop was next. I bought a PlayStation 4 and a couple of games. The vampires would be able to synthesize additional gaming consoles and software. Another six hundred dollars gone. I was burning through my operational budget so fast that if this summit went on for longer than a week, I would have to start panhandling to keep the lights on.

I saved PetSmart for last. I got my cart and turned left, past the tanks filled with schools of colorful fish to the row of glass cages holding cats from local pet shelters. The first cage held an fat, older calico cat sleeping with its butt pressed against the glass. No. Too old, too mellow, and completely different look.

The second cage held a small light brown ball of fur. Dark brown rosettes spattered the thick coat. I checked the card. Feistykins, three months old, female, friendly... From this angle she almost looked like a Bengal. I leaned closer.

The ball of fur sprang like a tiny tabby cannonball shot out of a canon and pounced on the glass. Big yellow eyes looked at me and fluoresced with brighter amber, catching the light. I put my finger against the glass and moved it back and forth. Feistykins batted at it with her paws. She didn't look like Grumpy Cat, but she definitely fit the bill on the adorable factor.

I moved to the only other occupied cage. A large gray cat looked back at me with big green eyes. His fur, thick and long, flared about his head in a Maine coon mane. There was something elegant, almost aristocratic about him, as if he were really a lion somehow condensed to house cat size. I checked the card. Count. Three years old, male, neutered.

The cat gazed at me. He didn't move. He didn't walk to the glass, but he definitely knew I was there, and he studied me carefully. His big eyes were mesmerizing. When I was younger, I used to read too much poetry. The lines from Byron's poem came to mind.

SHE walks in beauty, like the night
Of cloudless climes and starry skies;
And all that's best of dark and bright
Meet in her aspect and her eyes:

Byron wasn't writing about a cat, he was writing about his widowed cousin who had been in mourning when he met her. This cat wasn't black. It wasn't even female, but when I looked into those eyes, they made me think of the night and the starry sky. There was something witchy about him. Something hinting at a hidden mystery. That he sat there, confined in a small glass box, felt wrong and unnatural, like a bird with its wings tied.

"Looking for a cat?"

I almost jumped.

A middle-aged balding man in the PetSmart uniform khaki pants and blue polo shirt stopped by me.

The gray cat watched me. I almost asked for him. No, too old. "Can I see the kitten?" I asked.

"Sure." He unlocked the glass door, letting me into a private area that permitted access to the back of the cages.

Feistykins proved to be everything a kitten could be. She pounced on the feather toy, she pounced on the little kitten ball, she pounced on my leg, and when I put her on my lap, she purred and preened. Two minutes into petting, she decided she'd had enough and bit me. She didn't draw blood, but I felt the teeth. Well, if Grandmother Nuan wanted a cute, merciless hunter, this was probably the best we could do.

"I'll take her."

"Okay." The man handed me some papers to fill out. Five minutes later, Feistykins was safely contained in a small cardboard carrier.

"What about him?" I asked, pointing to the gray cat.

"Count? He's been here awhile. He isn't what you would call an affectionate cat. He doesn't suck up."

No, he didn't look like he'd suck up.

"He's got till tomorrow and then the shelter is taking him back. They've got to rotate the cats. If they replace him with someone less boring, that cat might get adopted."

"Thank you." I loaded Feistykins into the cart and moved on to the cat aisle. Cat litter, cat litter scoop, cat food, cat dish…

I'd never considered myself a cat person. I didn't really care for them. My mother had one, a big black fluffy cat called Snuggles. When I left the room for five minutes and came back, our dogs acted as if I was gone for ages. Snuggles mostly ignored us, including my mom who took care of him. The only time he deemed it necessary to notice our existence was when he was hungry.

Let's see, she would need a kitten collar too. And some toys. I plucked a long plastic stick with a feather on top. Before the summit pulled me out of my bored stupor, I'd read an article—you can really find out a lot of weird stuff when you spend your day surfing Facebook—that claimed cats didn't really love their owners, only manipulated them. They recognized their owner's voices and ignored them. They rubbed on their legs because they marked a new "object" in the room with their scent. And most of them didn't actually like getting petted. Besides, Beast probably didn't like cats.

Nobody would adopt him. He would just sit there in that cage with his starry-sky eyes. And tomorrow someone would come and take him back to the shelter.

This was a stupid idea.

I turned the cart around. The man who had helped me was feeding the fish.

"I'll take him."

"Who?" he asked.

"The gray cat. I'm taking him home with me."

I got home without further incident. I let the inn unpack the groceries from the car. I had errands to run. First I took the gray cat to my room and left him there in the carrier. He didn't look too freaked-out, but I didn't want to take chances. I would have to think of a name for him at some point, but right now I had nothing. Then I put on my robe, borrowed Arland's engineer, and set him to duplicating gaming consoles and controllers. Finally, I took Feistykins to the Nuan Clan.

I was greeted by Nuan Ara, who ushered me into their quarters. The entire Nuan Clan assembled in the room in a small semicircle with Grandmother resting on a luxurious divan.

"This is a kitten," I explained. "A very young predator. She doesn't look like Ennui predator, but she has a playful spirit. Right now she might be frightened, so when I open this carrier, she might escape. Do not chase her. She will hide and come out when she is ready."

I pried the carrier open, expecting Feistykins to take off like a bullet.

Seconds crawled by.

What if she'd died somehow in the carrier? Okay, where did that thought even come from?

The carrier shuddered. Feistykins stepped out and looked over the clan of bipedal foxes. The expression on her face said she was not impressed. She gave the gathering another derisive once-over, let out an imperious meow, and headed straight for the divan.

The Merchants formed a circle around the kitten, making cooing noises. I let out a breath, handed toys and the litter box to Nuan Ara with quick instructions, and went to see the noble knights of Holy Anocracy.

By the time the vampires were assembled, the inn had finished assimilating the new gaming consoles. I waved my hand and three huge flat-screens opened in the stone walls of the vampire quarters. The wall spat out sets of controllers.

"Greetings," I said. "House Krahr, House Sabla, and House Vorga, may I present *Call of Duty*."

The three screens ignited simultaneously, playing the opening of *Call of Duty: Advanced Warfare*. Soldiers in high-tech armor shot at targets, flew across the screen from bomb impacts, and walked dramatically in slow motion. Vehicles roared, Marines roared louder, and Kevin Spacey informed us that politicians didn't know how to solve problems but he did.

The vampires stared at the screens.

"This is a game of cooperative action," I said, "where a small elite force can triumph against overwhelming odds."

At the word elite, they perked up like wild dogs who'd heard a rabbit cry.

"The game will teach you how to play it. May the best House triumph over their opponents."

Arland reached for the first controller. I turned around and walked out, sealing the door behind me. Now their pride was involved. That should occupy them for a few days. Hopefully they wouldn't kill each other over it.

I made my way to the otrokars' quarters and asked Dagorkun to gather everyone in the common hall. Most of them were already there, lounging around the fire in the center of the room and drinking tea. Even Khanum was in attendance, brooding on her pillows strewn on the floor.

"Everyone is here," Dagorkun announced.

I flicked my fingers. An enormous screen slid out of the wall and turned black. A song started, softly. A football team burst into a stadium. The song picked up steam. Football teams clashed like two armies. Running backs streaked across the field. Receivers flew off the grass to catch impossible passes while defensive backs dove at them. Enormous linebackers tore at bodies, trying to crush the quarterback. Coaches screamed. Quarterbacks threw passes defying laws of physics. The very essence of the game was in that video, with all its failures, its brutality, and pure unrestrained elation of victory, and the song rose with it, loud and triumphant.

The otrokars stared, mesmerized.

"What is this?" Dagorkun asked quietly.

"This is football," I said.

Smaller screens opened in the side of the room as the walls under it released controllers.

"You can watch it on the big screen. Or..." I paused to makes sure I had their attention. "You can play it."

Madden's logo ignited on the two smaller screens.

"Football is a war game of land acquisition...," I began.

When I finally made it to my room, it was past six. Orro had yelled at me as I walked up to my room. Apparently everyone had spontaneously decided to reschedule the formal dinner to tomorrow night. There were kittens to play with, enemies to shoot, and footballs to be passed. That meant I could at least take a shower in peace.

Beast sat by the crate in my bedroom, looking scandalized.

"It's okay," I told her. "It's just an extra permanent guest."

I gently pried the carrier open. The gray cat stepped out on soft paws, looked about, and hid under the bed.

Beast whined at me.

"Not you too." I shook my head. "I had a rough day."

Beast whined again.

I went into my bathroom. Here's hoping soap and hot water would wash today off.

After the shower I climbed into bed and asked the inn to send a screen down. The ceiling parted, growing a screen on a thin stalk that tilted toward me.

"Resume recording," I murmured.

The emerald bounced on the screen. Otrokars and vampires walked past it, preoccupied with their own tasks. The big green gem lay forgotten like a cheap glass bauble.

"Fast-forward," I instructed. "Four times the speed."

The recording sped up. The otrokars and knights hurried about like actors from a silent movie, their movements exaggerated by the accelerated recording. An otrokar brushed by it. The emerald slid to the side. I yawned.

This would be so much more fun if Sean were here to make fun of it. He'd once called Arland Goldilocks and then told him he should try to get his woodland friends to help him if he got in trouble.

I pictured myself reaching into my mind, taking that thought out, and setting it aside. Sean Evans wasn't here. Maybe I could make a deal with myself. Once the summit was over, whichever way it went, I would go down to Wilmos's weapon shop and have a nice long conversation with Mr. Evans. Since he bugged me so much, I could ask him if he was planning on coming back in the near future. That way I wouldn't waste my time obsessing over…

The emerald vanished.

"Stop!" I jerked upright and almost collided with the screen.

The recording froze.

"Rewind at normal speed."

The screen blurred and suddenly the emerald popped back into existence on the floor.

"Stop. Play forward, one-quarter speed."

Slowly, part of the screen blurred slightly, moving toward the emerald. It wasn't an obvious, pronounced blur, more like someone had taken a smeared magnifying glass and passed it over the screen. I had never before seen anything like it. The inn's sensors weren't infallible, but they were pretty close.

The blur touched the emerald and the green gem vanished.

"Thermal imaging, same time block."

The screen blinked. A blob of yellow with a bright red center passed over the emerald. So whatever this was shielded the wearer from thermal imaging as well. It had to be some kind of device projecting a field that tampered with the inn's feed. My stomach churned.

Someone moved unchecked in my inn, and I didn't know how or why.

In my inn. In Gertrude Hunt.

I had to find out and fast. The lives of my guests depended on it, because while this was going on, any guarantees of security I promised weren't worth the hot air that came out of my mouth as I made them.

I stared at the distortion on the screen. *You want to play games? Fine. I will find you and when I do, you won't like what will follow.*

CHAPTER NINE

It was Sunday and we were back in the grand ballroom, watching the negotiations stall. Three days had passed since I discovered the tampering with the inn's recordings. I was no closer to finding the culprit. I still didn't know who took the emerald. The cat still hid. Once or twice, while half-asleep, I felt him on the edge of the bed, but when I woke up, he was always gone. I made sure he had water and food and I cleaned his litter box, but that was the extent of our interaction. I clearly failed at making friends. The otrokars and the vampires were still bored and irritable, despite the distractions I provided. And most importantly, the peace summit still made no progress.

The only thing I managed to accomplish was to ensure that Orro's banquet was scheduled and ready to go tonight.

At the far end of the grand ballroom, a large otrokar rose, his gaze fixed on a point behind me. I'd been reading up on the otrokars' warrior classes, and he looked like a basher to me. In battle, his kind wore the heaviest armor the Horde could provide and were fitted with arm guns that mounted over their shoulders and limbs and weighed over a hundred pounds each. Bashers were huge mobile guns. They punched through the enemy ranks while lighter warrior classes hid behind them and rained death on their opponents. This particular specimen was over seven and a half feet tall with shoulders that were probably too big for my front door. If he ever had to negotiate it, he'd have to turn sideways.

I turned so I could see the summit meeting taking place behind the transparent partition and keep an eye on the basher at the same time. At the negotiations table, the Marshal of House Vorga leaned forward, his fists on the table. When vampires confronted danger, they unconsciously tried to make themselves larger, like cats before a fight. Lord Robart positively loomed over the table, his face contorted by fury. The soundproof barrier robbed him of his voice, but he looked like he was screaming. Well, at least his fangs weren't bared.

The male otrokar started forward, moving deliberately, his head lowered slightly, his eyes unblinking, his gaze focused on Lord Robart with terrible intensity. Uh-oh.

Jack peeled himself from the wall by the partition and casually strolled down on an intercept course.

Khanum said something, her face projecting derision.

And there go the fangs.

A slim, hard-looking otrokar female smoothly moved into the big soldier's path. "Where are you going, Kolto?"

"I'm going to wring his neck," the large otrokar growled.

"First, you won't get through."

"Watch me."

"And if you did manage it, Khanum would rip off your balls and make you eat them. She's got it. If she needs our help, she'll call for it."

Behind the partition, Dagorkun said something, his pose relaxed, his arms crossed on his chest. The other two otrokars guffawed. The Khanum cracked a smile. Lord Robart did his best to propel himself and his high-tech armor into a massive leap, but Arland, Lady Isur, and the Battle Chaplain grabbed him and pulled him back. Nuan Cee put his furry head on the table, facedown. Lord Robart snarled, his fangs out, trying to break free.

This wouldn't end well, I just knew it.

"See, she has it," the female otrokar said. "And you're still in one piece."

The male otrokar frowned at her. "Why do you care?"

"I don't know." The female otrokar arched an eyebrow. "Maybe I have an interest in your staying intact."

She turned and walked away, joining a group of three other otrokars.

The male otrokar frowned again, his brain obviously trying to figure out why the female otrokar would be interested in the continued safety of his genitals. Then his eyes lit up. His expression turned speculative. Yes, she likes you, big dummy.

George made some sort of placating gesture and squeezed the top of his cane. The partition drained down, and Lord Robart marched out, his face still contorted with rage. Lady Isur and the Battle Chaplain chased him.

Arland bore down on me. "Lady Dina. We need privacy. He doesn't need to be around his people right now."

I unsealed the main entrance. "The front room and the kitchen are yours."

"My thanks." Arland raced after Robart.

I opened the side entrances and watched everyone pile out. Once everyone was secured in their quarters, I went into the kitchen.

Lord Robart sat at the table, his face murderous. Arland leaned on the wall next to him. The Battle Chaplain hovered nearby, his crimson vestments framing his big body like tattered wings. At the island, Orro chopped celery and carrots into small pieces, grimly ignoring the presence of the vampires.

I got out three mugs, dropped a bag of mint tea into each, and ran hot water from the Keurig into each one.

"We'll never make progress this way," Arland said quietly.

"Don't talk to me about progress," Robart snarled. "You want progress. You want to give them everything. Does your honor mean so little to you? Is that how far your House has fallen?"

Arland opened his mouth.

"This is why we haven't triumphed," the Battle Chaplain said, his voice deep and deliberate. "We would rather war with ourselves than our common enemy."

I used a teaspoon to fish the tea bags out, added some honey to each mug, and brought them over.

"Thank you." Odalon accepted his cup and sipped the tea. "Mint." He smiled with appreciation. "Delicious."

Arland took his mug. Robart pushed the mug away. "I don't want it. I need neither calming nor healing."

"You're being childish," Odalon said.

"Spare me your lectures. You're free to question my piety, but stay out of how I run my House."

Odalon sighed.

"May I ask a question?" I took another chair.

Robart stared off to the side, ignoring me.

"Of course, *Lady* Dina," Arland said, putting a particular emphasis on *lady*.

"My apologies," Robart ground out. "Please, ask your question."

"It's my understanding that Nexus has a single landmass. The Holy Anocracy holds a large portion of this continent to the north and the Horde holds an almost equal portion to the south. Clan Nuan holds a smaller portion to the east, but their territory is the best geographical location for the spaceport. Am I correct?"

"In essence," Robart grumbled. "The magnetic anomalies of Nexus make it difficult to build any permanent deployment structures. We are forced to drop supplies and troops from orbit via shuttles. Clan Nuan has the only functional gravity tube on the planet, which means they can transport goods and personnel in relative safety."

I had taken a gravity tube once. It was an enormous elevator that stretched from orbit to the surface and traveled at supersonic speed. The science behind it was magic and riding it had almost made me throw up.

"This is why Nuan Cee is seeking peace," Arland explained. "Nexus's main value is in the deposits of kuyo, the liquid mineral we require for our continued war effort. It's heavy. It's hard to mine and harder to transport. The Merchants wish to make money on the shipments of kuyo from Nexus. They know we'll be forced to use their facilities."

And knowing Nuan Cee, he would count every day he wasn't charging the Horde and Holy Anocracy an outrageous tariff as a day he lost money.

"We tried to overtake the gravity tube a few times, but we failed," Odalon said.

"They have Turan Adin," Robart said, his face grim.

The three vampires paused.

"Who or what is Turan Adin?" I asked.

"Turan Adin is a creature of war," Robart said and drank some of his mint tea. "He breathes and lives battle. Slaughter runs in his veins. Nexus was settled almost twenty years ago in Nexus time, and he has been there since the very beginning. He is the rassa in the red grass, the shirar in the deep water. The demon of that hell."

"We don't know where the Merchants found him," Arland said. "We don't even know what he is. But he's incorruptible and indestructible. He has run their mercenary

174

army for the past two decades. He learns, he adapts, he never tires."

"But as things stand, both you and the Horde can mine kuyo to use for your military needs?" I asked.

"Yes," Arland answered.

"Then why not just let things stand as they are?" I asked.

Robart stared at me. "You are not a vampire. You are not a knight."

Arland put his hand over his face.

"Then help me understand," I said.

"The land that the Horde holds is stained with our blood," Robart said, his voice barely controlled. "Only when they are gone can that stain be wiped clean. Would a surgeon remove half of a malignant growth and leave the rest, satisfied with what he already accomplished? Would a hunter skin half a carcass and leave the rest of the precious pelt to rot? We must kill them or drive them off that world. Anything less is a mortal sin. It is an ancient law. *Suffer none who would seek to stand on the ground you have chosen.* Thus the writs tell us."

"The Hierophant does not share your interpretation," Odalon said.

"The Hierophant saw fit to change her mind," Robart said. "But I did not change mine. My father died in Nexus's blood fields. The woman I loved more than life itself, the woman I wanted to bear my children, lost her life there. Her light..." His voice broke and he squeezed his fists. "Her light is gone. To look upon the Horde's territory on Nexus is to dishonor her memory. When I stand before the gates of the afterlife and my father and my almost wife meet me and ask if they were avenged, what will I tell them? That I was too tired of fighting? That I couldn't spare any more blood to be spilled in their name?"

"What will you tell the spirits of all who stand behind them?" Arland asked. "What will you tell them when they ask you why you threw away their lives in a fight we cannot win?"

"We will win." Robart punched the table. "It's a righteous war. A holy war!"

"It's logistics," Arland said. "Neither we nor the Horde can shuttle enough troops to Nexus to ensure a decisive victory. We lost two transports just last month. What will you tell the soldiers inside them? They didn't even get to taste the battle."

"They knew the risks," Robart barked.

"Yes, but they trust us to lead them into battle. They trust us to not waste their lives. I will not sacrifice any more of my knights on this pointless war."

"If you're too weak, then I will find another ally."

Arland strode to the Keurig and I heard the water pour. If he needed more tea, I would have gotten him some.

"Like House Meer?" Arland asked, opening the refrigerator. "The cowards who wouldn't even fight?"

"At least House Meer refuses to honor your pitiful attempts at peace," Robart said. "Their dissent is…" He inhaled.

I smelled coffee. Oh no.

Arland returned to the table with the mug. Judging by the color, at least a third of it had to be the hazelnut-flavored creamer from my fridge.

"Lord Arland." I sank a warning into my voice.

"What is this?" Robart looked at the cup.

"A drink for real men," Arland said. "I wouldn't recommend it. It doesn't suffer the unprepared."

Lord Robart turned to me. "I'll have what he's having."

"That is a terrible idea," I said. "The drink contains…"

"Here." Arland handed his coffee to Robart. "If you insist. I shall get another."

"No!" I reached for the cup.

Robart gulped the coffee. "This is interesting. It's delicious, but I'm awaiting that profound impact you promised me."

He drained half the mug.

Oh crap. Coffee had the same effect on vampires as alcohol on humans. He'd just downed an equivalent of half a bottle of whiskey.

"You know what your problem is, Arland?" His voice slurred slightly. "You're a... coward."

Odalon blinked.

Robart drank another mighty swallow. "All of you"—he waved his index finger around—"are cowards. We must be primal. Resolute. Like our ancestors. Our ancestors didn't need... weapons. They didn't need armor. They had their *teeth*."

He bared his fangs, clenched his right fist, and flexed his arm.

"Of course they did," I murmured, keeping my voice soothing. Maybe he would just sit here and tell us about his ancestors and that would be that.

"And they hunted their enemies." He finished off the mug and flipped it upside down on the table. He looked down at his beautiful armor. "This dung. I don't need this dung."

I knew exactly where this was going. "Grab him!"

Arland didn't move. Odalon stared at Robart, his eyes wide.

Robart hit his crest. The armor fell off him, revealing a black shirt and pants underneath. He yanked the clothes from his body. "To hunt!" Robart roared and shot out of the back door and into the rain.

Damn it.

Orro paused his chopping, rolled his head back, and let out several barking snorts.

"It's not funny. Arland!" I pointed at him with my broom.

"He needed it," Arland said, his tone unrepentant.

I squeezed the words through my teeth. "Go get him, my lord, before he hunts a car or a police cruiser and Officer Marais hauls him in for questioning."

Arland sighed and took off after Robart into the rain.

"Why do you always strip naked when you're drunk?" I asked Odalon.

"This happened before?" The Battle Chaplain's eyebrows crept up.

"Lord Arland drank some accidentally last time he was here."

"It must be the armor. We live in it, so we remove it only in the safety of our homes. If your armor is off, you are clean, safe, and free, probably well fed and possibly ready to meet your partner in the privacy of your bedroom." Odalon's somber face remained stoic, but a tiny mischievous light played in his eyes. "Did Lord Arland mention his cousin's Earthborn wife by any chance while he was indisposed?"

I kept a straight face. "Possibly."

"The universe is vast and we're its greatest mystery," Odalon murmured and followed Arland outside.

I sat in the front room, going through the recording of the phantom who stole the emerald. I decided that calling the thief a phantom was better than referring to him or her as the invisible blob. I'd reached some conclusions.

One, the phantom was definitely alive. It wasn't a machine. I'd managed to isolate a six-second video where I could see it move through the crowd based on a slight shimmer. The phantom moved to avoid people in its way, and it clearly stepped over other gems and gold on the floor, choosing to move through stretches of empty floor. If the phantom had been a machine, it would have to have reasoning abilities and it would have a complicated mechanism of locomotion. If it had simply rolled on wheels, I'd see things nudged out of the way.

When each delegation entered the grand ballroom, I had the inn scan them for weapons. I knew the otrokars had brought in a gun, although I hadn't expected them to actually fire it. The inn didn't register anything with advanced robotics or artificial intelligence or anything that had artificial legs.

Two, since the phantom was alive, he or she had entered the inn with one of the delegations. I would've felt an intruder.

Three, since the intruder was one of the guests, he or she would be missing from the crowd in the grand ballroom when the emerald was being pilfered. Problem was, Gertrude Hunt had recorded a wide-angle video that gave me a nice panoramic view of the crowd, but they bunched up too much in those crucial five seconds.

I checked the clock. We'd scheduled the banquet at nine. It was too late for me, a little late for the Merchants and the vampires, and a little early for the otrokars. The clock said sixteen minutes past three. Plenty of time. I groped with my hand for my teacup on the side table next to the sofa and touched something soft.

The cat sat on the side table.

We looked at each other.

Beast barked once, quietly.

The cat walked over the sofa's arm, stomped through my lap—he was surprisingly heavy—and rubbed against me. I stroked his head. He rubbed again, purring, walked to the other end of the sofa, and arranged himself on the blanket. He stretched, let out all the claws on his front paws, and began kneading the blanket.

I looked at Beast. She stared at me, her big round eyes puzzled.

The cat bit the blanket and made purring noises.

Okaaay. And that wasn't weird.

Caldenia strolled into the front room and took a seat on the chair across from me. Her Grace wore a dark purple gown with a severe high neck. Elaborate embroidery in pale lavender and gold decorated the length of the gown, spilling in beautiful rivulets over the expanse of the skirt.

Caldenia frowned at the cat. "Why is he doing that?"

I had no idea. "He's a freak."

The freak continued kneading the blanket and sucking on it.

My screen beeped. Dagorkun's portrait appeared in the left bottom corner.

"What may I do for you, Under-Khan?"

"Khanum wishes to share a tea. Will you be available in ten minutes?"

Being invited to share a tea was an honor and a privilege. Still, if it were up to me, I would've stayed on my nice comfortable couch.

"Please inform Khanum that I'm honored and will see her in ten minutes."

Dagorkun's image vanished.

"I will come as well," Caldenia said.

"If you wish, Your Grace."

"Oh, I do not wish. They're barbarians. A woefully unrefined culture." Caldenia rose. "However, I do not trust that brute of a woman to not poison you."

I dismissed the screen and it retracted into a wall. "Poison wouldn't be in the otrokar character. They favor direct violence."

"And that's precisely why I am coming. In matters of diplomacy and love, one must strive for spontaneity. Doing the unexpected often gets you what you want. It wouldn't be typical for the Horde to resort to poison, so we must assume they will."

We walked to the staircase, the doors opening as we approached the walls. "What possible reasons would they have to poison me?"

"I can think of several. The most obvious one would be to gain access to the rest of the inn. With you out of the way, they could ambush and slaughter the vampires."

"That would bar them from Earth forever." Not to mention that the inn would murder them.

Caldenia smiled. "And the hope for the peace between the Horde and the Holy Anocracy would perish with them. Of all the types of beings one finds oneself dealing with, the true believers are the worst. A typical sentient's psyche is a spiderweb. Pull on the right thread and you will get the desired result. Praise them and they will like you. Ridicule them and they'll hate you. Greedy can be bought, timid can be frightened, smart can be persuaded, but the zealots are immune to money, fear, or reason. A zealot's psyche is a tightrope. They have severed everything else in favor of their goal. They will pay any price for their victory, and that makes them infinitely more dangerous."

Caldenia's mind wasn't just a spiderweb, it was a whole constellation of spider nests. "So is there no way to subvert a true believer?"

"I didn't say that." Caldenia permitted herself a small smile. "At the core, they're often beings ruled by passion. Given time and proper enticement, one passion can be replaced with another. But it takes a long while and requires careful emotional management."

Dagorkun met us at the door. He nodded at me, pointedly ignored Caldenia's presence, and led us to the back where the Khanum sat on a wide covered balcony. A fire pit occupied the center, the stone of the balcony circling it in a broken ring, forming a round bench lined with orange, green, and yellow pillows. A thick blanket of gray clouds smothered the sky, promising rain but failing to deliver. The Khanum sprawled on the pillows. Her spacer armor was gone. Instead, she wore a light voluminous robe the color of blood, embroidered with turquoise birds, their plumage studded with dots of pure white, frolicking among sharp dark branches. Her face looked tired. Up close it was hard to ignore how huge she was. I looked like a child by comparison.

The Khanum regarded me from under half-closed eyelids. "Greetings, Innkeeper."

"Greetings, Khanum."

"Sit with me."

I took a seat across from her. Caldenia sat to my right.

The Khanum rolled her head and looked at her, her gaze heavy. "Witch."

"Savage." Caldenia smiled back, showing her sharp, inhuman teeth.

"We know of you," the Khanum said. "You've murdered a great many people. You've eaten some of them. You are a kadul."

A cannibal.

"An abomination," the Khanum said.

"You know what they say about abominations," Caldenia said. "We make the worst enemies."

"Was that a threat?"" Dagorkun's eyes narrowed.

"A warning." Caldenia folded her hands on her lap. "There is only one time to make threats: when you intend to negotiate. I do not."

A male otrokar came in, bringing a tray bearing a teapot and four cups. Dagorkun reached for it, but the Khanum took hold of the teakettle first.

"Khanum...," Dagorkun began.

"Hush," she told him. "It's been years since I last poured you tea. Pretend you are five for your mother's sake."

Dagorkun sat down to my left and watched as the Khanum poured everyone a cup. Caldenia picked up her cup, turned her left hand so the large amethyst ring on her middle finger faced the surface, and dipped it into the ruby-colored liquid.

The Khanum raised her eyebrows.

"It's an insult to question the Khanum's hospitality," Dagorkun said.

"Alas, I do not care." Caldenia glanced at her ring. A light blue symbol flashed on the surface of the beautiful stone. Caldenia picked up the cup and sipped it. I followed her lead. The tea, flavorful, spicy, and slightly bitter, washed over my tongue. I held it in my mouth, waiting for the familiar nip, and let it roll down my throat.

"You've had the red tea before," the Khanum observed.

"Yes, but not this variety." Most of the red tea I had seen was lighter in color, sometimes almost orange.

"This is wanla," the Khanum said. "Poor people's tea. You probably met the wealthier of our kind. They tend toward the paler teas. I like the tea my mother made. It's the one the Horde drinks after a hard march."

I took another sip. The Khanum wanted something. She wouldn't have invited me otherwise. Asking her about it was out of the question. I'd have to wait.

We finished the first cup in silence, and the Khanum poured us another.

"The blond vampire wants you. Can your kind and his mate?"

Thank you, Arland, for putting me into this lovely position. "It is possible, but I have no interest in such a relationship."

"Why not?" Dagorkun asked.

I smiled at him. "Because I have no intention of leaving my home, and Lord Arland would make a terrible innkeeper."

"You could go with him," the Khanum suggested.

"My place is here." I sipped my tea. "His place is with his House. His attention is flattering, but it doesn't interfere with my mission."

"And what is that?" Dagorkun asked.

"To keep you and them from killing each other."

An otrokar dashed onto the balcony, running backward, jumped and caught a football sewn from rough leather. He saw the Khanum. His eyes widened and he ran back inside. Dagorkun rolled his eyes.

"Should I purchase some helmets?" I asked.

"No," the Khanum said. "A few concussions would be good for them. It will settle them down." The big woman leaned back. "I do not understand you, Innkeeper. I understand the Merchants. They are driven by profit. I understand the vampires. They are our mortal enemy and they seek the same things we seek: glory in battle, victory, and land. I even understand the Arbitrator. There is power and satisfaction in shifting the balance of relations between many nations. What drives you, Innkeeper?"

"I want my inn to prosper. The more guests I have, the healthier and stronger is the inn. If the summit succeeds, it will be known that my home served you well."

"We know the Arbitrator approached other innkeepers to host this summit," Dagorkun stated. "They turned him down."

"My inn was uniquely suited for the summit," I said. "It's small and mostly empty at the moment. We specialize in dangerous guests."

"To take a job like this, one must have a strong motivation," the Khanum said. "What is yours?"

"I lost my family," I said. "They were taken from me. I've searched for them on my own and I failed. I want my inn to thrive and be full of guests, because sooner or later someone will walk through my door and I will see recognition on their face when they see the portrait of my parents downstairs."

The Khanum nodded. "Family. This I understand."

We drank more tea.

"It is the third of autumn," the Khanum said. "On our home world, summer is the time of drought and heat. Winter is a welcome respite; it is the time of mild weather and rains when the grasses grow. The third of autumn is the day we commune with our ancestors to celebrate surviving yet another year."

I didn't know much about the Horde's celebrations except that almost all of them were conducted outside.

"Do you wish to have an autumn celebration?" I asked.

"My people are restless," the Khanum said. "It would do us good."

I waited.

"The Arbitrator has denied my request."

Here it is. "He must've had valid reasons."

"He believes we are deliberately dragging our feet in negotiations," Dagorkun said. "He means to use our culture to pressure us."

"May I ask a question about the negotiations?" I asked.

The Khanum raised her eyebrows. "Yes."

"You control a large territory on Nexus. The Anocracy controls an equally large territory. Both of you may have to work with the Merchants to get shipments offplanet. Why not agree to peace?"

The Khanum reached into her robe and pulled out a small disk carved of something that looked like bone. She squeezed the sides and an image of an otrokar male appeared above it. He wore full battle armor. His face echoed both Dagorkun and the Khanum.

"Kordugan," she said. "My third son. He lies dead on Nexus. We never recovered the body."

Dagorkun looked down on his hands.

"I'm sorry," I said.

"Children die," the Khanum said, her voice resigned. "It is a fact of life. I've learned this again and again. It hurts every time."

"Then why not stop the dying on Nexus?" I asked.

"Because we do not negotiate," the Khanum said. "We conquer. When I look at the Anocracy's half of the continent, I see land. I see homesteads. I see families, our families, raising children, building lives, breeding cattle."

Dagorkun glanced at his mother. "Mother, cattle won't survive on Nexus. It's a barren rock. There isn't enough feed."

She waved at him. "That is beside the point. We expand, or like my son, we die. This is our way. This is the Anocracy's way. They stand in the way of our expansion. We must check them on Nexus. We must bloody them, break their spirit, and then launch an offensive. They hold seven planets. Seven fat, wealthy planets. That's enough land to support my children, and Dagorkun's children, and their children's children. Children must be born on the planet, with the earth under their feet, and they will be born on Nexus. That's what my son died for."

Right. Neither side was willing to see reason. I could understand why Nuan Cee was in despair.

"But if you oppose the peace so strongly, why agree to the summit at all?" I asked.

"Who says I oppose the peace?" The Khanum sighed, reached over, and ran her hand through Dagorkun's hair. For a second the seasoned warrior looked just like an eight-year-old human boy whose mother had kissed him in front of everybody as she dropped him off in front of the school.

"I told you what the Horde's policy dictates," the Khanum said. "My views are not relevant. My people wish to commune with our ancestors. We have long memories. Will you speak to the Arbitrator for us?"

The bargain was clear: if I intervened on their behalf, they would owe me a favor. They didn't need to promise me one. It was my duty to see to the comfort of my guests.

"I'll talk to George," I said. "I don't know how much influence I have with him, but I will try. Even if he is receptive, we may have to talk the vampires and Merchants into going along with it, which means we may have to make some concessions."

"We understand," Dagorkun said.

I rose and bowed. "Thank you for sharing your tea with me, Khanum. May your days be long and your sun weak."

The Khanum inclined her head.

Dagorkun rose and we followed him through the otro-kar quarters. Something didn't sit right with me about what the Khanum had said about the Horde's reasons for fighting. She delivered the lines perfectly, with just enough growl in her voice, but I had a feeling her heart wasn't in it.

Dagorkun stopped by the door.

I stepped through it. "Thank you for your hospitality."

"You're welcome."

The door sealed shut.

"Well, that was enlightening," Caldenia murmured as we descended the stairs. "She's desperate for the peace talks to succeed."

"You think so?"

Caldenia shook her head. "My dear, you must learn to observe. She is the general of this massive horde, but under all of it she is a mother who loves her children more than life itself. You and I both know who will lead the Horde's offensive on Nexus—it will be the son who now sits next to her. Remember that *National Geographic* documentary we watched last week, where the lions were trying to survive the drought? That woman is that old lioness trying to protect her last cub. She is fighting desperately to keep him alive, and she is losing hope."

She was right. It made perfect sense and it was so awful. The sadness of it took your breath away.

"This is marvelous," Caldenia said. "Press that lever and you can wrench her heart right out. You couldn't ask for a better weakness. You should take me to all your talks. They are so entertaining."

CHAPTER TEN

G eorge's hair, normally perfectly brushed and gathered into a ponytail at the nape of his neck, was haphazardly tied, with loose strands spilling around his handsome face. A trace of stubble graced his jaw. His cream shirt was slightly damp. When he met me at the door of his room, he looked slightly disheveled and mournful, like a man who had surrendered to his fate. Surprisingly, losing his elegant perfection catapulted him from merely shockingly handsome into outrageously seductive territory. I briefly wondered if I could find some excuse to send Sophie up here. I had a feeling she would really appreciate it.

I told him about the Khanum's request for autumn celebrations, and George did everything except listen to me. He tugged on his sleeve. He brushed his hair back. He scratched his stubbled jaw. He appeared generally to be distracted, but years of being an innkeeper's kid had taught me to watch the guests. George paid careful attention to everything I said.

"I attempted to shave and the faucet sprayed me with water," George reported when I finished. "Icy water. It's been three, no four, days since I've been able to take a hot shower. No, maybe three..."

Very well. "If you are asking whether you've been punished enough for cutting down my thirty-year-old apple trees, I'm sure we can work something out." I snapped my fingers for emphasis. Every faucet and shower head in the bathroom came on, spilling out powerful currents of steaming water. I let it run for three seconds and turned it off. "Also, if you could stop pretending to not listen to me, I would really appreciate it."

George abandoned his martyred expression. "There is a certain protocol when it comes to these things. A certain amount of back-and-forth that most people engage in. You simply bypass all the preliminaries. I can't decide if your directness is refreshing or frustrating."

"The more verbal dancing I do around a subject, the more opportunity I give you to argue," I explained. "Some guests tend to be very…"

"Manipulative?"

"Difficult," I said.

"But having a longer conversation also gives you the opportunity to learn more about the person," he said. "What buttons to push. What levers to pull."

"I'm not here to press buttons. I'm neutral by definition. My purpose is to provide shelter and comfort to my guests and see to their needs. I'm here to solve their problems while they are staying under my roof, and right now I would like to talk about the Khanum's request."

"Very well. Let's abandon the verbal gymnastics. It will go faster." George invited me to a sofa with a sweep of his hand. I sat, and he took a plush chair across from me. "Did the Khanum explain that the Horde signed a waiver prior to negotiations, indicating they were willing to suspend celebrations and religious holidays for the duration of the summit?"

"No."

"In fact, every participant of the summit has signed this waver." George's blue eyes were hard and crystal clear, their gaze focused. There was something sharp in the way he held himself now. He reminded me of a falcon watching a bird in a distant sky just before he launched himself into the air currents for the lethal dive, his talons poised for the kill. So that's what he really looked like. "The balance of power within the summit is very tenuous, and neither of the three participants is willing to relinquish any of it. If they see any opening at all, they will press their advantage. So if we now honor the Khanum's request, concessions will have to be made to appease the Holy Anocracy and the Merchants."

"In other words, they'll want a bribe," I said. Of course. "And whatever they ask for will result in additional complications."

"Furthermore, once we bring the celebration to the table, we can't back down. If the vampires, for example, make some outrageous demand in return for agreeing to the celebration, and we are unable to reach an agreement, in the otrokars' eyes, the Holy Anocracy will become the people who prevented the observation of a beloved ritual. One would think that given their history of mutual hatred, this one more small occurrence wouldn't matter. In reality, that hypothetical transgression will overshadow whatever bad blood they already have."

"They killed my brother, stole our planet, but most of all, they wouldn't let us have the autumn festival?"

"Yes. That's a peculiar quirk of the psychology of small isolated gatherings, which is why I chose this format and an Earth inn in the first place. When you take sworn enemies and put them together in a cloistered environment, provided the group is small enough, they experience the same events and develop similar attitudes, which gives them some common ground where previously there was none. It creates a 'we're all in this together' mentality, a camaraderie.

The vampires and the otrokars recognize their own emotions in their enemy: boredom while the proceedings take place, relief when they're over for the day, joy at the simple pleasure of a well-cooked meal. This commonality of circumstances and reactions fosters empathy, which is a precursor of any consensus. Right now this empathy is very fragile, and a conflict over the autumn celebrations has the potential to rip it apart beyond all repair."

"But if everyone makes a concession and consents to the celebration, wouldn't that show respect and tolerance of each other's religion and traditions? If the vampires and the Merchants show respect for the festival and observe it as guests, wouldn't it promote the feeling of empathy?"

"Assuming that celebration will happen, yes. But that's a big assumption. It carries a lot of risk."

I leaned back. "Unless I've gotten the wrong impression, the peace negotiations have stalled."

"You're not wrong." George grimaced.

"This could give them a boost."

"Or destroy any chance of peace."

"You are the Arbitrator. The decision is yours, but I would be willing to speak to all interested parties to see if I could get them to agree."

George studied me for a long moment. "What is your interest in all this?"

"Khanum and her people are my guests. They are stressed, and I want them to be comfortable. The autumn celebration will help."

"Is that all?"

That and the masked desperation in the Khanum's eyes that made me wince every time I recalled it. Remembering her on the couch, brushing at her son's hair and holding all her worry and sorrow in a steel grip, haunted me. I couldn't help with peace negotiations. I could do nothing to keep her son from going to war. But I could do this one small thing for her, and I would try to accomplish it.

"That's enough, isn't it?"

He thought about it for a moment. "You win. We'll take this risk. If you want to bargain with the vampires and the Merchants, you have my permission. But I want to be kept aware of everything."

"I will record our meetings and send the feed to your screen."

"Good. Do not agree to anything, Dina, before consulting with me. Make no promises. They will be held against you."

"I understand." I rose. "Thank you."

"You're welcome, although I'm not sure exactly what I'm being thanked for." George grinned, and his smile had a mordant edge to it. "This ought to be exciting. It's good to have some fun once in a while."

"You said yourself, this fun carries risk," I reminded him.

His smile got wider. "That's the best kind of fun."

"Absolutely not." If vampires had fur, Odalon's would've stood on end like the coat of an angry cat, so the Battle Chaplain would've doubled in size from the sheer outrage. "No, they can't have their pagan rite here, on this ground, where we must remain after it has been befouled."

I had gone to the knights first, because getting them to agree to the otrokars' festival would be much harder than bargaining with Nuan Cee.

"They have the same right to practice their religion as you do." I stood my ground. "You are all guests here and are on equal footing."

"Do you know what is involved in this heresy?" Odalon leaned toward me, all six feet and a few inches of him, his crimson vestments flaring. "They consecrate the ground. They dedicate it to their pagan deities. When I walk upon their unholy ground, it is with a battle hammer in my hand dripping with the lifeblood of the otrokars."

And here I'd thought he was the sensible one out of the whole delegation. "Would it help if I gave them a specific area to consecrate? Then you wouldn't have to walk on it and we could avoid bloody hammers."

Odalon sputtered. "How in the world would you do that? Do you intend to lift a section of the ground and float it in the empty air?"

"That is an option," I said. It really wasn't, but there was no reason to discuss the limits of my powers. "However, I was going to suggest digging a trench and filling it with running water. They are planning on calling specific earth spirits, and the running water would provide a boundary."

"This is blasphemy!" Odalon declared in the same way Gerard Butler had once roared "This is Sparta." Sadly, Odalon had nobody to kick into a bottomless hole for emphasis, so he settled for looking extremely put out.

"Let's not be hasty," Arland said. "So they want to celebrate. What's the harm?"

"So you don't object?" I asked.

"I do object," Arland said. "In the strongest words possible, but in the interest of peace, I'm willing to set aside my objections."

"Lady Isur?" I turned to the Marshal.

She frowned, tapping one finger against her lips. "I consented as well."

"What?" Odalon turned to her.

"I'm tired. My people are tired. These talks must conclude at some point. If this pagan dance helps the Horde get in line, so be it."

"I will not stand for this," Odalon announced.

"That's okay," Robart said. "We can outvote you."

Uh-oh. Out of the three Marshals, I had expected him to put up the biggest fight.

Lady Isur reached over and touched his cheek with her long fingers. "Strange, my lord. You don't seem to have a fever."

He glanced at her, surprised, almost shocked at her touch. For a moment he struggled with it, then recovered. "Let the savages have their celebration. But I want something in return."

Here it comes.

"I want to add guests to the banquet," Lord Robart said.

"Guests? What guests?" Arland's eyebrows furrowed.

"How many guests and of what sort?" I asked.

"I think three should suffice," Robart said. "They will be members of an old, respected House."

Vampires then. "Very well, I will bring this to the Arbitrator's attention. The final word is his." And he would likely say no. Increasing the number of vampires would just complicate the negotiations, especially if they were vampires Robart decided to invite.

"We shouldn't even be having this discussion," Odalon thundered.

"Robart, this is foolhardy at best." Lady Isur sighed.

Arland turned to her. "What House?"

"He means to invite House Meer," Lady Isur explained, as if to a child.

"Are you out of your mind?" Arland roared.

"Don't tell me my business, Krahr!" Robart stepped forward, baring his fangs.

Arland's teeth were already out on display. "How can you invite House Meer? They seek destruction of my House!" Arland snarled. "Of both of our Houses!"

"They are the true patriots!" Robart shot back.

"They are cowards. They refused to fight on Nexus so we would be weakened and they could pick over our bleeding carcasses. How can you consort with cowards? As of last night, they have been excommunicated."

"This is just getting better and better." Odalon shook his head in horror. "One wants to have a pagan ceremony, the other invites the excommunicated to it. Has everyone lost their mind?"

Robart stood his ground. "House Meer sacrificed their honor for all our sake."

"So help me, I will strangle him." Arland clenched his fists.

Lady Isur stepped between them.

"Explain it to me," Arland shot over her. "Explain to me how those sniveling worms have our best interests at heart while we are getting ready to spill our blood in their place."

"This rotation does nothing except drain our blood," Robart said, emotion clear on his face. "I wish I could make you see. Only a concerted offensive can end this war. We must throw all our might into it."

Arland shook his head. "And you suppose the Kair, Dui La Kingdoms, and the Harat will just stand by and wait at our borders patiently, like docile livestock, while we do this? Or have you signed some peace treaties on behalf of the Anocracy when I wasn't looking?"

"How can you be so dense?" Robart growled. "Do you not understand that we must reject the Hierophant's directive and abandon the Warlor—"

"Stop!" Odalon thrust his hammer against Robart's chest. "Stop, Lord Marshal, before you add treason to your heresy."

"I withdraw my consent to the celebration," Arland said, his eyes dark.

"You can't. You've given your word." Robart smiled at Arland and Isur. "You both have given your word."

Arland bared his teeth.

"Anytime!" Robart pushed forward.

"Enough!" Lady Isur barked. "You may be Marshals, but I'm the Bitch of Eskar. Do not make me show you how I earned my name."

Robart took a step back.

Arland turned and stormed out of the room.

The Battle Chaplain turned to leave as well.

"Odalon!" Robart called.

"I'm going to pray," Odalon said, pronouncing each word with crisp exactness. "I'm going to pray for me, for this gathering, and most of all for you, and hope for divine mercy or we'll all end up on the icy plains of Nothing."

He walked out.

Lady Isur faced Robart. "Your passion does you credit, but take care. Do not permit your grief to allow you to be used."

Robart shook his head and left.

Lady Isur looked at me. I looked back at her.

She exhaled. "He is a demon on the battlefield."

"Lord Robart?"

She nodded. "However, he badly needs a woman with a cool head to channel all that fire before it leads him astray."

She walked away as well, leaving me standing by the exit. Well. I suppose it could've gone worse.

I left the Holy Anocracy's quarters and paused to open a screen to George, mentally preparing myself for a no.

The Arbitrator sat on the couch. My new cat sat next to him, looking very regal. I wondered how he got into George's quarters.

"I find their terms agreeable," George said.

What? "Why?"

That "why" slipped out before I could catch it.

"Because, as I suspected, the greatest impediment to these negotiations is House Meer. I want to meet my opposition out in the open, assess them, and dismantle them before they can do further damage."

For a soft-spoken, seemingly mild man, George could be chillingly cold-blooded I decided as I walked to the Clan Nuan's quarters. The Merchant of Baha-char met me in his common room where he reclined on a divan. As I outlined my proposal, the kitten ran out of the side room, followed by a group of Nuan Cee's relatives in brightly colored clothes.

"Why do you think the summit is failing?" Nuan Cee asked me.

"It's not my place to offer an opinion."

"I insist."

"It's failing because among the three of you, none understands how the people from the other factions feel," I told him honestly. "If you only knew the true price each of you is paying for the war, you would agree to end it."

Nuan Cee sighed, watching as the kitten ran back and forth while his clan collectively tripped over their feet in a comical fashion. "I fear you're right. What concessions were made to the Holy Anocracy?"

"They asked to have guests for the banquet following the rite."

The kitten stood up on her hind legs and batted her paws at the leading fox. He made a grab for her, and the tiny beast dashed to the side and climbed the curtains. I pressed my lips together so I wouldn't giggle. After being in the presence of four upset vampires roaring at the top of their lungs, this was almost too much to take.

"How many guests?"

"Three."

"I'm inclined to be generous."

Out of the mouth of a Merchant, there were no more dangerous words.

Nuan Cee toyed with the tassel on the corner of his pillow. "I will also add a guest. Just one. An employee."

"Is there anything else?" That was too easy.

"No."

"I will relay your terms to the Arbitrator."

"Thank you."

I carefully picked my way through the room, trying to avoid the kitten-chasing mob. After allowing three guests for the Holy Anocracy, George had no reason to deny what looked like a modest request from Nuan Cee. The autumn celebrations were going forward. The Khanum should be pleased. And if I could make this a little bit easier for her, I had to try.

I just hoped I hadn't completely ruined the peace summit by my meddling.

CHAPTER ELEVEN

O rro raised his head to the sky, opened his mouth, and let out what could only be described as a primal yell. Since he was holding a butcher knife in one hand and a sharpening stick in the other, the effect was very dramatic.

I waited.

"Is he always like this?" Gaston asked me quietly.

"I think so."

Orro stood frozen, seemingly lost to his despair.

I counted in my head. One, two, three...

Orro turned to me, his eyes intense. "How long?"

"You have to delay the banquet for an hour to allow for the otrokars' celebration," I said.

"One? Hour?"

"Yes."

Orro swung his stick and knife. "I have fish. Delicate fish. I have soufflé. I have... I can do one hour. But no more!" He waved the knife for emphasis. "No more. Not one minute, not one second, not one nanosecond, not one attosecond more."

"Thank you."

I walked into the front room, Gaston following me.

The Arbitrator's delegation had, for some reason, decided to appropriate my front room despite the perfectly adequate space in their quarters. George was absorbed in his reader. Jack and Sophie were playing chess. Given that I was terrible at chess, I had no idea who was winning. Her Grace had artfully arranged herself in a chair by the window and indulged in a cup of hibiscus tea and her tablet. Judging by the small smile on her lips, Caldenia was reading something with a lot of smut or a lot of murder.

"Attosecond?" Gaston asked.

"I'm guessing it's a very, very small fraction of a second," I said.

"One quintillionth of a second," George said without raising his head from his reader.

Jack pondered him. "Have you started memorizing random crap again to amuse yourself?"

"No, I'm connected to the wireless," George said. "I googled it."

The otrokar shaman emerged from the hallway, wearing a tattered black cloak. His long black hair, tinted with a hint of purple, spilled over the fabric. Combined with his skin, a deep bronze with an almost green undertone, the hair made his pale green eyes startling on his harsh, angular face.

"Greetings, Ruga." I inclined my head. "Are you ready to inspect the site?"

He nodded.

I stepped outside, Gaston and the shaman in tow. I had a feeling George had assigned Gaston to me, because he'd been trailing me for the past half hour.

Dagorkun had informed me they would need a clearing that was at least five akra long and wide, which roughly translated to a square with a side of thirty-five point two yards. I would have to appropriate part of the new land for it. After we took down the alien assassin last summer, I used part of the money I had earned from House Krahr to purchase another three acres. The plot sat in the back of the property, past the orchard, on the north side, securely cushioned from view by dense oaks and cedars. Fueled by the boost of Arland's, Sean's, and Caldenia's presence, the inn had rooted through the new land almost overnight and spent the past seven months or so making it its own. That provided me with a large enough area for the otrokar festival.

The new land had only cost me fifteen thousand dollars, primarily because it housed a bat cave and couldn't be zoned for building. The cave itself opened a few hundred yards to the east, outside my property, and if the peace summit succeeded, I would buy it. The bats could prove very useful.

I stopped and surveyed the lot. Small gnarled cedars rose above the grass, flanked by some bushes. I had never liked the Texas cedars. They always looked really dry and starved of water with their rough trunks, and just to add insult to injury, every winter they spat out clouds of yellow pollen so thick it blanketed the hoods of the cars in fine powder overnight.

"This is wrong," the shaman said. "There are too many trees. There is no water and the ground is too uneven."

I inhaled and let my magic flow.

The soil around the cedar trunks softened. Ripples pulsed through it like waves from a stone cast into a pond. The trees shuddered and sank into the ground whole, twisting as they were sucked into the soil. No sense in wasting the wood. The otrokars would likely need some for the festival. The inn would prepare the logs and absorb what was left afterward for its own purposes down the road.

Gaston's eyebrows rose. The shaman frowned.

Obeying my push, the ground smoothed out. A foot-wide trench formed along the perimeter of the clearing.

Rocks, stones, and pebbles, most pale sandstone, rose like mushroom caps from the depth of the ground to line the bottom of the trench. I raised the south end of it about eight inches to create a slope. A long garden hose snaked its way from the house. A second hose connected to the first, and its end dropped into the trench. Water spilled onto the rocks and obediently flowed down the newly made stream bed. I walked along the trench, adjusting the height as needed.

The shaman stepped over the trench, reached inside his cloak, and produced a pouch made of scaled hide. He whispered something, opened the pouch, and spilled bright red powder into the air. For a moment the red cloud lingered, suspended by some invisible force, and then the individual particles fell, sinking into the soil. A subtle change came over the area. I couldn't see any difference with the naked eye, but now the land enclosed by my artificial stream felt slightly odd. It still belonged to the inn, but now it also responded to the shaman's magic.

"Are there any additional adjustments you would like me to make?" I asked.

He shook his head. "This will suffice. I have work to do here before the festival can begin."

"Do you require wood for the fires?"

"Yes."

A pile of cedar logs rose from the ground.

I inclined my head. "Gaston will keep you company so there are no incidents."

The shaman spared me a look. "I now stand on the land of my ancestors. There are things in this life I fear. Vampires are not one of them."

"All the same, I would like Gaston to stay with you. Please let me know if there is anything else you require."

I walked away. I had more preparations to make. Lord Robart's guests from House Meer would need their own small set of rooms. Putting them in with the Holy Anocracy's delegation would be asking for trouble.

Red curtains or blue curtains? I peered at the guest suite for Nuan Cee's "employee." When I'd pressed Nuan Cee for specifics about his guest, he played dumb. I tried dropping subtle hints, then more obvious hints, until finally I straight-out asked what sort of furniture I should provide for the new addition to his delegation. His answer was "large," after which he informed me that he was too tired to continue the conversation and needed to retire.

Large as in human large? Vampire large? Nuan Cee large? Which large were we talking about? First Sophie, now this. This new thing with guests arriving but not bothering to explain to me their species or any preferences was getting really annoying.

I caught myself before my irritation tainted the room. I had settled on a very basic set of furnishings, light bamboo floor, and beige walls. The room desperately needed color, but I would have to add it on the fly. With my luck, his guest would turn out to be a Ravelian slug and I would have to coat the whole room in crude oil.

"It will have to do," I told Beast.

A chime sounded in my head. Lord Robart's guests were about to arrive. I checked the time. We had less than fifteen minutes before the celebration was set to start.

Time is a funny thing. When you have a headache, five minutes seems like an eternity. When you're trying to prepare for the otrokar celebration, make two additional guest suites, one for the vampires and the other for the Merchants, and pacify a melodramatic seven-foot-tall hedgehog-like chef convinced that his fish will become inedible because it has to wait an extra hour in the refrigerator, three hours go by in a blink.

I hurried to the front room. The sun had set, the day burning down to purple embers in the west. Twilight claimed the streets, painting the floorboards of the hallway in cool blue and purple. We had less than fifteen minutes before the celebration started. I made it just as George walked down the stairs. He was wearing an indigo doublet that set off his pale hair. Jack followed him, dressed in dark brown leather.

"House Meer is incoming in ten minutes," I told them.

"Good." George smiled. It wasn't a nice smile.

The magic of the inn tugged on me. Something was happening in front of the building. I stepped to the window. The long stretch of Camelot Road rolled out before turning, and on the corner, half-hidden by the enormous prickly pear the Hendersons refused to trim, a police cruiser waited. Oh great.

"Problems?" George asked.

"Officer Marais's intuition never fails."

George glanced at his brother. Jack shrugged and pulled off his shirt, exposing a hard, muscled frame.

"Jack will take care of it," George said.

That's what I was afraid of. "Please don't hurt him."

"The guy is ruining your life and you want me not to hurt him." Jack's pants followed. He kept going, and I kept my gaze firmly on his face.

"Officer Marais isn't trying to ruin my life. He's trying to do his job and keep the neighborhood safe."

"Fine, fine." The last shred of clothing landed on the floor. "I'll be back in time for the fireworks."

Jack stretched and then his body broke apart. Fur spilled out. For a moment he almost appeared to be suspended in midair, then his body twisted, crunched, knotted on itself, and a large lynx landed on my floor.

Okay. That was certainly interesting. What the hell was he? He wasn't the Sun Horde, that's for sure.

"Could you open the back door please?" George asked.

The back door swung open and the lynx shot out through the kitchen and into the night. Something banged. A screech echoed through the inn.

"It is enough I put up with the dog. Must I have cat hair in my food as well?" Orro yelled.

He'd missed his calling. He should've become a Shakespearean actor instead.

Beast barked, clearly offended.

"My apologies." I turned to the wall. "Screen please. Front camera feed, zoom in three hundred percent."

A screen sprouted on the wall, giving me a detailed view of Officer Marais's car and its owner, who was leaning back in his seat.

Something thumped the cruiser. It rocked on its wheels.

Officer Marais sat up straight.

Another thump.

Another.

Officer Marais swung the door open and stepped out, illuminated by the glow of the nearby street lamp, one hand on his gun. He stepped around the car and checked its rear.

The crape myrtle bushes in the yard across the street rustled.

Officer Marais turned smoothly and stepped away from the car. The bushes rustled again, shivering, as something moved away from the car toward the streetlight.

Marais followed, his steps careful.

A lynx emerged from the bushes and sat on the pavement.

Officer Marais froze, his hand on his sidearm. His face told me he was calculating his odds. He'd walked too far from the car. If he turned and ran, the lynx would catch him.

Now what? If Jack attacked, Marais would fire, I had no doubt of it. "Your brother might get shot."

"Jack is a man of many talents," George said.

Well, that didn't answer anything.

The lynx stretched his paws out in front of him, turned, and flopped on the road on his back like a playful house cat.

Some tension left Officer Marais's stance. The line of his shoulders softened.

Jack rubbed his big head on the pavement and batted at the empty air with his paws.

"Hey there," Marais said, his voice hesitant. "Who's a good cat?"

Jack rolled over, sauntered over to the nearest bush and rubbed his head on it.

"Good cat. You're a big guy, huh. Did you escape from someone's yard? People should have more sense than to own wild animals like that." Officer Marais took a careful step back.

Jack whipped about. His furry butt pointed at Officer Marais, his tail went up, and a jet of pressurized cat spray drenched Marais chest.

Oh no.

"Aaah!" Marais leaped back and jerked his gun up, but Jack had vanished as if he were never there.

"Sonovabitch!" Marais shook his left hand, which was dripping with cat urine. "Damn it all to hell."

His face stretched as if he had just taken a gulp of sour milk.

He looked down on his chest and gagged. "Oh Jesus."

He tried to hold on to his composure. His chin quivered. He gagged again, bent over, and dry heaved.

I didn't know whether to laugh or to feel bad.

"Oh sweet Jesus." Officer Marais straightened and marched to his car, his face contorted. The cruiser's lights came on as the engine roared to life and the big car tore out of the neighborhood.

George smiled. "I told you—many talents."

I stood on the edge of the landing field as a crimson drop fell from the sky and melted into thin air, leaving three vampires in its wake. Vampires got bigger and more grizzled with age, not taller or fatter, but bulkier, as their bodies gained more and more hard mass. The three knights before me were massive. Where Arland's and Robart's armors were works of art, the newcomers' armor was a work of art designed to communicate the fact that its owner had a nearly unlimited budget. Ornate, customized to fit, it turned each of them from a living being into a mobile, lethal fortress. They stood there scowling and showing their fangs, and I had a strong feeling that this would not end well. The one in the front carried a huge axe. Behind him, on the left, a vampire with an old scar across his face brandished a blood mace, and his friend on the right, with hair so pale it looked almost white, had equipped himself with a sword that had a wickedly sharp, wide blade.

"Greetings to House Meer," I said.

Next to me Robart had a deeply pleased look on his face. He was the only Marshal who'd come to meet them. Two of his knights waited nearby, their faces grim, looking like they were ready to repel an attack at a moment's notice. Apparently Lord Robart's affinity for House Meer wasn't shared by those under his command.

The oldest knight opened his mouth. The biggest of the three, his mane of jet-black hair streaked with gray, he was clearly the leader. It was strange to think in a several decades, Arland would look like that.

"Greetings, Innkeeper," he said, his voice a deep growl.

"Lord Beneger," Robart said.

"Lord Robart," the leader answered.

No standard, no display, no ceremony. Vampires thrived on ceremony. House Meer was here, but they were making it clear they weren't visiting in an official capacity. My hand tightened on my broom. I had only seen vampire delegations do this four times, and every single time it was done so the House could deny it had sanctioned the actions of its members. I would not permit a massacre in my inn.

"Follow me." I led them through the back of the house to the balcony overlooking the festival grounds. Arland, Lady Isur, and the rest of their vampires occupied the far right side of the balcony, House Vorga the middle, and Nuan Cee's clan took up the far left.

Below us the otrokars were checking piles of wood. They had arranged the logs I provided into a bonfire at the south end of the circle created by my stream and made four smaller piles along the water. The bark on some of the logs was red and purple. They must've brought some of their own wood.

The scarred knight from House Meer looked down on them and spat on the balcony. "Blasphemy."

He spat on my inn.

I smiled as sweetly as I could. "Next time you choose to spit, my lord, the stones under your feet will part."

The scarred knight glared at me.

"We are guests here, Uriel," Lord Beneger said. "My apologies, Innkeeper."

Apologies or not, the next time Lord Uriel decided to hawk up some phlegm, he would regret it.

The otrokars formed a ring around the festival grounds. While we spoke, the night had snuck in on soft cat paws, turning the eastern sky a deep, beautiful purple. Twilight claimed the clearing, the light of the sunset diluted by encroaching darkness. Shadows deepened and grew treacherous, the wind died down, and the first hint of the stars studded the sky.

The otrokars' shaman stepped into the circle drawn by my stream, entering from the north. He wore only a long, layered leather kilt. Strange symbols drawn in pale green and white marked his exposed torso. His hair streamed loose about his face. Some strands were braided with a leather cord decorated with bone and wooden beads.

Fire burst in the two piles on his left and right all on its own. He kept walking, the lines of his muscular but lean body oddly beautiful. The fire jumped to the other two piles, then to the bonfire. An insistent drumbeat sounded, growing more and more urgent as the three otrokars on the edge began to play big bloated drums. A wild, eerie melody of pipes that hadn't come from any wood or grass born on Earth issued a challenge, the simplest kind of music brought to life by a sentient being's breath. The shaman turned his head, his long dark hair flying, spun like a dervish, and began to dance.

The otrokars clapped as one, picking up the rhythm of the drums. The shaman whirled and twisted, his movements born from the grace and speed of a hunter closing on its prey, wild and strangely primal, as if every layer of civilization had been ripped away from him and what remained was a creature, fruit of the planet that birthed it, as timeless as life itself. It was impossible to look away.

The otrokars began to sing, a simple, exuberant melody. I couldn't understand the words, but the meaning was clear. *I live. I survived. I'm here.*

Breath caught in my chest. I realized with absolute clarity that one day I was going to die. One day I would no longer be here. All the things I wanted, all my thoughts, all my worries—all of it would be gone with me, lost forever. There were so many things I wanted to do. So much I still wanted to see. I had to hold on to it. I had to hold on to every short second of life. Every breath was a gift, gone forever to the cold stars the moment I exhaled.

I wanted to cry.

The symbols on the shaman's body glowed, weak at first, then brighter and brighter. The flames of the fires turned pale yellow, then olive, then a bright emerald green, matching the radiance of the shaman's markings. The wood no longer fueled it; the blaze raged on its own.

Shadows rose among the otrokars, translucent silhouettes without features, silent and standing still.

The shaman twisted, bending backward, his supple body nearly parallel to the ground, and suddenly a simple wooden staff was in his hand. He spun the staff, turning it into a blur, planted it into the ground, and clawed at the sky with his free hand. The glowing coals from the bonfire rolled to him, forming a narrow scorching path to the blaze.

The shaman froze, poised on his toes, leaning back slightly, rigid, every muscle in his body tight, like a genius ballet dancer frozen in a moment just before the leap. His eyes glowed deep purple, otherworldly, as if the distant planet itself stared through him. He held out his left arm to the side.

The Khanum emerged from the shadows and came to stand next to him. She wore a simple tunic. Her feet were bare. The shaman's hand clamped her shoulder.

A wave of translucent purple dashed through the green light of the coal path. A shadow appeared in the heart of the bonfire.

The Khanum stepped onto the coal path and walked quickly to the blaze. With every step, the shadow became clearer. Arms formed, the lines of the shoulders and the neck streamlined, hair sprouted, and features formed in the oval of the face. A young otrokar man stood in the flames. He looked like Dagorkun.

They were so close now she could almost touch him. The Khanum stood still on the coals, one hand raised, as if trying to touch her dead son. Her bare feet burned, but still she refused to move.

Dagorkun moved in from the side and took his mother by her hand. The shadow in the fire nodded to his brother. Dagorkun nodded back and gently led the Khanum away, back to the others. The shadow melted into the light.

I realized I was crying.

Another otrokar stepped to the shaman. A second wave of purple, a second shadow, another trip down the coal path. A woman this time, older, wearing the otrokar armor.

One by one the otrokars came, each finding another loved one in the fire. Dead wives, dead husbands, fallen parents, children taken before their time... Some only stayed for a brief glance, but most lingered, enduring the pain for a chance to see someone they'd lost one more time.

Finally the last otrokar stepped aside, letting the ghost of her past fade into the light. The shaman moved, his staff drawing a complicated pattern in the air. An otrokar woman began to sing, her voice soft but rising, a challenge to the stars above us.

The shaman thrust his staff into the ground and opened his arms.

The fires turned white. Tiny sparks swirled within them like ghostly fireflies.

The woman's voice rose, stronger and stronger, her song holding the darkness at bay like a shield.

Fear not the darkness
Fear not the night
You are not forsaken
We remember you

The fire exploded. Thousands of white sparks floated through the air, swirling, drifting among the otrokars. The shaman held out his hand, letting the glowing dots brush against his skin, and smiled.

The myriad of glowing lights floated up, pulled to the sky by some invisible current, and rose high, toward the greater universe beyond.

CHAPTER TWELVE

Four long tables stood in the main ballroom, arranged into a rough letter *m*: one table across for the Arbitrator, the heads of the delegations, and special guests, which included Caldenia and Sophie, and three longwise, with about twenty-five feet of space between each to make sure nobody happened to trip and accidentally fall into a slaughter. We put the otrokars on the left, the Nuan Clan in the middle, and the Holy Anocracy on the right. I took a position to the left of the main table. I was starving, but food was out of the question. I had asked Orro to save me a plate because this banquet would require my complete attention. The tension in the air was so thick you could cut it with a knife and serve it with honey for dessert.

The three delegations took their places, the leaders arranged at the main table on both sides of George, who sat in the middle. One seat, next to Nuan Cee, remained empty. Cookie's seat at the Merchants' table was orphaned too. Nuan Cee had sent him to wait in the field in the back for his guest. I still hadn't found the emerald. With everything that had happened, the search for the phantom thief had been pushed aside. If everything went well, I would get on that tonight.

George rose in the center of the main table. "I was going to make a long, inspiring speech, but everyone is clearly hungry. I have visited the kitchen and the chef has outdone himself, and I have very little willpower left after all these strenuous negotiations. Thank you for being here. Let's eat."

Everyone applauded and stomped in approval. The tables sank into the floor and reappeared, bearing a variety of starters. Orro stepped through the doorway.

"First course," he announced. "Spicy tuna tartare in a cone of miso, spring vegetables in a cucumber wrap, and vine-ripened tomatoes with basil and mozzarella."

He stepped back. I glanced at the table. He had somehow twisted tuna tartare into tiny cornucopias; the cucumber wraps looked like delicate blossoms filled with bright, paper-thin slices of something red and green; and the vine-ripened tomatoes were sliced into wedges, stuffed with basil and mozzarella, and drizzled with something that smelled tangy and delicious. My mouth watered. The delegates fell on the delicate starters like starved wolves onto a lame deer. The food was disappearing at an alarming rate.

The magic tugged on me. Someone had just landed in the back field. Nuan Cee's guest had finally arrived. I reached out with my magic and sensed Cookie and the guest moving toward the house.

The tables sank down. We were going much faster than expected, but the guests were devouring the food. A moment passed and the dining tables reappeared, filled with more dishes.

"Pasta course," Orro announced. "Agnolotti with fennel, goat cheese, and orange."

The fennel had cost me an arm and a leg and so had the cheese, but Orro had refused to compromise on the pasta course. It had to have fennel, it had to have the expensive cheese, and that was that. Well, at least if they filled up on pasta, it would make them full and happy and less prone to casual murder.

At the vampire table, the three newcomers with Lord Beneger had barely touched the food, instead they sat wrapped in hostility like it was a winter cloak. On the otrokar side, Dagorkun, a smaller female on his left and a huge hulking mountain of a male on his right, were watching Beneger very carefully, keeping their food intake light.

There would be trouble. I could feel it.

I just had to keep them from attacking until the main course. Orro had made pan-seared chicken. I had no idea what he had done to it, but the smell alone stopped you in your tracks. I had happened to walk into the kitchen to check on things just before the banquet, and I couldn't recall ever having such an intense reaction to cooked chicken before in my entire life. Orro was a wizard. Finding ingredients that didn't set off digestive alarms in five different species would've driven me crazy. He'd not only managed that but had turned what he found into culinary masterpieces. Too bad he would leave after the summit. I would miss him, and I wasn't sure what I regretted losing more—his great food or his dramatic pronouncements.

"Main course! Pan-seared chicken with golden potatoes."

Beneger surrendered to his fate and attacked the chicken. At the far end of the table, Caldenia put an entire drumstick in her mouth and pulled it out, the bone completely clean. Sophie, wearing a lovely seafoam-green gown, watched her in morbid fascination.

The smell was too much. If I didn't get some of this chicken, it would be a crime.

Cookie and Nuan Cee's guest reached the back door. I opened it for them and made sure they had a straight shot to the ballroom. At my feet Beast sat up. Apparently the new intruder smelled odd.

"Easy," I murmured.

Beast wagged her tail.

Cookie appeared in the doorway and scampered in, adorably fluffy. The creature behind him was anything but. Seven feet tall, he wore armor, but not the rigid high-tech metal of the holy knights. No, this armor was made with maximum flexibility in mind. Obsidian black, it coated him, mirroring the muscles of his body, thickening slightly to reinforce the neck and shield the outside of the arms and the chest. At first glance it looked woven, like high-tech fabric, but when he moved, the light rippled on it, fracturing into thousands of tiny scales shimmering with green. It sheathed him completely, flowing seamlessly into clawed gauntlets on his huge hands and angling into a semblance of boots on his feet. A charcoal-gray half-tabard half-robe draped the armor, embroidered with a rich green pattern. The tabard left his arms free and narrowed at the waist, where it was caught by a decorative cloth belt and flowed down. It split over his legs so a single long piece hung down in front while the rest of the fabric obscured his sides and back, falling to his ankles, its hem tattered and frayed. The tabard came with a hood that rested on the newcomer's head. I looked into it.

He had no face.

Darkness filled the hood, an impenetrable, ink-black darkness that hovered there like a living thing. It was as if the creature himself had no muscle or bone but was formed from jet-black cosmos and held together by his armor alone.

Everyone froze.

"*Turan Adin*," Lord Robart whispered to my right.

A torturous moment of silence stretched.

"Oh for the love of all that is holy," Lord Beneger roared. "He is but one man! You sniveling cowards, I'll do it myself!"

He leapt over the table as if he weighed nothing. Turan Adin halted, waiting.

Oh no, I don't think so. The walls of the inn erupted with its smooth roots.

"No!" George barked at me. "Let it happen!"

Damn it, I was getting sick of being yelled at in my own inn.

Beneger's two knights charged after him. The huge vampire lord got there first. His blood axe whined, primed, and came down in a devastating blow, so fast I barely saw it. Turan Adin sidestepped. It shouldn't have been possible, but somehow he dodged the axe that should've annihilated him, and struck out with his right hand. His claws punched straight through the reinforced neck collar of Lord Beneger's ornate armor. The vampire lord froze, all of his powerful kinetic momentum checked, broken on the slimmer form of Turan Adin like the rage of an ocean shattering on a wave breaker. A faint gurgle broke free of the huge vampire's mouth. Turan Adin tore his hand free, a clump of Lord Beneger's esophagus and flesh caught in his claws, opened his hand, and let the bloody chunk fall to the floor. The vampire lord took a step forward and collapsed onto the floor, facedown. Blood spread on the mosaic image of Gertrude Hunt.

With a vicious roar, the two remaining vampires of House Meer fell onto Turan Adin. He danced between them as if he were vapor. A short black blade appeared in his hand. He hammered it into the back of the left vampire's head, right where the neck joined the skull, let go, spun around his victim to avoid the other knight's blow, pulled the blade free as the injured vampire crumpled to his knees, and sank it into the remaining vampire's left side, slicing through the armor between the ribs and up.

Ruah, the otrokars' swordsman, jumped onto the table and dashed along it toward Turan Adin. Sophie sprinted across the floor toward him, her gown split apart on one side as the secret seam had come open. The swordsman saw her. His eyes narrowed. He changed the angle of his charge, running straight for her. His blade flashed with orange and Ruah shot past Sophie, his sword a blur, and halted five steps behind her. If Sophie had moved, I missed it.

Ruah took another step. The top half of him slid off and landed on the floor.

The banquet hall erupted as the vampires and otro-kars charged at each other. The Nuan clansmen pulled out razor-sharp daggers and formed a protective circle around the grandmother.

I tapped my broom to the floor.

Suddenly the grand ballroom was calm and quiet. Everyone who had managed to jump over their table and land had sunk into the floor up to their noses. Everyone who had been in midair was stuck to the wall, held there by the inn's roots. Only the leaders, Turan Adin, and Sophie remained standing.

"This is good," I said. "I like this. Nice and quiet." I turned to George. "This is the last order I will tolerate from you. Tell me no again and you will join them."

It took me twenty minutes to sort the guests into their respective quarters and confine them there until everyone calmed down. That left me with leaders and corpses.

I turned to the Khanum first and pointed at Ruah's pieces. "You've spat on my hospitality," I said quietly. She could've ordered Ruah to stop and didn't.

The Khanum's face took on a dark red tint as blood rushed to her skin.

"Under normal circumstances I would force you to leave this house, but I'm bound by my agreement with the Office of Arbitration."

"Think of a boon," the Khanum said. "We will atone."

"I will," I promised her and turned to Robart. "Are you satisfied?"

He drew back. "I didn't..."

"You invited them here. They came like bandits, without their standard, without declaring the honor of their House. They came with one purpose: to do violence and cripple the negotiations beyond repair. You knew this and you did nothing to stop them."

Robart winced.

"Now four people are dead. Elderly and children have been put in danger."

Robart took a step back. I was so angry my voice cut like a knife. I should've stopped—this was beyond the limit of my duties, but I was furious.

"Congratulations. You did it. You let House Meer pull your strings like a puppet. Now your people will keep dying on Nexus while House Meer attacks House Krahr. Every vampire who is killed there, every spouse who weeps alone, every child who is robbed of a parent, all of that is on your soul. Enjoy."

Robart opened his mouth.

"We will make amends," Lady Isur promised.

I ignored her. I was going to let everyone have a piece of my mind. "Mr. Camarine."

George snapped into a coldly regal stance. A few days ago I would've cared. Right now, not so much.

"People died in my inn because you stopped me. The reputation of Gertrude Hunt is irrevocably damaged."

George opened his mouth.

"Guests are dead on the floor!" I snapped. "In my inn! Everything I worked for, everything I stand for, is ruined. No amount of money will make this right. My professional integrity is compromised. I allowed this to happen because you wanted to play games."

George opened his mouth.

"Do not speak to me," I told him. "You may be the Arbitrator, but I am still the innkeeper."

I pivoted to the shaman and the Battle Chaplain. "You will conduct the rights to appease the spirits of the fallen and to shepherd their souls into the afterlife. Cleanse this main hall of the stain of their deaths. Then you will take the bodies of your dead. Bury them, set them on fire, deliver them to their families, do whatever it is that must be done. You have tonight."

The shaman and the Battle Chaplain looked at each other.

"At the same time?" Odalon asked.

"Yes. No special provisions will be made. I'm done tip-toeing around your customs. I have honored your people's wishes, and they spat in my face. Deal with it."

I turned to Turan Adin. "My apologies for the poor reception. Please follow me. I have quarters prepared for you."

I led him out of the hall. My future was in shambles. It would be really difficult to come back from this disaster.

We passed the kitchen, and through the doorway I saw Orro curled into a ball on the floor. Oh no.

I rushed into the kitchen and dropped by him. I couldn't see head or feet. He was just a ball of spikes.

"Are you injured? Orro?"

No response.

"Orro?"

A muffled voice came from somewhere within the ball. "What is the point of my existence?"

Not wounded. At least not physically. I breathed a sigh of relief, sat on the floor, and gently patted the dark fur between his spikes. "Don't talk like that."

"This was to be my comeback."

"It still is. That chicken smelled like nirvana. I never saw so many beings eat so fast. Caldenia was licking her fork. You even got sworn enemies to forget their revenge for a few moments."

"I didn't even get to the dessert. I had a whole cavalcade of desserts. I didn't even serve the palate cleanser after the main course. I am a failure." His voice quivered with real despair.

I glanced at Turan Adin. He waited by the wall, a silent shadow.

"No, you're not. You're the best chef I've ever met. Years from now nobody will remember that some people got killed, but they will remember that chicken."

"You think so?" he asked softly.

"I know so. People push aside unpleasant memories and remember the good things. Your food makes people happy, Orro." I glanced at the wall by me and held out my hand to the inn. "I need the gift now."

The wall parted and spat a gift bag at me. I caught it and rustled the gold foil decorated with a bright red ribbon bow, wishing curiosity would get the better of him. I had bought this gift during my grocery trip and had the inn hide it. I'd planned to give it to him after the banquet.

"I bought these for you. They will help."

"Nothing can help."

I carefully plucked the tape holding the edges of the bag together. I had sealed it, hoping the contents would be a surprise. The tape came off on one side and I pried the edges of the bag open.

The sound of sniffing emanated from the ball. "What is that scent?"

"It's a gift for you." I held the bag up to him and waved it around, letting the smell drift. "Delicious fruit."

"I don't want it."

"I bought it special for you. I've been through so much today already. You don't want to hurt my feelings, do you?"

The ball shifted and unrolled into Orro sitting on the floor. I handed him the gift bag. He looked at it cautiously, sniffed the gap between the bag's edges, pulled it apart, and extracted a mango. The red-and-green fruit lay on his palm. He pricked the mango with his claw, peeled back a thin ribbon of the fruit's skin, and licked the bright yellow inside.

His needles stood on end with a quiet rustling.

"What is this?" he whispered.

"Mangoes." My father always said mangoes with a Quillonian were a sure bet. I hadn't realized how much of a sure bet.

Orro licked the fruit again, looked at it, and suddenly bit into it, shredding the yellow pulp. He'd wolfed down half a mango before he realized I was still there and froze, pieces of mango on his whiskers. "Don't see me."

"I won't," I promised. I reached out and gently patted his furry cheek. "You are the best chef in the galaxy."

He blinked.

I got up and left the kitchen, motioning to Turan Adin to follow.

I climbed the staircase, aware of Turan Adin walking silently behind me. His presence prickled the skin on my neck, as if he were woven together of high-voltage wires humming with live current. I had screwed up his room. It didn't fit him at all.

"I apologize for the delay," I murmured.

"It's fine."

I almost jumped. His voice was low-pitched, more of a deep snarl than any kind of voice a human throat could make.

"I'm sorry I had to kill within your inn."

"It's fine." Wait, what? It wasn't fine. Why did I say that? "It's been a long day for all of us. You must be tired. Our accommodations are probably more modest than what you have been used to."

Oh yes, that was so subtle. Here, let me insult my own inn because I can't figure out any other way to get you to tell me your room preferences.

"I'm used to war," he said quietly. "Anything you offer me is better than what I have now."

Said in a different tone of voice it might have sounded like grandstanding or an attempt to gain sympathy, but coming from him it was a simple, factual statement. I heard so much in those words: weariness, regret, grief, acceptance of inevitable violence, and an urgent need for distance. He was tired, bone-weary, and he wanted to be far away from the death he caused. The need to step away from it rolled off him. No innkeeper worth her salt could've missed it. He needed a retreat, and I would make one for him. That's why I was the innkeeper.

He was definitely male. He was also Nuan Cee's employee and a vital one, so he would be used to luxury, but more than that he wanted to be at peace. To be clean.

I feverishly moved things around in his room. We were almost to the door.

"Is the reputation of your inn irreparably damaged?" he asked.

"How much do you know of Earth's inns?"

"I have been a guest before."

"Then you know that our first priority is to keep the guests safe. I have allowed the Arbitrator's orders to direct my actions because I believed his goal was peace between these people. I know these people now. I understand how much the war hurts them. I became emotionally involved, and it compromised my ability to think clearly. Now some guests are dead. I don't trust George anymore, but worse, I don't trust myself. The fault is mine. I bear the ultimate responsibility."

And right after I was done here, I would go to the lab and throw myself into work, because if I stopped to consider all the ramifications of tonight, I would explode.

The door to his room swung open. I stepped aside.

Panels of rough fabric the color of beech wood sheathed the walls, framed by narrow polished wooden planks. The top of the wall was painted a soothing sage, the same color as the vaulted ceiling, with the kind of finish that put one in mind of parchment. A polished bamboo floor echoed the wooden accents on the walls, its boards the color of amber honey. A large platform bed stood against the left wall, simple and modern, yet retaining strong square lines. The bedspread was gray, the slew of pillows white edged with sage and gold. The fabric panels ended on both sides of the bed, letting the sage finish of the ceiling flow down to the floor, and an elaborate square Celtic knot formed from varnished bamboo decorated the wall. Two bedside tables flanked the bed, simple rectangles of nine square drawers, stained nearly black, then distressed so the pale golden grain of acacia wood showed through. The door to a private balcony stood wide open, offering a hot tub and a view of the orchard.

It was a tranquil room, high-end yet masculine, peaceful and clean without being sterile. Stepping into it was like entering a refreshing lake after a hard sweaty run.

"My deepest apologies," I told him. "I'm sorry you were attacked in my inn. I'm sorry I didn't keep you safe."

"Thank you," he said quietly.

The wall parted and a tray slid out, offering a plethora of food from the banquet: the starters, the drinks, the desserts in tiny cups, and in the center, the pan-seared chicken. Orro must've recovered enough to put a plate together.

"The best chicken in the galaxy," Turan Adin said, a hint of something suspiciously resembling amusement in his voice.

"Of course," I told him. "We only serve the best to our honored guests."

I stepped outside and quietly closed the door behind me.

⚜ ⚜ ⚜

The trick to finding an invisible thief is making him or her visible, which sounds like the most obvious conclusion in the world. Teaching the inn to recognize the faint blur of the thief's presence and target it was a lot harder.

I raised my head from the screen. I was sitting in my lab under the main floor of the inn. In front of me, the inn had formed a niche in its wall—five feet wide, five feet deep, and roughly nine feet tall.

"And go," I murmured.

A holographic projector in the wall of the niche conjured up the close approximation of the blur. The wall split and a jet of mist erupted over the blur. The niche's walls looked exactly the same.

"Lights," I murmured.

The light died. A black UV lamp came on, rotating slowly. Its beam swept the niche. Once-sterile walls glowed with bright blue.

"Perfect."

My screen blinked and changed into an image of my front room. George and Sophie were looking around as if they had lost something.

"What is it?"

The two of them spun around, back to back, identical neutral expressions on their faces. My voice had emanated from the walls. Usually I didn't do this because it was bad manners and guests tended to react badly to disembodied voices echoing through their living spaces, but I was still annoyed.

"We came to check on you," Sophie said.

Wasn't that sweet? I could tell them to piss off. Unfortunately, I was still an innkeeper and they were my guests to whom I would afford every courtesy even if it made my insides explode from the strain of containing my rage.

I waved at the inn. A set of stairs formed in the wall and I walked up into the front room. The floor flowed closed behind me.

George and Sophie looked at me.

"I'll get us some tea," Sophie said and went into the kitchen.

"She made you come down here to talk to me." I took a seat on the sofa.

"Yes." He lowered himself onto a chair opposite me.

"And you humored her. Her feelings are important to you, so you weighed the odds and decided that whatever plan you have wouldn't be injured too much by having this conversation with me, and here we are."

"Yes." He leaned back, his handsome face somber. She must've told him he had to be honest.

"Everything you have done since you arrived here, every word, every expression and every action, has been carefully calculated. You've destroyed the alliance between Robart and House Meer, isolating him from his peers. To Arland and Isur, he is damaged goods and to House Meer he is no longer an asset. He's an embarrassment, a witness and facilitator of their dishonor. He will be desperate to make peace now. House Meer is huge and House Vorga is one-fifth of its size. If the knights of Meer choose to set aside the shame of Beneger's failure and pursue House Vorga, Meer will swallow Robart's House whole and barely notice. Robart has no choice but to throw his lot in with Arland and Isur now and pray for a strategic alliance. On the flip side, House Meer is dishonored. They sent three of their better fighters and they couldn't take one man. They look weak and pathetic. Together with their excommunication, this will make them hard-pressed to form any alliances at all."

"The region will be more stable for it," George said, matter-of-fact.

"Then you've murdered the pride of the Horde in front of the otrokars. I saw Sophie's face. She lives for the challenge. You knew that the moment you showed her Ruah's image, she would target him and kill him. You didn't check the Horde's hubris, you annihilated it."

"Yes," George said.

"Now the vampires are desperate, and the Horde is desperate. Both are humiliated. Both are indebted to me and the peace talks are in shambles. All part of the plan?"

"Yes."

If he said yes one more time, I would brain him with something heavy.

"And my inn is an unfortunate casualty of this process?"

"Perhaps."

"Are you done?"

"Not quite."

"What else is there? You could also make the Merchants desperate. Is that next?"

"Yes," he said.

"George, stop with single-word answers. You came into my inn and you used me and Gertrude Hunt in the worst way possible. I deserve to at least know the final objective of this terrible mess."

"It's not a mess," he said. "It's a carefully steered ride. And the objective has always remained the same: to do the impossible and broker peace on Nexus."

I leaned forward. "Where is my place in this?"

"You're in the very center of it," he said. "You and the inn. Everything that happened has been designed for its impact on you."

"To what end?"

"I can't tell you that. You have to trust me."

"That is the one thing I will never do again. You can't just play with people's lives."

"I never play." A hint of frustration twisted George's face. "I examine my objective very carefully and I weigh everything I do against the benefits attaining that objective will bring. I'm intimately familiar with death. It's been a constant companion since childhood. I take no one's life for granted—not yours, not Ruah's, not even Beneger's. To avoid murder, I will go so far as to endanger myself and my objective, provided that the level of risk to my goal is acceptable, and my threshold of acceptability is a lot higher than you might believe. I resort to killing only when it becomes absolutely necessary, and you can be sure that when I take a life, it is because I have examined all my options and had no choice. But some events are greater than the people who bring them about, and so I will do what I must to set them in motion. It's almost over, Dina. You will understand soon. I promise I won't drag it out."

He rose and walked away.

Who the hell had I let into my inn?

Sophie glided over from the kitchen and set a cup of steaming tea in front of me. I tasted it. Chamomile.

She sat in the same chair as George.

"Do you know what he is planning?" I asked.

"No. I know he is conflicted about it. He calls me his conscience even though, of the two of us, I'm more violent, at least at first glance."

"No," I told her. "You kill quickly and with mercy. George is merciless."

"If one can be compassionate and merciless at once, he is that. George was always a contradiction." Sophie drank her tea. "What will you do?"

"I'll do what I was hired to do. I gave my word. I won't back out now, but I will no longer let myself be used."

Sophie smiled. "I bet he's counting on that."

CHAPTER THIRTEEN

I woke up because the nameless cat was staring at me. His big round eyes shone like two moons, catching the morning light slipping through the curtains.

I raised my hand. He pondered it for a few seconds, then slowly moved forward and rubbed his soft head against my palm. For some inexplicable reason, it made me feel better. The cat rubbed against me again and settled on the bed to knead the blankets. I read on the Internet that some people called it making muffins. It seemed oddly appropriate. Judging by his diligence, he would totally bake me muffins if he could.

I slid down to the floor.

"Beast?"

The little dog shot out from under the bed and jumped on me, licking my face. I hugged her. "Who's a good doggie? Beast is a good doggie!"

At least Beast loved me. No matter what I did, Beast thought I was the greatest owner in the history of the universe. Sadly, I couldn't just stay up here and play with her all day.

I got up, brushed my teeth, took a shower, and got dressed in my innkeeper garb, complete with the blue robe, accomplishing the tasks on autopilot. Sleep had helped my body, but not the rest of me. I felt exhausted, emotionally and mentally wrung out.

"Main ballroom, please."

A screen offered me the view of the main ballroom. The Battle Chaplain and the shaman sat on the floor with about fifteen feet of space between them. They were talking. Their facial expressions didn't seem hostile. The bodies of the three vampires had been placed into stasis chambers that looked a lot like coffins and had given rise to many Earth vampire legends. The body of Ruah had been wrapped in layers of cloth with ritualistic runes on it.

I made my way downstairs. Both of the religious representatives had decided to ship the corpses offworld. Ruga, the shaman, wanted Ruah to be buried with his family. Odalon had written a communique to House Meer. He read it to me as we walked through the orchard, the pallet with the dead trailing behind us.

"It is with great regret that I must inform you that Lord Beneger and Knights Uriel and Korsarad have fallen victim to Turan Adin, having attacked him as he entered the dining hall during dinner."

"Like cowards," Ruga added on my left.

"Fallen victim?" Vampires saw themselves as predators, not prey. That was a scathing insult.

"Indeed," Odalon smiled, baring his fangs. *"Their resistance lasted but a few breaths, and despite our most valiant efforts, they couldn't be saved."*

The laughter burst out so fast I had to clamp my hand over my mouth before I snorted.

"Even the intervention of an otrokar swordsman failed to make a difference as they were dead within moments of their ill-fated charge."

I glanced at Ruga.

The shaman shrugged. "It's not my communique."

Odalon grinned. *"I have performed the rights of Absolution and Passing through the Veil and have stood vigil for the required hours. I can only hope that my years of serving the Most Holy through thought and action and the blood of my body and that of my enemies spilled onto the fertile battlefields in the name of the Holy Anocracy are sufficient to recommend the souls of your knights to Paradise. You will find the recording of the incident with Lord Beneger."*

I chuckled. "So how hard did you beg the Most Holy to allow them to enter Paradise?"

"Only as hard as my integrity required." Odalon smiled. "What do you think?"

"That is the nicest 'Here are your dishonored dead, piss off and don't come back' letter I have ever heard," I told him.

"I helped him with it," Ruga said.

I felt someone's gaze on me. To our left, Turan Adin stood on the balcony. When I designed everyone else's quarters, I made sure they all saw the orchard but jumping into it from their balconies would've landed them in different spots in it. Since Turan Adin made everyone lose their mind by his mere presence, his balcony actually opened here, near the landing field. He wore his armor and tabard. His hood was up, but he was looking at us.

Ruga growled quietly. Odalon glanced at Turan Adin, and for a moment the otrokar and the vampire wore identical expressions.

"That creature disturbs me," Ruga said.

"You are not alone in that," Odalon told him.

"Because of how he kills?" I guessed.

"No." Ruga grimaced. "Because he is desperate."

"We are all desperate," Odalon said. "Nobody wants to go back to Nexus."

"Yes, we are desperate, yet we still have hope the fight will end."

"True," Odalon said. "There is darkness there."

I glanced at him.

"A true spiritual advisor is more than a priest," Odalon said. "We are the link between human and holy. We devote ourselves to service, and that includes not just the spiritual but also the emotional needs of our congregation. We were chosen and drawn to our vocation because of our empathy."

"We are similar," Ruga said. "We seek to peer into the soul of the person and heal the frayed edges."

That explained why the two of them had hit it off. Put two empaths into the same room for a few hours, and sooner or later they would naturally try to reach out to each other in an effort to understand how the other person feels.

"When I look into his soul," Ruga said, glancing back over his shoulder at Turan Adin, "I see conflict."

"Desperation is a catalyst that forces us to act," Odalon said. "It summons the last reserves we possess in an effort to extricate us from danger. This is why we are here at this summit. We are so desperate we are willing to negotiate with our sworn enemy. It pushes us to limits we normally cannot reach."

"Desperation is a fire," Ruga added. "It burns bright but it must have a chimney, an outlet."

"A chimney?" Odalon's eyebrows crept up.

The shaman rolled his eyes. "Fine. Desperation, as exhibited by that creature, is basically a prolonged lower state of fight-or-flight response. Where the fight-or-flight shot of adrenaline is a reaction to the actual manifestation of danger, desperation is the result of a perceived future danger. It primes the organism, forcing it to actively seek an avenue of escape before the danger actually manifests, resulting in a complicated cascade of hormonal inter-actions. You get higher metabolic rate, an entire slew of glands functioning at a greater output, obsessive thoughts, and so on."

I stopped and pinched myself.

"I know," Odalon told me. "When I discovered he has an advanced degree in microbiology, it was quite a shock to me as well."

"It's not a healthy state of being," Ruga continued. "You are not designed to function in a state of desperation for a prolonged period of time."

"It's a short-term metabolic burst," Odalon added. "The body will seek to vent some of that built-up potential. If you are under a great amount of stress, you might have a panic attack, for example."

"Turan Adin is desperate, but he is also trapped," Ruga said. "It rolls off him. To go back to my earlier metaphor, if desperation is a fire, his fire is raging inside a stone bun-ker. I don't know what is keeping him where he is—if he is indebted, if he is disciplined, if he feels he is there for the right cause—but whatever it is, it has created a deep-seated conflict within his psyche."

"He won't be able to sustain that kind of pressure," Odalon said. "His body and his soul desperately want to escape, but his mind is keeping him trapped. He is tired and he's subconsciously looking for an escape. When he realizes that there is only one escape route available to him, he'll take it. He'll kill himself in six months."

"I would go as far as eight, but yes," Ruga said.

"It makes him incredibly dangerous," Odalon said, "because he doesn't care. He has no thought of self-preser-vation beyond the basic instincts of his body."

"He will never take his own life. He will try to die in battle," the shaman added. "And I do not want to be on the battlefield when he decides that it is his last day."

"That's horrible," I said.

"War is horrible," Odalon said. "It ruins people."

"War on Nexus is especially horrible," Ruga said.

"Why?" I asked.

"Modern war is, in an odd way, merciful," Odalon said. "Our technology permits us to precision-bomb strategic targets. When casualties occur, they are typically swift."

"Death from high-density beam bombardment takes point three seconds," Ruga said. "It is a loss of life, irreversible and irreplaceable, but it is a death without suffering. Advanced weaponry doesn't function correctly on Nexus. Orbital bombardment is out of the question because environmental anomalies prevent accurate targeting. Trying to pound your enemy with artillery is pointless as well."

"We've had weapons explode," Odalon said. "There is a record of a concentrated artillery assault in the first year of the war. The projectiles disappeared and thirty minutes later materialized above the House that fired them."

"I remember reading about that." Ruga smirked.

"It is an up close and personal war, fought with savage weapons," Odalon said. "At first when you're young and dumb and you hear about it, you think it will be glorious. That you will be like the hero of old, ripping through the ranks of your enemy. Then you find out what six hours of fighting with your sword is really like. The first hour, if you survive, is exciting. The scent of blood is intoxicating. The second hour, you are injured but you keep going. The third hour, you realize you've had your fill of blood. You want to be done. You want off the battlefield. In the fourth, you notice the faces of people you kill. You hear their screams as you hack off their limbs. It is no longer an abstract enemy. It is a living being that you are ripping apart. It is dying by your hand, right there in front of you. In the fifth, you bleed and vomit, and still you push forward, punishing your body and soul. In the sixth, you collapse finally, grateful that you survived or simply numb. Everything smells like blood and the smell of it makes you ill. You're hurting and you try to keep your eyes open, because if you close them, you might see the faces of those you killed, so you look upon the battlefield and you see that nothing was gained and, as the medic is patching you up, you realize you must do it again tomorrow."

It sounded like hell.

"That was good," Ruga said.

"Thank you," Odalon said.

"We've become hopelessly civilized," Ruga said. "We are not suited for that kind of war. I don't think our ancestors were even suited for it. They died much easier than we do, so a single long battle could decide the course of a war. It takes a lot more damage to kill one of us now, so every evening all those who are still breathing end up in recuperative tanks, and a few days later, they are back out again. Endless battle. Endless war."

"Endless suffering." Now I understood why Arland's face had changed when he mentioned it.

"Yes," Ruga said. "And now there is no hope for peace."

"I wouldn't say no hope," Odalon said. "That is rather bleak."

"Your people attacked the Merchants and my people attacked the Arbitrator." Ruga sighed. "Mark my words: this is the beginning of the end."

We were walking back from the landing field when Turan Adin jumped off his balcony. He did it very casually, as if clearing the thirty-foot drop was like stepping down the stairs. The vampire and the otrokar at my side went for their weapons.

"May I walk with you?" he asked me in his quiet, snarl-tinted voice.

"Of course." I looked at the two clergymen. "Please excuse us."

Odalon and Ruga hesitated for a long moment. "As you wish," Odalon said finally. "We will go on ahead."

They walked on. I waited until they were a short distance ahead and turned to Turan Adin. "Was there something specific you wanted to discuss?"

"No."

Maybe he just wanted some company. "I was going to take a few minutes and sit in my favorite spot to collect myself. Would you like to join me?"

He nodded.

I led him to the left, past the apple trees to an old overgrown hedge. I made my way through a narrow gap and waited for him. A small pond sat in the horseshoe clearing, bordered by the hedge. Lily pads floated on the surface, and two large koi, one orange, one white with red spots, gently moved through the shallow water. A small wooden bench waited by the pond. I sat on one end. He sat on the other.

We sat quietly and watched the koi.

"Did you make this?" he asked.

"Yes. When I was growing up, my job was to tend the gardens. It's harder here, in Texas, because of the water restrictions, but the inn collects rainwater."

"It's nice," he said.

"Thank you. I'm hoping to work on this more in the summer. Make it a little bigger. Maybe plant some flowers over there and put a hammock up so I can come here with my book and read…"

He jumped off the bench and left. One moment he was there, and the next I was alone. I felt him moving back to the inn, inhumanly fast. He had jumped up, scaled the wall, gotten up to his balcony and disappeared into his rooms.

What did I say?

I sat by myself for another minute or two. The serenity I was looking for refused to come.

The inn chimed. The otrokars were trying to get my attention from their quarters and something was happening in the stables.

I sighed, got up, and headed for the stables. Inside, Nuan Sama, Nuan Cee's niece who had helped Hardwir repair Officer Marais's car, crouched by one of the donkey-camel beasts. Jack sat on the bench, watching her. At Nuan Cee's request, I had given her clearance to come to the stables every day to tend to the animals. Usually either Jack or Gaston escorted her.

"What is it?" I asked her.

She brushed at her blue and-cream-fur with her paw. "Tan-tan is feeling poorly."

The donkey-camel looked at her with big dark eyes.

"Is she sick?"

"No. She is just old." Nuan Sama sighed. "This is her last trip I think. I come and visit her when I can, but she is… Sometimes creatures just get old."

"Is there anything I can do to make it easier on her?"

"Could you increase the oxygen in the stables?" Nuan Sama looked up at me.

I couldn't fix anything else, but at the very least I could fix that. "Would twenty-three percent do?"

"That would be perfect. Thank you! It will let her breathe easier."

"Done." I made someone's day better. Today wasn't a complete loss.

The inn chimed again. The otrokars were really persistent. I called up a screen in the nearest wall. Dagorkun's face filled it.

"The Khanum asks you to share her morning tea."

I didn't want to share tea. I didn't want to play politics or be smart. I just wanted to go to the kitchen and get a cup of coffee. I would need backup. "Thank you. I will be right up."

I waved at the screen, calling up the covered balcony where Caldenia liked to have her breakfast. Her Grace was in her favorite chair, impeccably dressed in a complicated cobalt hybrid of a dress and a kimono embroidered with gold and red flowers.

"Good morning, Your Grace. Would you mind accompanying me to Khanum's morning tea?"

"Of course not. I will be right down."

I dismissed the screen and left the stables to meet Caldenia by the stairs.

The otrokars' quarters were unusually quiet. A somber-faced Dagorkun led Caldenia and me to the balcony once again and stood behind his mother, who sat in her robe on the bright pillows. This time a flame burned in the circular fire pit, sending up a cloud of spicy smoke. I recognized the scent—jeva grass. The otrokars burned it for good luck before a long journey. The Khanum stared into the flames, her eyebrows furrowed. She didn't acknowledge Caldenia's presence.

I took a seat on the circular couch. "Are you leaving?"

"Tomorrow evening,"

"Why?"

"The peace negotiations have failed." The Khanum narrowed her eyes. "There can be no peace now."

"I don't understand," I said gently. "What changed?"

"We were embarrassed and humiliated."

So were the vampires, but pointing it out in quite those words wouldn't be the best strategy. "The Holy Anocracy struck the first blow."

The Khanum sighed. "Yes, but now we are both in a position of weakness. We are here." She raised her hand, holding her palm parallel to the ground. "The Merchants are here." She raised her other palm a few inches higher.

"The Merchants want peace. Without peace, there is no profit."

"It's not that simple," Dagorkun said.

"We are a democracy," the Khanum said. "The men and women who are here are all distinguished warriors. They are the best seeds of the crop, and they lead specific factions within the Horde. Had the peace treaty been ratified, each otrokar would've added the weight and value of his or her reputation to it. It is their reputations and their honor that would've made our agreement binding. My people were given a simple order: to never initiate violence while they are under your roof. Ruah disobeyed it. It reflects badly on his commanding officer. On me."

Dagorkun winced.

"I came here to negotiate, and I was unable to control the people under my command. Because of this happening, we, as a delegation, are no longer united. A decision of peace, a decision of great gravity and significance, must be unanimously approved. And now, since my honor has been tarnished, I would need that unanimous vote more than ever. Without a united vote, the treaty will hold no weight with the rest of the Horde."

A male otrokar approached us, carrying a platter with a pot of tea and four cups. He placed it on the table, inclined his head, and left. Dagorkun poured the dark red liquid into the cups. The Khanum watched him, her face impassive. She had wanted the peace treaty to succeed so much. My heart was breaking for her.

"Is there any hope for peace? Any at all?" I asked softly.

She shook her head.

"I don't like debts," the Khanum stated, her voice flat. "So before we go, I would ask that you name the price of our restitution for our transgression."

I sipped my tea.

A puff of mist erupted from the floor of the balcony and within it for a briefest of moments I saw the faint outline of the phantom thief's body.

My muscles locked. My body turned hard, as if I'd suddenly become steel, and I crashed onto the floor. The air vanished. I struggled to inhale and couldn't. My lungs sat in my chest like two boulders, unable to expand.

"Dina!" Caldenia lunged to me.

I couldn't look at her. My eyes wouldn't move.

Poison... I've been poisoned.

The inn screamed, its wood creaking and groaning, reaching for me. I shoved at it with my magic. *No!* If it touched me, the poison would spread. I couldn't kill Gertrude Hunt.

"You poisoned her!" Caldenia snarled, her sharp teeth rending the air.

Breathe, breathe, breathe... My body refused to respond.

I'm dying...

The balcony parted under me. I fell through it, down, and landed on the table in the kitchen, right between George, Sophie, and Jack. Pain slapped my rigid back. Above me, through the hole in the fabric of existence, Caldenia screamed, "She's been poisoned!"

"Dina!" Sophie cried out.

I saw Turan Adin. He was there and then he vanished.

I couldn't even gasp. My mouth wouldn't move.

George's face, pale, his eyes wide open, swung into my view. The tip of his cane was glowing, projecting information in front of it, scrolling with dizzying speed.

Not enough air…

"Not again!" Orro howled. "No, no, no…"

"Fix this," Sophie ground out through her teeth. "Fix it now, George. This is going too far."

"I can't. This wasn't part of the plan."

"Do something!"

"I'm trying," George growled. "The database doesn't know this poison."

This is it, flashed in my head. *This is how I am going to die.*

The inn wavered around me, warping, its roots stretching to me.

No!

"The inn can heal," Caldenia called out. "Let it heal her!"

"No," George barked. "If the inn forges a connection with her, the poison can spread."

Thank you. Thank you for looking out for Gertrude Hunt.

I sent my magic out, letting it brush the walls. *I love you. You are the best. You will be okay.*

Wood snapped, cracking, as if something within the inn tore itself apart.

Shhhh. It will be okay. You will be okay.

I wish I could've found my parents. I wish I could have seen Sean one last time...

The light was fading. I couldn't even close my eyes. I would die with them open.

Turan Adin filled my view. Nuan Cee's furry muzzle appeared near me.

"I have your word?" the Merchant said.

All went black.

CHAPTER FOURTEEN

I opened my eyes.

The room was dim, the light soft and muted, coming from the setting sun. The ceiling looked familiar. I was lying on the couch in the front room. And I was still alive.

I inhaled deeply and felt my chest rise, then fall. The air flooded my lungs, so sweet. Such an easy, small movement. I would never again take it for granted. I sent my magic out. It whispered through the rooms, testing the connection, and Gertrude Hunt sighed in relief.

I was still alive.

The thought made me smile. I stretched a little and wiggled my toes. Someone had taken off my shoes. I turned my head slightly. The room was empty except for Turan Adin. He sat in a chair, his head inclined, his face hidden behind the empty blackness. Beast lay on his lap, her eyes closed.

The smile vanished from my lips. In all the time I'd owned Gertrude Hunt, there'd been only one person besides me who could hold Beast on his lap.

I slipped off the couch. Turan Adin raised his head but didn't move. I walked over to him, my bare feet making almost no sound on the floorboards, reached out, and touched his hood. It retracted, folding as it slid to settle over his back. For a moment I saw a lupine head armed with monstrous jaws, and then it melted in a blink. Sean Evans looked at me with his amber eyes. His hair was shaved down to stubble. A ragged scar cut across his forehead, slanting to the left, interrupting his eyebrow and chewing up his cheek. Another scar snaked its way up his neck on the right, breaking into a tangle of smaller scars near his ear. What kind of injuries could they have been that the Merchants' medical equipment couldn't knit him back together?

His face was hard, so much harder than I remembered, as if any hint of softness had been bled out of him. His eyes were haunted. He looked at me and through me at the same time, as if he were expecting a distant threat to appear on some far horizon behind me. The cocky, funny guy was gone. I was staring war in the face and it was looking back at me.

Oh no.

I reached out and touched the ragged scar on his cheek with my trembling fingertips. He leaned into my hand, like a stray dog who's been on the run for too long, desperate for any crumb of affection. Painful heat burned my eyes and fell on my cheeks. Beast whimpered on his lap.

"Why?" I whispered.

"I owed a favor to Wilmos," he said, his voice quiet. "I said I wanted a challenge. Turan Adins don't last. The Merchants just keep recruiting more when the latest one bites the dust. As long as you match the height, the armor takes care of everything else. I signed up for six Nexus months and got there two days after the last Turan Adin died."

"Sean…"

"The Army wasn't hard for me. Everything I did on this planet was easy. What my parents went through was beyond anything I ever tried. It was a test. I wanted to know if I could do it. If I was good enough to survive like they did. If I was someone they could look on with pride. I wanted the training wheels off."

Six Nexus months, that was barely two months our time. "Why didn't you leave? Your contract ended."

"There are civilians in the spaceport and the colony." His voice was ragged and low. "Children. Our resources are stretched too thin. They would be overrun. They need me."

He was trapped. Sean's parents were alpha-strain werewolves, designed and genetically engineered to protect the escape gates against overwhelming force as the rest of population evacuated their dying planet. Sean was born with the drive to protect, the kind of drive that overrode everything else. Repelling the siege of the spaceport must've felt right to him, so right, and once he started, he couldn't stop. His very nature trapped him there.

That's why he'd fled from the pond. He knew that he would go back to Nexus. He would never see the pond in summer. He would never see me again. He would never cook another barbeque in my backyard and sneak bones to Beast. I would never hear him crack another joke. He…

Nuan Cee had said something just before I passed out. He said, *"Do I have your word?"*

Ice shot through me. "What did you promise Nuan Cee to save me?"

Sean smiled. "Nothing I regret. You're alive. It makes me happy."

"Sean?"

He didn't say anything.

I spun around and dashed up the stairs to the Merchant quarters.

I found Nuan Cee sitting alone in the front room. The huge screen on the wall was glowing. A recording of some Merchant festival played, its sound muted to a mere murmur as foxes in bright garments twirled long ribbons while dancing through the streets.

"I've been expecting you," he said quietly.

"What did he promise you?"

"Lifetime of service," Nuan Cee said, his voice mournful. "A life for a life. A fair trade."

No. No, I don't think so. Sean Evans wouldn't die for me. I had to save him now. I came over and sat on the couch.

I looked at the screen. The festival recording melted, obeying my push, and a different image took over the screen. Massive tree trunks twisted between the spires of gray and white stone, each branch as wide as a highway, bearing clouds of blue and turquoise leaves. Pink flowers bloomed on long indigo vines. Golden moss sheathed the trunks, catching the rays of bright sun. A massive feline predator, its fur splattered with rosettes of black and cream, made its way down one of the branches, keeping to the shadows, its massive black claws scratching the moss lightly.

"I once asked my father how the lees became the dominant species on their planet," I said.

Nuan Cee winced. Few knew the true name of the Merchants' species, and outsiders weren't supposed to say it out loud, but I was past the point of caring.

The predator kept moving down the trunk. The view slid down to a spot below where, tucked into a crook between a small, thin branch and the massive tree limb, a single fox sat, gathered into a tiny ball. His blue fur was striped with white and black paint. Compared to the predator, he was tiny. The feline beast could swallow him in two gulps.

"After all, you are so small and your birth planet is so vicious."

The feline beast smelled the air. He was almost to the fox.

"Do you know what my father told me?"

On-screen the fox's bright indigo eyes opened wide.

"He told me to never trust a lees, for they are smart and crafty and when their negotiations fail, they kill to get what they want."

On the screen the small fox shot out from under the massive tree branch, leaping into the air, a blow gun at his lips. A tiny dart shot out and bit into the fur of the feline hunter. The beast shuddered, wracked by convulsions, struggling to stay on its feet. The fox landed next to it on soft paws and yanked a dagger from the sheath at his waist. His black lips drew back, baring savage teeth. His muzzle wrinkled. A deranged light flared in his eyes. The fox fighter fell on the convulsing beast, stabbing its throat again and again, flinging blood everywhere in a frenzy. There was nothing refined about it. Nothing civilized or calm. It was a pure primordial bloodlust, brutal and violent.

Nuan Cee looked away from the screen, averting his eyes.

"I had seen the shape of my poisoner. It was short. Short like a lees. Then you showed up with an antidote to a poison that couldn't be found even in the Arbitrator's extensive database. One of your people tried to kill me."

"It wasn't sanctioned."

"The inn marked my poisoner."

Nuan Cee winced.

"Why did you do it?"

"It wasn't done on my orders, and I will punish the one responsible. Someone used my image disruptor, but I don't know how. It is very expensive, and I am the only one who has one. It was completely secure and it is untouched in my quarters. I had used it only once."

He'd used... "You took the emerald?"

"Yes. I was wearing the disruptor that night under my clothes. Everyone was so busy, and it took mere seconds."

"You've abused my hospitality."

Nuan Cee sighed. "We did. We are indebted to you. The favor you owe me is forgiven."

I was so sick of trading favors. "Let him go."

"No."

"Nuan Cee! The debt you owe me is greater than any favor. You broke the rules of hospitality. You broke your people's treaty with the Innkeepers of Earth. You should've healed me anyway because I am an innkeeper, and when the others find out about it, you will be banned. Sean didn't know that, and you took advantage of him."

"Yes. His bargain with me is separate from your bargain."

"Let him go."

"I can't. Anything but that."

"Why?" I snarled.

Nuan Cee spread his paws. "There have been forty-two Turan Adins since the war on Nexus began. Some lasted mere days. He's been on Nexus for a cycle and a half. You don't even know how special that is. He's too good. He lasted longer than even the original one. I was terrified because he refused to sign another contract. He said he would walk as soon as we found a replacement. But now he will stay. All will be well."

"All won't be well. Nexus is killing him."

"It will eventually. But until then, he will lead our defenses."

"Release him. This is what I want."

"No. Ask anything else."

"Damn it, don't you have a crumb of conscience? Is there any drop of kindness in your soul, or is it all just cold dark greed?"

Nuan Cee bared his teeth. "There are three thousand of our people on Nexus. There are families and children. He is keeping them alive."

"What the hell were you thinking, putting children on Nexus in the first place? Move them out."

"Don't you think I would if I could? They have no place to go. They are not welcome anywhere."

The realization hit me. The Kuan lees, the cast-outs. He had staffed Nexus colony with the exiles.

Nuan Cee turned away and waved at the screen, his paw limp. "Archive number ten twenty-four."

A long procession of foxes appeared on the screen, moving one by one into a shrine, carrying little lanterns.

"In our society, family is everything. Clan is everything. When I look back, I should see the line of my ancestors stretching through time, long and unbroken. It is they who give us strength and wisdom. Our clan. Our pack. Our past and the wealth of our clan's deeds. When one of us commits a crime, when he or she is found weak or unworthy, they are cast out. Such is the way of the forest. Only the strong and the useful survive. The cast-outs are cut off from their clan. They have no shrines. They can't pray to their ancestors. They can't ask for solace or guidance. Their children grow up adrift, not knowing where they come from, branches severed from the tree of their clan and family forever. Some don't even know their fathers. They have no home. They're not welcome anywhere. My father was a Kuan. He was a criminal and the son of a criminal."

Grandmother stepped out of the shadows and came to sit on the couch, quiet as a ghost.

"And when my mother fell in love with him and her clan paid a fortune, the worth of a small planet, to include him into our clan, he had a choice. He could go with my mother and cut off all ties with his clan or he could stay an outcast. My father's mother told him to walk away from her and his sisters and to never look back. His own mother. She gave up her child so he could have a better life." Nuan Cee's voice shook. "I don't know my other grandmother. She is gone now. Her soul is floating out there, lost and gone, crying out for the light, and I can't even light a candle in a shrine to help her find her way. I am a cripple. I have not been able to bring myself to sire children, for they will be crippled like me. They will not know half their family."

He swiped the tears from his eyes. "It took me decades to wrestle away the rights to Nexus. It is rich. I had offered a third of the profits we'll reap to the Clans Assembly. A royal sum. In return, they let me settle the exiled ones on Nexus. They let me forge them into their own clan. They will receive dispensation to raise their shrines."

His eyes shone. "Their children won't have to wonder if they are just specks of dust in the nothingness. They will be connected. They will light their candles and speak to those who passed on. That's why the exiled ones volunteered to come to Nexus, knowing they could never leave and that for the rest of the galaxy, where time moves slower, they will be dead long before anyone else they know. They left what little they had behind and trusted me to bring them there. They cannot leave now, because they have no place to go."

He had brought thousands of his people to Nexus and now they were stranded, trapped between the grinders of two armies.

"I must have peace to turn a profit. And now the peace treaty is dead, and the least I can do is keep them safe for as long as I can. You cannot have Sean. Ask me anything but that. If he leaves, my people will die."

He would never let Sean go. Sean would return to Nexus and die there. I had to save him. I had to do something. Anything.

"What if there is peace?"

"There won't be. The otrokars are ready to leave, and the Anocracy is torn by their feud."

My mouth had gone dry. I licked my lips. "Here is my bargain: you owe me. If I get the peace treaty signed, you will let Sean go."

Nuan Cee shook his head.

"You're wrong," Grandmother said, her voice quiet.

I nearly jumped, I'd never heard her say a word and had almost forgotten she was there. Nuan Cee turned, startled.

"We have caused her an injury," Grandmother said. "We owe her a great debt. We owe her parents a debt after everything they have done for us."

Nuan Cee bowed his head. "As you wish. If the peace treaty is signed and upheld, I will release Sean Evans from my service. That will wipe the slate clean between us. You have my promise. I swear on the honor of my ancestors."

That was the best I could get. I had to find a way to bring them together and convince them to end this insane war. Desperation wrapped around me like a noose. How in the world would I do that? I didn't even know where to start. I was numb and terrified at the same time. I had to move, go, do something, but all I could do was sit. Everything else seemed too hard.

We sat in the quiet gloom, watching the procession of foxes at the shrine.

"There is only one thing I don't understand," I said. "Why did you take the emerald?"

Nuan Cee sighed again. "Because I was young once and foolish, my father did something to me to save me from myself. It is a thing within the clans that adults know and children learn when they become adults. The young are so rash, so desperate to make their own money and leave their mark on the galaxy. Couki is very bright, and that keen intelligence will get him into trouble. He will inherit a sum of money when he comes of age. He will use it, hoping to prove he has what it takes to be a Merchant. The bazaars of the universe are full of greedy sharks and he is smart, but too inexperienced to swim with the worst of them. The brighter they are, the faster they lose the money. Left on his own, he will become bankrupt within months. It will take him another five cycles or so after he reaches the age of maturity to pay back the emerald and the interest. Time enough for him to learn and mature and for the clan to absorb his small mistakes and keep him from making big ones."

"Nuan Cee was a very bright child," Grandmother said with a smile. "He almost bankrupted the entire clan twice before his twentieth birthday."

They trapped their young adults, forcing them to remain with the family. "Do you do this to every smart child?" I asked.

"Yes," Nuan Cee said.

I rose. I had a couple of things I needed to verify.

CHAPTER FIFTEEN

The full enormity of my task mugged me right outside the Merchants' door. I made it midway down the curving staircase and sat down on the stone steps. How the hell was I going to fix this?

I wished desperately, with all the intensity of a terrified five-year-old in trouble, that my parents were here. I wanted advice. I needed reassurance. *What do I do, Mom? Dad? How do I handle this? They all want peace but can't bring themselves to actually agree to it, and now Sean will die on some hellish planet fighting a war he never wanted to win.* He'd signed his life away to save me. Looking into his eyes was like watching ashes rise from a funeral pyre. The vampires hid in their rooms, the otrokars were getting ready to leave, and the Merchants had tried to poison me.

How do I fix this mess…

I wanted to rage. I was so angry, and I'd been keeping it inside me for so long. All the sources of my fury, all the people who'd caused it, they were my guests. They'd lied to me, they'd appealed to my kindness and then taken advantage of it, they'd insulted me, they'd treated me like I was an idiot, and they'd tried to murder me. It was my duty to keep them safe. It was the very essence of who I was, but universe help me, I wanted to collapse the inn on top of them and bury them. It would make me happy.

A pressure built in my chest, a dense, insistent ache. A tear wet my cheek, made of distilled stress. I fought it back, but the pressure ground on me from the inside. I was ready to burst. Either I cried now or I forced it down, which meant I would have to cry later, probably at exactly the wrong moment.

I was alone. Nobody would hear.

I took a deep, shuddering breath and let it go. The dam inside me broke. All my stress and pain came out with the flood of tears. I cried and cried, and my sobs sounded like snarls. I cried because I didn't know what to do, because I'd almost died, because the anger inside me tore at my soul, because Sean had sacrificed himself for me, and because I wanted my parents to hug me.

Gradually my sobs began to die down. I felt tired but light. My head was clear.

A thin tendril slid out of the wall and brushed my cheek. I looked at it. A tiny white bud formed on the tip of the thin branch and opened into a little star of a flower with tiny turquoise stamens in the middle. A faint, honey-sweet aroma drifted up.

The poor inn was trying to make me feel better.

I inhaled the aroma. It washed through me, sweet and delicate. That's right. I was an innkeeper. I had seen the universe and survived it. I would survive this too. I would fix this.

I stroked the branch with my fingers and whispered, "Thank you."

If only all of them were as sensitive as Gertrude Hunt. The inn always felt what I felt...

It hit me like a freight train. George, you bastard. You conniving, manipulating bastard.

He knew. The Arbitrators' database was one of the most comprehensive in the entire galaxy. He did his research, figured it out, and then he set about finding an innkeeper he could manipulate into doing it. He must've approached some of us straight on, which is why everyone turned him down. No innkeeper would do this unless their back was against the wall, and mine was.

Hell, he told me exactly what he intended to do during our very first conversation at the inn. I just hadn't understood it. He'd laid it out and now it all made sense.

Was Gertrude Hunt even strong enough? Was I strong enough?

I needed information. I had only seen it done once in my whole life, and that was when my mother used our inn to get a murderer to confess. There had to have been others. I got up and went down into my lab.

Two hours later, I had my answers. The good news was that Gertrude Hunt was definitely powerful enough to handle it. The inn's roots were deep. It was possible. But it would have to go through me. I was the weakest link in this chain. As long as I held up long enough, it was possible. My books didn't cover the past eighty years, but they did reach back three centuries from that point. The bad news was that four out of six innkeepers who'd tried it during that time went mad in the process.

Lousy odds.

I tried desperately to find another way. Any other way at all. I came up empty. It was this or failure.

If I did it, I would have to do it fast. The otrokars would leave tomorrow evening, and everything had to be ready by then. All of my guests would actively resist it too. All the favors I'd collected wouldn't be enough. I had to restore my influence and authority as an innkeeper, or they would never submit to the process. Right now I was an innkeeper who'd been poisoned in my own inn, like a bartender who got his ass kicked in his own bar. I had to solve my own poisoning, hit them with it fast, and then dump the rest on them before they had a chance to really think about the possible consequences.

The identity of the poisoner wasn't the problem. I could assemble all the Merchants together, turn out the lights, and the guilty party would light up like a Christmas tree. But that wasn't impressive. I had to figure out who had done it and why so the big reveal would be an icing on the cake.

Twenty-one centuries ago Lucius Cassius, censor and consul of Rome, had asked, "*Cui bono?*" To whose benefit? Every crime had come to pass because someone had something to gain by it, whether it was money, fame, or emotional satisfaction. I had to figure out who would benefit from my death.

I found a pen and a piece of paper and began writing my thoughts down.

Guests who wanted peace had nothing to gain. If I died, the negotiations would end. This included the Arbitrator. His ultimate goal was peace as well.

Guests who wanted war had nothing to gain either. The negotiations were in shambles as it was, and my death, while it definitely would put a final nail in the coffin of peace talks, carried risks. It would be investigated, and the guilty party would be barred from Earth. Why risk it when the summit had broken down so completely?

The Holy Anocracy had no reason to want me dead. First, Arland and Lady Isur liked me. I was an instrument of Robart's punishment shortly after his arrival, but he had much bigger concerns right now. I wasn't directly involved in the brawl that took place in the dining hall either.

The otrokars owed me a favor, but it wasn't enough of a burden to risk my death, especially not so obviously, by serving me tea. Not to mention that sharing tea was a sacred tradition. Poisoning it spat on one of the cornerstones of their society.

The Merchants owed me a favor too, and more importantly, they wanted Sean to sign away his life. But Nuan Cee had no way of knowing that Sean would offer to trade his life for mine. We'd had no contact in the past six months, except for that one time at Wilmos's shop. Sean never reached out to me, never sent me any letters, and never expressed any feelings for me. The only way Nuan Cee would be aware of Sean's possible motive for sacrifice would be if Sean told him that he cared for me. I hadn't known Sean for very long, but the few days that we did spend together put us through a pressure cooker and I knew him well. Sean wouldn't share his feelings. If he truly loved me, he would keep it secret.

I stopped and squeezed my eyes shut. Sean Evans had traded his life for mine. That probably meant he loved me. Okay, I would have to deal with that later. Not now. Now I had to save him.

I looked at my paper. Unless Sean confessed his love for me to Nuan Cee in a heart-to-heart talk—and Sean just wasn't that kind of a guy—the Merchant had nothing to gain through my death. Even if Sean had betrayed his feelings somehow, there still wasn't any guarantee that putting me in danger would get the Merchants their lifetime contract. If I did die and the Merchants' involvement was discovered, the Nuan family would be barred from Earth, and that was a hefty price tag. Killing me simply didn't make financial sense.

I stared at my paper. Nobody had anything to gain from my dying. I was an innkeeper, a neutral party. It's not like I was some criminal mastermind or a former tyrant with a constellation of bounties on my head...

Oh.

Well. That made complete sense.

I walked into the kitchen wearing my innkeeper robe. Beast shot out from under the table and bounced around my feet. She must've abandoned Sean, because he was alone in his room. Orro slumped motionless in his chair. He saw me, and then my world turned dark and furry, and powerful limbs squeezed all the air out of my lungs.

"Let her go, dear," Caldenia called out. "You will crush her."

Orro released me, and I sucked in a hoarse breath. Quillonian hugs weren't for people with weak bones.

"Wonderful to see you moving around," Caldenia said.

Orro retreated to the chair and turned away, suddenly embarrassed.

"Did you save the kettle?" I asked.

Her Grace raised her eyebrows. "Do you take me for an amateur?"

She stepped to the island, where a cake stand waited covered by a metal hood, and lifted the cover. The kettle, still filled with ruby tea, waited on the stand.

"Sadly, we are still unable to identify the poison," Caldenia said. "Orro offered to taste the tea, but of course the Arbitrator refused to allow him to put himself in danger. But the Khanum provided us with another pot and I can tell you that there are definite chemical differences between the two liquids."

"So the entire kettle was poisoned?" Just as I thought.

"It appears to be so. This was either very calculated or extremely sloppy."

Or due to inexperience or desperation. "Thank you."

"Whatever I can do to help, dear."

I went to George's quarters and knocked on the door. He opened it. Behind him Sophie sat on the couch next to Gaston. Jack leaned against the wall in his favorite pose, one foot propping him up.

"I know," I told George.

An understanding showed in his eyes. "It is the only way," he told me.

"You are despicable."

"I will have to live with that," he said.

"Yes, you will. We'll revisit this later. I need to know when the Merchants were notified that the peace summit would be held here, in Gertrude Hunt."

"On 2032, Standard," he said.

The Standard galactic year had five hundred "days" of twenty-five "hours" each. The days were divided into four "seasons," each a hundred and twenty-five days long. The first of the four digits identified the season, the next three identified the day. Today was 2049 Standard. "You didn't give them much warning."

"No," George said.

"Good. I will be back in a couple of hours. Keep the peace while I am gone."

"Where are you going?" Gaston called out.

"To see the weapon merchant," I told him and shut the door.

Wilmos's shop was an island of calm in the chaos of Baha-char. As I stepped into its cool depth, the soft, lilting melody of a now-dead planet wound about me like fragrant smoke from an incense burner. Gorvar, Wilmos's huge lupine monster, lay on the floor, sprawled on a pelt of long golden fur that no doubt once belonged to some ferocious creature. Gorvar glanced at me with his orange eyes but decided moving wasn't worth the trouble. I didn't present enough of a threat.

Wilmos emerged from the back room, wiping his hands with a rag.

"You sent him to Nexus."

"I've been expecting this conversation." Wilmos pointed at a horseshoe-shaped couch. "Let's sit."

I sat. "You said he was your life's work. Then you sent him to Nexus to die."

Wilmos growled under his breath. Yellow light rolled over his irises. "I didn't send him. I tried to talk him out of it."

"Not hard enough."

"It wouldn't have mattered. It was the impossible job. The one that killed every creature that took it. He had to have it."

"Why?"

Wilmos sighed. "It's complicated."

"Try me."

The old warrior leaned forward, his eyes dark. "Soldiers aren't born. They are made. Under the right conditions, most people can be forged into soldiers. They follow orders, they respect the chain of command, and when occasion calls for it, they will perform heroic deeds for the good of the many. But at heart those soldiers hope there is no war. Given a chance, they prefer to avoid combat and, if forced to go into battle, they fight so they can eventually go home. Sean isn't just a soldier. He is a warrior. War is a thing he does as naturally as you breathe. It draws him like flame pulls the night insects to itself."

And then they die, burned by the flame. "But why this war? Why not any other war, the kind with an expiration date?"

"Because he wanted the roughest job I had, and when I offered it to him, it had an expiration date. A six-month tour. He was supposed to come home ages ago."

Wilmos dragged his hand across his face. "As to why he did it, there are many factors. His parents are one. He wanted to know that he could stand shoulder to shoulder with the two people who sacrificed so much to bring him into this world. In some way, if he proved to himself and to them that he could cut it in the roughest war, it would mean that everything they went through to give him life was worthwhile. He wanted to make them proud. His own sense of self-worth was a factor. He wanted to be able to look his reflection in the eye and prove that all his skills and power meant something. You want to be the best innkeeper you can be. He wants to be the best soldier he can be."

Wilmos shrugged his massive shoulders. "I was a contributing factor to this. I told him to his face that he was the pinnacle of my work. That's a hell of a lot of expectation to put on someone, and if I wasn't old and stupid, I would've recognized this. He wanted to show me what he was capable of. Sean hates to disappoint. You were a factor."

"Me?"

"I asked him if he was leaving anyone behind. He said he'd met a girl with stardust on her robe, and when he looked into her eyes, he saw the universe looking back."

"He said that?"

"He did. The blood of Auul flows through him. We were warriors and poets, often both. I asked him if he thought this girl would wait for him, and he said he wasn't sure."

Wilmos sighed. "How do you think he felt when he met you? If I give you an obscure sentient species, I bet you can tell me their favorite color. You walk the streets of Baha-char and bargain with Merchants, you open doors to planets thousands of light-years away, and you use complicated technology like you grew up with it, because you did. He knew nothing except what he'd learned on Earth. You weren't equals."

"But I never wanted him to…"

"I know. He knows too. He wanted to learn everything in a hurry. He learned, all right. If you ever have trouble with an armored rover or your particle cannon, he'll fix it for you."

"I don't want him to fix my rover. I want him to come home."

Wilmos dragged his hand across his face again, as if trying to wipe away the pressure. "He wants to come home too. But he was designed to withstand a siege and protect civilians, and everything he has known since he was born—his parents' moral code, the military training, and his service—all of it reinforced that core programming. That idiot Nuan Cee loaded Nexus with exiles. There are whole families there, hiding out in the colony bunkers. Sean couldn't walk away from them. Biological programming isn't everything, but you can't discount it either. In this case, his programming aligns with his ethics. That's a powerful urge."

"Sean Evans won't walk away from someone who needs his protection." I had learned that when our neighbors were attacked.

"Yes," Wilmos said. "It's about doing what he believes is right. Beings depend on him for their very survival. He already proved whatever he set out to prove. He is the best there is. He lasted a year and a half on a planet where seasoned mercenaries died in days. He doesn't have the manpower to win, but he sure as hell isn't backing down. He is what we envisioned when we created his parents."

I exhaled. "He traded a lifetime contract to save me from dying when I was poisoned."

Wilmos grimaced. "It doesn't surprise me."

"It surprised the hell out of me. Wilmos, we spent a week together. One week. We flirted. We kissed once. Where is this... devotion coming from?"

The veteran werewolf studied me for a long moment.

"What?" I asked.

"I'm trying to figure out a way to explain it and not screw things up between the two of you. I've done enough damage as is."

"Why don't you just say it straight?"

Wilmos took a deep breath. "You're young." He made some uncomfortable motions with his hands, as if he were trying to juggle something and failing. "Just... try not to take it as a blow to your ego. When the night is long and dark, you picture dawn in your head and you wait for it. It sustains you and gives you hope. In a war you search through your memories and you find that one thing, that anchor that tethers you to home. You are that to him. You are everything that is clean and peaceful and beautiful. You are someone who would cry if she heard he died. Soldiers do this. Sailors and long-range space crews too. Men, women, doesn't matter. We all wish for someone at home who might be waiting for us. It's not always fair to those who stay behind, but that's the way it is."

Gorvar rose and trotted over and Wilmos patted the big wolf's head.

"Sean is no fool. He knows there wasn't anything solid there, but he thinks there might be if he ever made it off Nexus. He thinks there is a chance. When he fought his way through that dark night, covered in gore and with no end in sight, he thought of you. He thought of coming home and seeing you smile. You are worth living for. You kept him going. He couldn't let you die, Dina. I knew this was a long shot. I hoped that if worse came to worst, you'd let him down gently so he had some piece of a heart left. Now it doesn't matter anymore. He will go to his fate knowing that he kept you out of harm's way, and he will be perfectly content."

"He won't be going anywhere. I'm going to save him," I told him. I would deal with being Sean's dawn later. Now I had to keep him alive.

"You can't." Pain brimmed in Wilmos's eyes. "The only way to save him is to bring about peace on Nexus. It is impossible. I know the Arbitrators are trying, but it can never be. They've been enemies for far too long. That's why the Office of Arbitration gave it to some greenhorn Arbitrator nobody ever heard of."

Nice to know this was George's first try. I leaned forward. "You said yourself I have stardust on my robe and the universe in my eyes. I want to save Sean. After I save him, I'll decide if I am going to give him a chance or not. Right now that's still up in the air."

Wilmos's eyebrows crept up.

I met his gaze. "I'm not an angel who will soothe all his wounds, I'm not his dawn, and I'm not his perfect sweetheart who is waiting for him to come home from the war. He'll figure it out very quickly, if he doesn't know that already, and then he will have to decide if he wants to let go of that and work on getting to know the real me. But none of this can happen until I pry him out of the Merchants' contract. Are you going to help me or not?"

Wilmos stared at me for a long time. "What do you need?"

I passed him a piece of paper. "There are many bounties on this person."

Wilmos glanced at the name and raised his eyebrows. "Yes."

"I need to know if any of those contracts came off the market after 2032 Standard."

"I can check that."

"And I need the psy-booster."

Wilmos leaned back. "The psy-booster has to be fed with life energy."

"I know."

"It's agony. One of the worst pains known to a human."

"I know."

Wilmos thought it over. "Okay. I hope you know what you're doing."

So did I.

After the heat of Baha-char, the cool interior of the inn was more than welcome. And I could finally stop rolling the bag. The psy-booster wasn't something I wanted close to my skin, so Wilmos's dealer had packed it into a large wheeled bag. The bag was cumbersome and made for an easy target. I had dragged it through a mile's worth of Baha-char streets, worrying that some enterprising thief was going to make a play for it. But I was finally home. I strolled through the hallway with the bag rolling behind me, and opened a screen to George. "Meet me in the grand ballroom."

He nodded.

This wasn't going to be a pleasant conversation, but I didn't really care.

I walked to the back of the ballroom. Where would be a good place…? To the side? No, I'd want them to be in a circle around me. I stopped in the center where the mosaic floor offered a depiction of Gertrude Hunt circled by a stylized broom. This had to be the best spot.

A hole opened in the center of the mosaic, small, but growing larger and larger, swallowing the mosaic pieces. That was okay. I would redo it later.

George walked into the ballroom.

"So this is your first assignment," I said.

"Yes."

The hole was now three feet wide. Good enough. I raised my hand, coaxing one of the inn's bigger roots out. Thinner roots wouldn't work. They were capillaries, and I needed a nice thick vein, a direct access to the heart of the inn. This would take a while.

"Was this supposed to be a feather in your cap? Your first assignment, which you must accomplish without any regard to the cost to everyone else?"

"Feathers are for people who seek recognition," George said. "Recognition does not matter to me."

"People don't seem to matter to you either. You came here and appealed to my trust. You pretended to know nothing about the inns or how they work. Then you systematically manipulated events and chipped away at my resolve until you brought me to this point."

"You wouldn't have reached it unless you were desperate," he said.

"Yes. Did you know Sean was Turan Adin and he and I have a history?"

"Yes. There was a chance that his presence would give you that final push. Nuan Cee was growing increasingly frantic. His back is against the wall. Both the Holy Anocracy and the Horde are martial cultures, and the lees are not. The prolonged war is harder on them than on any of the others. Ancestral worship is so ingrained in the lees' society they've killed each other over the privilege of taking care of their elders. Nuan Cee is half-exile; his obsession with forging the cast-outs into a clan has dominated his business strategies for the past twenty years. He did take the time to cover his tracks, but when you examine his financial maneuvering with his ancestry in mind, the pattern emerges quite readily. When he finally acquired the rights to Nexus, it must've felt like a triumph. Finally he could make his people whole. He jumped the gun with colonization. It was quite possibly the most emotion-driven decision of his entire career. Then he saw it all fall apart."

"He put his own people in danger."

George shook his head. "He thought he was doing the right thing. But without peace, there is no clan, no shrine, no closure. He wanted to bring Turan Adin into the negotiations because he is their biggest weapon. I just needed to give him an excuse. With the negotiations breaking down and the Khanum's eldest son having died on Nexus in the past year, she would need the Autumn Festival. It was her only chance to see her son again. She would do almost anything for it. So I suggested to Robart that sometimes people do not truly understand the situation until they had a chance to see it through their own eyes. His budding alliance with House Meer was tenuous; he was blinded by grief over his beloved. House Meer understood this and placed very little confidence in him, so when he offered them a seat at the metaphorical and actual table, they jumped on the chance and sent three of their finest to ruin the negotiations before Robart came to his senses."

"When?"

George arched his eyebrows. "When what?"

"When did you suggest that to Robart?"

"On the second day of the peace summit."

I stared at him.

"It was the kind of seed that needed to be planted in advance. Robart is a sensitive man, possessing an unfortunate combination of nobility of spirit and a certain inborn belief in the fairness of the world. His instincts tell him that if only he does the right thing and makes sure that everyone around him does the right thing, life will respond in kind and reward him for his efforts. He is a more sophisticated version of the proverbial knight in shining armor who believes that if he slays the evil dragon, he will rescue a beautiful princess who will love him forever and they will live happily ever after in their castle. He worked so hard, he had fought his way past the dragon, but his princess is dead and his castle stands hollow and empty. He's come to learn that life is a bitter bitch. She is inherently unfair. She took his happy future and crushed it, grinding it into dust. That realization is too much for him; he is emotionally volatile, swinging from one extreme to the other. A man in that emotional condition isn't able to make quick, reasoned decisions. I had to give him time to process the nudge, until his emotions finished churning. Meanwhile, the interaction with his opponents began to foster some sympathy in him. He had come here with the desire to burn everyone and everything to the ground, and yet here he was, feeling compassion toward his enemy. This created a conflict within him, one he wasn't capable of resolving, so he did what I suspected he would do—he reached out to his allies, hoping that they would assess the situation and point him in the right direction, eliminating his doubts. He came to the inevitable conclusion that the Meer should witness the summit for themselves."

He couldn't possibly be human. No human being could calculate the odds that far in advance.

"The rest fell into place," George said. "The poisoning was a wild card, but it worked in our favor. Given a choice, I wouldn't have poisoned you, Dina. It was too risky. I need you for the final act to this drama, and I am genuinely fond of you. For all my ruthlessness, my friends are very dear to me. That's why I have so few. I try not to form friendships."

"Because you might have to kill people you know?"

He nodded. "Yes."

A thick root slid out of the opening in the floor, wrapped in a network of thinner shoots. I let it rise about three feet and opened the bag. A round white jewel sat inside, as big as a soccer ball and rippling with all the fire of a diamond. The thinner roots bent toward it, scooped up the gem, and pulled it to the main shoot, wrapping tightly around it, forming a cocoon. The psy-booster was in place. Hopefully Gertrude Hunt would bond with it in the next few hours.

"I understand the Khanum, Robart, and Nuan Cee." I shook my head. "I still don't understand you."

George sighed, his handsome face resigned. "Very well. I owe you that much."

He raised his walking stick and gently tapped it on the floor. A huge projection burst out of the top of the cane, curving in front of us, taking up almost an entire half of the ballroom. Jagged mountains thrust through the barren brown and green soil, their yellow cliffs reflecting the light of a green sickly sun, puncturing the sky like an infected wound. Nexus. Hot during the day, cold at night, ugly at all times, yet hiding immense mineral wealth just beneath its crust.

"I was five when my grandfather died," George said. His voice was hollow. "He was a pirate, a swordsman, and a vagabond. He told great stories. He was the best grandfather a child could have. Our mother was dead, our father had abandoned us, so it was just my older sister, Jack, me, and my grandparents. So when he died, I was very sad."

On the screen George walked into the desolation of Nexus. He wore plain pants and a simple white shirt. His loose blond hair streamed around him. His face was serene and so beautiful... He was almost angelic, a strange haunting mirage conjured up by a planet wishing for something other than a wasteland.

George's voice was soft, intimate, the kind of voice that reached deep into your soul. "I was so sad that I called him back to life. Everyone thinks the dead rise as mindless monsters. It is always that way for necromancers. The dead rise without the burdens of their past lives, without a mind, and without pain."

I sensed what was coming and braced myself.

"The thing that came back wasn't my grandfather. It had claws and fangs. It devoured stray dogs. But it could speak and it knew my name. It remembered me. It remembered how the man it used to be died. It remembered the pain of his passing and it mourned the love he had lost."

The other George kept walking. The jagged cliffs parted and a vast valley, its floor rough and uneven, stretched before him. He was utterly alone.

"When the Office of Arbitration gave this assignment to me, I reviewed all the files and found I couldn't understand this war. Anyone with a rudimentary grasp of strategy and tactics could see that it was unwinnable by any of the factions. It devoured resources, time, and lives, and the longer it went on, the weaker everyone involved became.

Why would these three nations, all pragmatic, all used to weighing the odds in battle and in trade, hurl themselves at each other, dying for years in a war they couldn't win? Why continue this senseless slaughter at such a terrible cost? It made no sense."

On the projection George stopped. His blue eyes blazed with a pure white light. He raised his right hand, his fingers pointing up like claws.

"I couldn't understand it, so I went to Nexus."

A wind stirred his hair, growing stronger, tugging at his clothes.

"You see," he said, his intimate voice filled with regret, "the living lie. They can't help it. They lie out of kindness, necessity, and self-interest. But the dead always tell the truth."

On the screen the ground broke around George's feet, as if the dry crust of Nexus's desert turned liquid.

"So I went to Nexus and I asked them."

Bodies rose, some rotting, some skeletal, but all reaching to him, hundreds and hundreds of corpses, their limbs held out as if pleading, and then I heard it, a muted, desperate wail, coming from hundreds of creatures at once, so terrible I wanted to clamp my hands over my ears and run.

"They say the dead have no memories and know no pain." George's voice was barely above a whisper, but somehow it was louder than the pleas of the corpses. "It's not that way for me."

The dead cried out, louder and louder, grabbing at George's clothes, begging. George stood in the center of this maelstrom, his eyes brimming with pain. Tears wet his face. He wept and the dead cried with him.

"I understand them now. They fight because they cannot stop," he said, his voice somehow reaching me despite the wails. "They have buried their friends and lovers in that ground. It is watered with their blood, and they have nothing to show for it. The idea that those they lost died for nothing is too painful and frightening to contemplate. It's not a war of the living, Dina. It's the War of the Dead. Trust me when I say this: the dead do not care. I can call on their last memories and feelings, but they're not the same beings they were during their lives. They are echoes of the dying minds. They have no soul."

On the screen white lightning tore out of George. The corpses fell as one. He stood alone.

"Those who remain have forgotten they are alive. They think they have more in common with their fallen than with their enemy. Nothing could be further from the truth. I know the difference between life and death. Two live beings from the opposite boundaries of the galaxy have infinitely more in common with each other than the living and the dead from the same family."

The real George, the one next to me, touched his cane, and the projection vanished.

"The war on Nexus has to stop," he said. "It won't be ended by noble means, because if good intentions, compassion, and meaningful dialogue could've solved this, peace would've been reached already. Sometimes to stop something this terrible, you have to do something equally terrible in return at a great personal cost, and that terrible thing can't be done by one of the principals in this conflict. They must be able to walk away clean, united and guiltless, or the peace won't last. Someone must remind them that they are still alive. Someone must bear the blame and the rage that will bring. I am that someone. I take full responsibility for tomorrow. I forced it to happen. I'm sorry that you must also be involved. It is unfair that I used you. Nobody will ever know what you have done or what it will cost you. Your name and mine will be forgotten quickly, but we will both know and remember what we have done and why it had to be done. The psy-booster runs on magic. I will fuel it for you tomorrow."

He turned and walked away, leaving me alone on the mosaic floor.

A while ago I told Sophie that George was merciless. She told me that he was compassionate and merciless at once, a contradiction. I understood now. There was no contradiction. George was merciless to himself. At the end of this, everyone, including me, would look for someone to blame for the pain and the suffering that lay ahead. We'd need a target, and he'd willingly painted a bull's-eye on his chest. He took it all on himself, because the dead wept on Nexus when he returned their memories. He would take all the guilt and carry it away with him, absolving me because he had forced my hand. He had even done it a moment ago when he told me he had used me.

I would have to watch him very carefully tomorrow. He would give as much of himself to the psy-booster as he could. I didn't want George to die.

Chapter Sixteen

I stood just beyond the door, watching the grand ballroom through a one-way mirror the inn had made for me. The hall shone tonight, the constellations on its ceiling bright, the floor all but glowing. The Holy Anocracy stood on the right in full armor, shoulder to shoulder, like a phalanx of ancient warriors using their bodies as shields. Across from them the Horde waited grim-faced, arranged in a wedge formation with the Khanum in front, a huge basher on her left, and Dagorkun on her right. Clan Nuan crowded on the left as well, some distance from the otrokars, shielding their matriarch with their bodies. Turan Adin in full armor stood between them and the Horde.

The wagons were circled, the weapons were primed, and the faces were grim. They eyed each other, ready for the violence to erupt, and they glanced at the four-foot-high bud growing from the center of the floor. The bud's thick green sepals remained firmly shut.

My parents would be ashamed of me. Here were the guests of my inn. They had stayed at Gertrude Hunt for almost two weeks, a place where they were supposed to be protected and safe, yet they expected to be attacked at any moment. If the Innkeeper Assembly ever saw this, Gertrude Hunt would lose all her stars. There was no helping it now.

George stood by the bud, his handsome face solemn. The gold embroidery on his soft brown vest, the color of whiskey, glinted weakly in the light. His people had taken positions behind each of the factions: Jack stood behind the vampires, Sophie behind the Horde, and Gaston behind the Merchants. He had discussed it with me prior to the meeting, and when I asked for his reasoning, he told me that Gaston had natural resistance to poisons, Sophie had a strong psychological impact on the Horde, and Jack apparently had a lot of practice fighting soldiers in armor.

I ran through my mental checklist: Beast and the cat securely locked in my bedroom and the inn wouldn't let them out, the sound dampeners activated, the street-facing facade reinforced. Yes, that was everything. You could set off an explosion in the grand ballroom now, and nobody outside the inn would hear a single sound.

A rustle of fabric announced Her Grace's arrival to the bottom of the stairs. She wore a dark green dress with a silklike sheen, cinched to one side at her waist with a jeweled clasp and spilling down into a long skirt with a train embellished by glittering embroidery. Long, matching gloves covered her hands and arms. A luxurious fur collar, dark hunter green with individual hairs gradually changing color to bloodred at their tips, framed her shoulders. Black and green eight-inch spikes protruded from the collar, biological weapons of some long-dead alien predator. Matching small spikes decorated her elaborate bejeweled hair brooch. A necklace of emeralds, each the size of my thumbnail and framed in small fiery diamonds, graced her neck. She looked every inch exactly what she was: a ruthless, cunning animal of prey, armed with razor-sharp intelligence and unhindered by morals.

Caldenia saw my robe. Her eyebrows crept up.

Under ordinary circumstances, an innkeeper was an unobtrusive shadow, readily identifiable if the guests looked for her yet drawing no attention to herself. Our robes reflected that: gray, brown, dark blue, or hunter green, they served as our uniform. We had no need to impress. A bit of embroidery along the hem was as far as embellishment went. Yet once in a while, an occasion required that the full extent of our power had to be communicated. Today was that kind of day. I wore my judgment robe. Solid black, it swallowed the light. It pulled you in, and if you looked directly at it for too long, you would get the strange sensation that you were plunging into a bottomless dark well, as if someone had reached deep into the abyss, scooped out primordial darkness, then spun and wove it into a fabric. Lightweight and voluminous, the material of the robe was so thin that the slightest air current stirred it, and even now, without any perceptible draft, its hem moved and shifted as if some mystic power fanned it. The robe was impenetrable. No matter what sophisticated scanner a being might employ to augment their vision, I would appear the same, a specter, a chilling cousin of the Grim Reaper, my face hidden by my hood so only my mouth and chin remained visible. The broom in my hand had turned into a staff, its shaft the color of obsidian. I was no longer a person. I was an embodiment of the inns and innkeepers.

There were few universal principles in this world. That most water-based lifeforms drank tea was one. That we fear what we cannot see was the other. They would look at my robe, trying to discern the contours of my body, and when the abyss forced them to look away, they would search for my eyes trying to convince themselves I wasn't a threat. They would find no reassurance.

"Well," Caldenia said. "This should prove interesting."

"Stay by my side, Your Grace."

"I shall, my dear."

The wall parted before me and I strode into my ballroom. They'd all had their show. It was time for mine.

The weak murmurs died. Silence claimed the hall, and within it I glided across the floor without a sound. As I moved, darkness rolled across the floor, walls, and ceiling, a menacing shadow of my power. The light dimmed. The constellations died, snuffed out by my presence. *Watch me as I end your universe.*

I reached the bulb. George didn't step back, but he thought about it, because he unconsciously leaned back, trying to widen the distance between me and him. The darkness rolled behind me and remained there, an antisunrise blocking out the stars. Caldenia took a spot behind me on my left.

Nobody said a thing.

The floor parted in front of me, and a thin stalk of the inn lifted a platter supporting a glass teakettle half-filled with wassa tea. The light within the platter set the teakettle aglow, making the tea sparkle like a precious ruby. Or like blood.

The Horde stiffened. Nuan Cee visibly braced himself.

"There is a killer in this inn." My voice rolled through the grand ballroom, a too-loud whisper charged with power. "A killer I will now punish."

"By what right?" The question came from the vampire side. I had ratcheted the pressure to the limit. All of them were already on edge. If I weren't careful, they would erupt.

"By the right of the treaty your governments signed. Those who attack guests within an inn lose all protections of their homeland. Your status, your wealth, and your position do not matter. You are in my domain. Here, I alone am the judge, the jury, and the executioner."

I turned, my robe moving lightly along the floor, and began to circle the teakettle. A projection spilled out of the ceiling: me sitting on the divan, Dagorkun serving the tea, Caldenia picking up her cup.

"One of you made an effort to move through the inn unseen. One of you employed a device that hid his or her image."

The tension was thick; I kept waiting for it to crack like a thunderclap.

"This device was stolen and duplicated. The original was returned to its owner. The duplicate was used to allow someone to poison the tea in this kettle."

The ruby-red tea shone once, responding to the light.

"Who?" Arland demanded. "Who brought the device?"

"I did," Nuan Cee said.

"You!" the Khanum snarled.

The darkness flared behind me like a hungry beast ready to devour. They fell silent.

"There are only three motives for murder. Sex. Revenge." I paused. "And greed."

A contract appeared on the projection, huge, almost nine feet tall, hanging like a banner from the ceiling. On it odd symbols lined up into words next to an image of Caldenia.

"Less than a day after the location of this peace summit became known, this contract went off the market," I said. "Someone had taken the job."

The symbols mutated into general galactic script, showing a number large enough to buy a small planet. Jack whistled in the back.

"Cai Pa?" Caldenia blinked. "You mean to tell me this comes from that sniveling worm of a magnate who decorated his palace with jewel-eyed portraits of his horrid family? After two decades, he still wants me dead over a casual remark?"

"Yes."

Caldenia put her hand over her chest, her gloved finger-tips barely touching her skin, leaned back, and laughed. It was a rich, throaty laugh, showing off the forest of triangular, sharp teeth inside her mouth.

Everyone stared.

"After all these years, I've still got it." She chuckled.

"The question is, why poison the entire kettle?" I said. "Three people would have drunk from it, and all three would have died. The consequences for all factions involved would've been dire."

I paced back, passing my hand above the kettle. It pulsed with a bright spark in response.

"An experienced assassin would've selected the time and place of his strike carefully. An experienced assassin would've weighed the risks and realized that such a crime wouldn't go undiscovered or unpunished. The esteemed Nuan Cee is an experienced assassin, cunning, smart, and disciplined. He wouldn't have taken that risk."

I turned back. The motion of my walking was enough to keep my robe shifting, as if stirred by some mystical power, and I needed as much impact as I could get.

"No, this assassin was someone who hadn't had a lot of practice. Someone inexperienced. Someone young. Someone desperate and easily tempted."

Nuan Cee's lips trembled, baring a hint of his teeth. He just put it all together.

"Tell us, esteemed Merchant, what is the unspoken custom of your clan when a bright member of your family is about to reach adulthood?"

"The clan takes measures to make sure that the young one stays bound to the family for a while longer," Nuan Cee said through clenched teeth. "It is done to preserve the family's wealth."

"Just like you have done with Cookie?"

The projection showed a close-up of the emerald vanishing into thin air.

Cookie gasped.

"Yes," Nuan Cee said.

"You arrange for a child approaching adulthood to make a mistake, a mistake that puts them in debt to the clan, which they then have to repay?" I had to really break it down so everyone got it.

"Yes."

"And how many years of service does Nuan Sama owe you?"

The Nuan Clan parted as every member simultaneously stepped aside. Nuan Cee's niece stood alone in the circle of her family members.

"Nuan Sama had made some additional mistakes," Nuan Cee ground out. "Her debt to the clan is substantial."

"It wasn't me." Nuan Sama smiled. "Why would I do such a foolish thing? I love my clan. I have no desire to leave."

Wow. That was some serious chutzpah.

"When Hardwir repaired the vehicle with the molecular synthesizer, you were asked to assist him. You're an expert in age sequencing."

I turned to the vampires. I had already interrogated the engineer before the gathering. I knew the answers to the questions I was asking.

"What did Nuan Sama suggest before you began the repairs?"

"She said that we should try it on a complex piece of equipment to make sure the results were optimal," Hardwir answered.

"Did she provide such a piece of equipment?"

"Yes."

"The esteemed engineer misunderstood," Nuan Sama said. "I brought him a part from our ship."

"You brought me an image disruptor," Hardwir said. "We duplicated it, and then you took both of them away."

"It is his word against mine," Nuan Sama said.

"There were only three people besides the otrokars who knew the Khanum had invited me to her tea," I continued. "Me, Her Grace, whom I called directly after I received the invitation, and you."

"The honored innkeeper has no way of knowing I was the only one," Nuan Sama said. "After all, the honored innkeeper couldn't even tell her tea was poisoned."

Nice. "When you dropped the poison into the kettle, you felt a puff of wind. Did you not wonder what that puff might have been?"

Nuan Sama shook her furry head, the many silver hoops in her ears gently clinking against each other. "I was never there."

"That puff was a dye," I said. "The inn marked you. Shall we see if your fur is stained?"

A lamp sprouted from the ceiling. She didn't wait for the light. Nuan Sama leapt straight up, flipping in the air as she tried to clear the crowd of her clansmen. A furry blur shot toward her. They collided in midair and landed back in the circle of the clansmen, her uncle next to her.

Pawed hands grabbed her as her relatives rushed to restrain her.

"You took a contract not sanctioned by the family?" Nuan Cee's voice was mournful.

"I did," she snarled.

"Why?"

"Why?" Nuan Sama's voice rose, shaking. "Why? Do you need me to tell you why? I've been an adult for four years. I want my freedom. I want my money, the money that was rightfully due to me on my majority, the money you and the rest of them stole from me. You've trapped me and you work me like I'm some indentured servant. Can't you see you're suffocating me? I can't even breathe the same air as you. It's poison to me, Uncle."

The floor under Nuan Sama's feet turned liquid. She began to sink. The foxes frantically tried to pull her out. Panic broke what little composure Nuan Sama had left.

"Uncle!" she cried out.

Nuan Cee spun toward me. "No!"

"She belongs to me," I said, loading all my magic into my creepy voice.

Nuan Sama had sunk to her knees. She was screaming and whimpering now, making sharp fox noises as her family tried desperately to pull her free.

"She will be punished!" Nuan Cee cried out.

"I know," I told him. "It won't be quick or easy."

"A favor from the Merchants is worth more than the life of one unskilled assassin." Caldenia murmured next to me. "I assume you have a plan, dear?"

"Yes."

Nuan Cee pivoted to Sean. Turan Adin shook his head. Yep. I didn't think so. According to Wilmos, nothing in Sean's contract obligated him to serve as a bodyguard to spoiled rich girl assassins.

The floor reached Nuan Sama's hips. Desperation vibrated in her voice. "Help me, Uncle! Help me!"

Nuan Cee turned to me. "Yes. Whatever it is you want, yes."

I flicked my fingers. The floor solidified, trapping the fox in place. I needed a visual aid in case Nuan Cee developed second thoughts.

"What is this?" The Khanum's eyes narrowed.

I heard the buzzing sound of a blood weapon being primed. The vampires were ready to rumble.

"The Holy Anocracy, the Horde, and the Merchants. All of you are responsible for spilling blood within these walls. All of you owe me a debt. I am calling it in. It's time to settle your accounts."

"What do you want?" Lady Isur asked.

"Your memories." I touched my staff to the bulb. The fuzzy green sepals peeled back. Delicate, translucent flower petals unfurled, hair-thin and glowing with pale green near their base, then turning transparent, and finally darkening to a magenta toward the tips. Long, whiplike stamens, coated in soft blue light, stretched from within the flower, reaching and twisting, and inside, in the whorl of petals, the psy-booster glittered.

"You want to take our memories?" Dagorkun asked.

"Not take. I want you to share them with me."

"You don't know what you're asking," the Khanum snarled.

"I do." *You know why I am asking it. Your reason is standing right there next to you.*

George stepped forward, undid the clasp on his wrist cuff, and rolled the sleeve back, exposing a scarred, muscular arm.

"You do not want this," Robart said, his voice suffused with so much sadness. "You do not want to experience my memories, Innkeeper."

"Yes, I do. This is my price. Your honor demands you pay it. If you do not, there will be consequences."

I had no idea what those consequences would be, but it sounded impressive.

George rolled back his other sleeve.

"Very well." The Khanum's face was terrible. She stepped forward.

I shook my head. "No. Him." I pointed my staff at the shaman.

Ruga's eyebrows crept together. He walked forward and stopped before me, corded with dry muscle, his charms and totems hanging from the belt of his kilt. Odalon shouldered his way through the vampires and came to stand next to Ruga, resplendent in his crimson battle vestments.

I looked at the Merchants. Nuan Cee started forward.

Grandmother made a quiet noise. He stopped almost in midstep. Grandmother turned in her palanquin. The foxes carrying it lowered it to the ground. She rose within it and stepped out onto the floor.

Clan Nuan let out a collective gasp.

The elder fox crossed the floor and stood next to Odalon. I had the spiritual leaders of every faction.

"Form a line behind your faction," I said. "Leaders at the very end."

The grand ballroom rippled as vampires, otrokars, and Clan Nuan formed three lines behind their spiritual representatives.

"Hold out your hands and take the hand of the person in front of you and behind you. Skin to skin."

Metal slid as high-tech gauntlets fell away. Grudgingly they obeyed.

I looked to the back where the Khanum, Arland, and Nuan Cee stood, each the end of their line. "Complete the circuit."

The muscles on the Khanum's jaw stood out as she clenched her teeth. Arland's face might have been made of stone. The gauntlet slid off his hands. He held out his hands, one to Khanum and the other to the Merchants. The Khanum gripped his fingers. Her expression was terrible. On the other side, Nuan Cee took Arland's hand. Robart, the next in line behind Arland, turned and clasped his left hand on Arland's bare forearm, locking his fingers on Arland's wrist.

"Sorry, my friend," he said.

Arland braced himself. They thought they knew what was coming. They had no idea.

George held out his arms.

I pushed with my magic. The glowing stamens reached out, fastening around his arms. A muscle in his face jerked. He would feel the pain immediately. When the booster actually began drawing on his magic reserve, the agony would be excruciating. I glanced at Sophie. She nodded. We had made a deal, and I was counting on her to stick to it.

I planted my staff into the floor. It opened, unfurling into three long flexible metal branches. The branches shot to the three beings standing in front of me and clasped their free hands.

This would hurt. This would hurt so much.

I looked up, past the people gathered behind me to where Turan Adin stood alone on the floor. He walked toward me and grasped my shoulder with his clawed hand. We stood together, locked into a single living circuit.

"Do not let go," I said, speaking to all of them. "If you do, you may not survive."

I thrust my hand into the flower and pressed my palm against the psy-booster. Obeying my command, the inn reached out with a tendril and anchored my hand.

The magic of the inn swelled behind the flower and ripped through me like a gust of incredibly powerful, painful wind. It dashed down the chain, splashed against the leaders, and dissipated.

Was that it? That wasn't so bad, but now nothing was happening...

I felt magic swelling behind the flower, like a tsunami, rising higher and higher. Before I had a chance to prepare myself, it crested and tore into me.

Pain exploded inside me, erupting into a starburst of red-hot needles. Tears wet my eyes. I tried to take a breath and a cascade of memories hit me. Robart screaming at the top of his lungs, screaming and screaming as he looked across the battlefield and watched the otrokar's axe carve into the woman he loved. I saw her arm fall from her body, saw the bloody stump where it had been, and at the same time I saw her kissing Robart in a garden, her eyes luminescent with love. I *felt* it. I felt her love; I felt how much she cared. *She would do anything for me. I would do anything for her. In my darkest moments, she was there. She would... They were cutting her apart and there were too many between me and her, and I was reaping and slicing, but she was too far. She was screaming for me. She was screaming for my help, and I could do nothing. Her face... Oh stars, her face... Please, please Divine, I will do anything. Anything. Take me. Take me instead. Take me instead, you fucking bitch! The axe carved into her neck and I screamed. I screamed, because the pain burst out of me and if I didn't let it out, it would tear me apart.*

The memories kept hammering into me like nails into a coffin. Nuan Cee weeping over the small furry body of a fox baby in his arms, bent over and wracked with grief. Sean in his rooms alone, visions of blood and death... Odalon comforting the dying; Ruga walking through a makeshift morgue, hand over his mouth; Grandmother Nuan weeping... We were screaming. We were crying and wailing in one voice, battered by the pain and loss.

Another memory punched me like a bullet to the heart. A little otrokar boy trying to walk, unsteady on his feet, teetering, a very serious expression on his little face as behind him a huge otrokar got down on his hands and knees. The boy, my boy, was walking toward me. Big round eyes. *That's right. Oh! He fell right on his butt. Pick yourself up. That's right. That's my boy. You will grow up big and strong. You will grow.* The little boy morphed into a slender adolescent with the same round eyes, full of laughter. He dashed across the yard, leapt onto a rukar's back, and kicked his mount into a sudden gallop. *Come back here! Clean your room! His father laughing in the corner. Are you going to let him get away with this?* The little boy morphed again and here he was my son, strong broad shoulders, proud face, and still those eyes, those big green eyes amused at the world, looking outward and seeing only the promise of adventure. He wore the leathers of our people, and he was looking at me over his shoulder. Don't go. Take off your armor and come back. Come back to me, my precious one, my son, my little one. He vanished, jerked out of existence. No longer there, as if all those years never happened. There was a gauntlet in my lap. A bloody gauntlet. *That is all I have left of my son.*

The memories kept coming. Lovers, brothers, sisters, children, parents, I lost them over and over, I mourned them, my grief so raw it cut me from the inside. The waterfall of memories pounded against my soul, shredding it.

I can't. Too much. Too much. I can't.

How can you live through this? How can anyone live through this?

I can't!

Make it stop. Make it stop, please.

Please. I beg you.

Stop!

The magic vanished. A single image burned before me, a field of bodies under a bloody sky, and then it too dimmed to nothing.

The inn released my hand, and I collapsed to the floor. Next to me George was panting. His nose and eyes bled. Sophie stood by him, her sword in her hands, the severed stamens of the flower melting into nothing on the floor. We'd agreed that when George neared his limit, she would end it.

All around me people curled on the floor. Some wept, some buried their faces in their hands. A huge otrokar was rocking back and forth.

I licked my dry lips. My voice came out rusty. "Stop it."

Across the room the Khanum stared at me with haunted eyes.

"You can stop it. You can do it today. Right now. No more. Please, no more."

I stood on my back porch, smiled, and watched the long line of the otrokars depart into the night. The Merchants and the Holy Anocracy would follow. Half an hour later and the inn would be almost empty.

It took the three factions less than an hour to hammer out a peace agreement. Nexus had been split along the existing boundaries, with both Horde and the Holy Anocracy surrendering a stretch of territory to create a demilitarized demarcation zone, a no-man's-land that would keep them separated and hopefully minimize the incidents. Clan Nuan's territory had been expanded at the cost of the otrokars and vampires. In return, Clan Nuan cut its export and import prices by sixty percent. The agreements had been signed, spat upon, and marked with blood. Everyone had made painful concessions. Everyone stood to reap great benefits. Everyone would have a hell of a time trying to sell the treaty back home, but at least all those present were united in their satisfaction with the arrangement.

Now they were leaving. Such was the way of an innkeeper. Guests came. Guests left. I remained.

The otrokars were moving fast. I couldn't blame them. Everyone had been traumatized by the joining, but at least nobody went mad. Sophie had severed the link just in time. I didn't want to contemplate what would've happened if she let it go on for another minute or two. I would have nightmares for weeks as it was. George was standing to the left of me, pale as a sheet, and both his brother and Gaston hovered near him. He'd almost fallen twice already, and they were ready to catch him. I had offered him a chair, but he refused.

The Khanum and Dagorkun were the last in the line. They halted before me.

"Your parents," Dagorkun said quietly. "We saw your memories."

Oh no. I'd hoped that wouldn't happen. I had directed the inn to search for the most traumatic experiences connected to Nexus. The only experience I had connected to that planet was when my brother Klaus and I landed there six months after our parents disappeared. We were combing the galaxy trying to find them, and the pain of their disappearances had been so raw. I couldn't recall thinking of them during the link, but I must've done so, and now every guest in the inn who had been connected to Gertrude Hunt had seen deep into a private place in my soul.

Well, I did it to them. It was only fair.

"We will keep our eyes and ears open," Dagorkun said.

"Thank you," I said.

The Khanum looked at me, reached out, and crushed me to her in a bear hug. My bones groaned. She let go and they went off, through the orchard toward the shimmering tunnel leading to a faraway place.

The Merchants followed, including Nuan Sama, who was wrapped in what looked like a space-age straitjacket. I had given her back to Nuan Cee. The Merchants could deal with her crime. I had a feeling taking a contract unsanctioned by the family was going to cost her much more than whatever tortures I could level on her.

Clan Nuan departed one by one, heading toward their ship in the field. Cookie walked by me, grinned, and showed me a big green gem clutched in his paw. So, the emerald was returned. Clan Nuan would have to find some other way to entrap their young adults. I had no doubt they would think of something.

Grandmother passed me in her palanquin, favoring me with a nod. Nuan Cee nodded to me as well, and I nodded back. The next time I went to Baha-char to seek a Merchant, I would have a rough time bargaining, but some things couldn't be helped. Maybe I would shop at his competitors. Stranger things had happened.

The Holy Anocracy was the last. They moved past me, huge in their armor. Lady Isur and Lord Robart walked together, side by side. As they passed me, Lady Isur gently touched Robart's forearm. He glanced at her and put his hand over hers. Maybe there would be something there in the future. Who knew?

Arland was the last of the line. He lingered by me.

"Here we are again," he said. "I'm leaving."

"And I'm staying."

"Lady Dina…"

"Your people are waiting for you, Lord Arland."

He smiled, showing me his fangs. "Until next time then."

"Until next time."

"He has feelings for you," Sophie said softly.

"He likes the idea of me," I told her. "In practice, both he and I know this would never work."

I turned to George.

"It is our turn," he said.

"Yes. Congratulations on your first successful arbitration."

"It wouldn't have been possible without you," he said.

"You're right. It wouldn't have been."

George offered me a smile. The impact was staggering, but I was now immune.

"I suppose I am now banned from the inn."

"Well, you've broken my apple trees, deliberately inflicted emotional distress on me and my guests, and manipulated me into a dangerous magical ritual that could've cost my sanity. Unfortunately, as much as I would like to ban you, the Office of Arbitration is a valuable ally. So Gertrude Hunt will welcome you again, should you need our hospitality. At triple your current rate and an ironclad contract that you will sign before I let you set one foot into my inn."

George laughed. "Very well. Our bill has been settled."

I had checked the account an hour ago. My account showed a lovely new balance, complete with a hundred-thousand-dollar bonus marked as "apple trees." The payment had been processed through a complicated system of the innkeeper network. It would stand up to scrutiny as long as all my taxes were filed properly.

"To borrow from the Marshal of House Krahr, until next time," George said.

Yeah. Hopefully not too soon.

The top of his cane shone with bright light, and the Arbitrator's people vanished.

I sank into my patio chair and sighed. The inn had sprouted lights shaped like grape clusters from the roof of the porch, and they bathed the space in a soft light. Finally. Everyone was gone.

The door swung open and Caldenia emerged onto the porch. Her Grace wore a light green kimono-style robe. She took the chair next to me. Orro followed and loomed over me, a seven-foot-tall, spiky shadow.

Oh. Right. He had to leave too. The kitchen would feel so empty and quiet without him. But there was no way I could afford him.

"I do believe you let the Arbitrator off too lightly," Caldenia said.

I smiled.

Her Grace raised her eyebrows.

"I entered his name into the Problem Guests database, complete with the description of the apple incident. The next time he attempts to find an inn on Earth, he will find it exceedingly difficult. In fact, I'm pretty sure that he will have to return here. It's frightening how high you can raise a price of a room when you are the only Innkeeper willing to take the guest in."

Caldenia grinned.

I turned to Orro smiled at him. "Thank you so much for your help, Orro. I couldn't have done it without you. You managed the impossible."

He continued to stand over me without saying a word.

I raised my hand. The brick wall of the inn parted and a small datacard popped into my hand. I offered it to him. "This is your payment and some endorsements for you. It's not much, but it is the least I can do."

"Please, dear." Caldenia glanced at Orro. "She obtained testimonials from the Khanum of the Horde, three Houses of the Holy Anocracy, Clan Nuan, and myself. That is enough recommendations to rejuvenate your career."

Orro moved. His hand shot out, blur-fast. A tiny cupcake landed on the table in front of me, decorated with a swirl of bright yellow cream and a tiny flower made from fondant. The delicate aroma of mango filled the air.

"For me?"

He nodded.

"Thank you."

He made a harrumph-like noise and moved again. I looked down at the grocery-store flier deposited on the table. He'd circled a sale on strawberries and cherries.

"I need these things. I cannot make breakfast with thin air."

I blinked.

"And dinner. I will need these." He flipped the page and pointed to pork chops.

"Orro, I can't afford to keep you. You're a Red Cleaver chef. I barely even have guests..."

His chest swelled. His needles stood up, making him even larger. "This is an inn. An inn needs a chef. You can't afford not to keep me. You don't even have a gastronomic coagulator!"

"Orro…"

"If I leave, you would ruin this kitchen." He raised his chin. "I have spoken."

He turned, went inside, and slammed the screen door behind him.

I remembered to close my mouth.

"Oh thank the stars." Caldenia exhaled. "No offense to your cooking, but the thought of going back to it was causing me actual anxiety."

I licked the icing on my cupcake. It was delicious. Mmmm, mango.

"Where is your werewolf?" Caldenia arched her eyebrows.

An hour ago Sean and Nuan Cee had walked out into the dark night. I watched as the armor melted off Sean Evans and his body slimmed down to his human form. He took a deep breath, looked at the moon, handed his armor to the Merchant, and walked away.

"He'll come around," I told her and licked my cupcake again, savoring the taste. "I'm sure of it."

"Things he has seen. Things he has been through. I've had affairs with men damaged by war. It is an uphill battle. You do realize this will be exceedingly difficult?"

"I know," I told her.

"Very well." Her Grace leaned back. "At least this will be interesting to watch. One must do something for entertainment around here."

I laughed and ate my cupcake.

EPILOGUE

The Innkeeper Directory lay open on my lap, a plain book issued by Innkeeper Assembly. Nothing special, except for a fact that it listed all the inns on the planet. It came out monthly. By now the news of the disaster at Gertrude Hunt would've spread. Guests died on inn's grounds. I braced myself. I would lose at least half a star. Maybe more. With the inn at two and a half stars, any drop in rating might as well be a death sentence.

It was Thursday night. The sky behind my windows was dark.

I had spent the past three days sleeping, stuffing my face, and sleeping some more. Nightmares came and went, fading remnants of the Nexus memories, but I accepted them. I knew why they were there, I didn't have to wonder what they meant, and it made things easier. I just had to wait them out, like the pain of a healing wound.

I've been dreading the Directory's appearance. Here it was. Nothing I could do about it.

I held my breath and flipped to the *News and Changes* section. The name Gertrude Hunt stood out in bold, indicating changes. Two and a half stars.

What?

Maybe they didn't know. No, they had to know. It's not like you could've hidden something as huge as the Peace Summit between Anocracy and the Horde.

I scanned the small footnote under the entry.

The Office of Arbitration thanks Gertrude Hunt for their hospitality and their unwavering support in most extraordinary of circumstances. We look forward to our next visit.

Cold sweat broke out on my hairline. An endorsement. It was an endorsement from the Office of Arbitration. The Office didn't do endorsements. That was like getting a public thank you from the British Royal Family. Under ordinary circumstances, it would've catapulted my rating up an entire star, but it remained the same.

They knew, I realized. The Innkeeper Assembly knew I had screwed up, but the public thank you from the Office Arbitration carried so much weight, they chose to ignore it.

George saved my rating.

I remembered to breathe.

I won, I realized. Gertrude Hunt got a boost from the guests, our bank account got a boost from the Office of Arbitration, and we had kept our rating. I grinned.

I won.

The inn chimed, announcing a guest.

I reached out with my magic. The newcomer felt familiar.

The still-nameless cat and Beast looked at me. I made big eyes at them. Well, how about that?

A knock sounded. I got up and opened the door.

Sean Evans stood on my porch. He wore jeans, running shoes, and a plain gray T-shirt. The scars still crossed his face, and his eyes were still dark with memories. I searched them for the hopelessness I had seen before and I couldn't find it.

"Hi," he said.

"Hi."

"It's '80s night at the Sims Theater," he said.

Sims was our local answer to a movie and dining. It came equipped with small tables, and once you ordered from a menu, a speedy and nearly invisible crew of servers would deliver your food while you watched the movie.

"What's playing?" I asked, keeping my voice light.

"*Big Trouble in Little China.*"

I grinned.

"I have two tickets," he said. "Would you like to come?"

"I would." I grabbed my purse from the table and stepped out. "I think I totally deserve a night off."

"Lucky for me."

Behind me, the inn shuttered itself. It would be okay for a couple of hours.

We walked down the long driveway to a Range Rover parked by the street. I liked this. I liked walking next to him.

"So what did you tell the neighbors about your absence?" I asked.

"I told them the truth. I took a job in a faraway place to make some money and broaden my horizons."

We reached the car. Sean peered at the side street and swore.

A brief wail of a siren cut through the night, and Officer Marais's cruiser slid out of the side street and stopped next to us, facing in the opposite direction.

Oh no.

"Is there a problem, Officer?" Sean asked.

"We have a movie to catch," I added.

Officer Marais rolled down his window. "I had a five-day training session in Houston last week. I don't like leaving my family alone overnight, so instead of them flying me, every day I drove to Houston and back."

"That's a long trip," Sean said. His voice was deceptively calm. We were off the inn's grounds. If he snapped and yanked Marais out of the cruiser, there wouldn't be much I would be able to do to stop him.

"Two hundred and seventy miles every day," Officer Marais said. "Plus all the driving around Houston. I put fourteen hundred miles on my odometer."

"That's very nice," I said.

"I'd gassed up on Monday before going to Houston."

Aha.

"I'm still at a quarter of a tank."

Oh shit.

"It's great what the Dodge Charger is doing with fuel efficiency these days," Sean said, his face calm.

Damn it, Hardwir.

"Sure. This isn't over." Officer Marais smiled, showing his teeth. "Enjoy your movie."

The cruiser slid past us and drove into the night.

THE END